THE COILED THRONE

MYRANDA RAE

CHAPTER 1

Turning the key, my engine makes a clicking sound, and then the gears grind.

"Oh, no. Not tonight, Rhonda. I really can't take it." I pet my steering wheel, hoping a bit of affection will fix this. Not only does the thought of walking home fill me with dread, but I absolutely cannot afford car trouble right now.

Mentally preparing myself to be let down, I turn the key again.

Whirring, cranking, sharp grinding.

Shit.

"Ok, Rhonda. I made exactly fourteen dollars and twenty two cents tonight. I'm supposed to pay rent in three days and I'm still a few hundred short. Please, I beg of you. Don't do this to me." I close my eyes and lean forward, resting my head on the steering wheel while I say my desperate prayer.

Turning the key, hoping against all rational reason, the engine turns over, clunking a bit but turning on.

"Oh, thank you!" I peel out of the empty parking lot onto the empty street.

The only perk of working the graveyard shift is the traffic free commute. Everything else about it is absolutely awful. My grand total for a week of shifts is ninety two dollars and forty six cents in tips.

Sinking into my seat, I focus on driving, not how I'm supposed to afford food, or gas, or rent.

Looking up, I search for the moon. It's extra dark tonight, eerily so. I've lived here my entire life, nothing about this place scares me. Tonight, I feel like a stranger in my hometown.

As I putter down the road, a chill comes over me. It's too cold for August. Even in the early morning hours, this is unusually chilly.

Pulling up to one of the two stop lights on the main street, it turns yellow, then red as I approach.

Of course it does. Why would the light stay green for the busier direction in the middle of the night when there are no other cars on the road?

Tapping my fingers on the steering wheel, I wait. And wait. And wait.

This is so ridiculous.

"Come on!" I throw my hands up. "There isn't anyone over there! Who are you green for?"

I feel desperate to get home. Once I'm there, this lingering feeling will go away.

Looking left, then right, then left again I search for a bored local police officer out trying to meet his ticket writing quota. The last thing I need right now is a ticket.

When I'm positive that there's no one else out here for miles, I creep out into the intersection running the red light.

My radio buzzes crinkly static coming through my speakers, cutting off the peppy eighties song that was playing.

My anxiety spikes. "Come on, Rhonda. We're almost there."

Leaving the Main Street behind, I drive on the long, dark highway toward my shitty apartment—a studio above my elementary school principal's garage. My life is so pathetic.

Groaning, I spin the dial to find another radio station. The knob breaks off in my hand.

"Sorry, girl." I cringe, trying to push it back into place. Rhonda requires a delicate touch. While I'm fumbling with the dial, trying to fix it and drive at the same time, I hear a sound, like a high-pitched whistle, that makes me swerve.

My car skids into the irrigation ditch that lines the ditch.

A blinding white light flashes, three times in rapid succession. My vision is spotty, and my head is spinning.

There is a boom, like a bomb going off, and the ground shakes.

The shaking only lasts for a second, but it was like it came from below me, like something exploded out of the ground.

Using my body weight, I lean my shoulder into the car door, trying to push it open. It's stuck in the thick, soupy mud my car is rapidly sinking into.

Using the hand crank, I roll my window down and pull myself out. I'm knee deep in mud and long grass when I'm covered in something falling from the sky.

Stumbling and coughing, I climb out of the ditch.

It's dirt.

Dirt is raining down on me.

But just as suddenly as it started, it stops. I'm left in silence. There isn't anyone around for miles. I'm so confused.

Was it a bomb? Or did I get into an accident with another car?

There weren't any other cars.

None of the pieces fit together into a scenario that makes any sense at all.

Covered in dirt, grass, and mud, I stare up at the sky. "What the hell?" I try to wipe my face, but every part of me is filthy. It's like trying to clean with more dirt.

A sound from the field behind me catches my attention. There's a crater. A huge circle of displaced dirt dipped into the ground.

As I walk toward it, I can see that there's something in the center of it. The closer I get to it the clearer it becomes that it's a person. A man. He's shirtless, and there are strange tattoos all over his back. They look like scales that move up from below the hem of his pants and fade as they reach his shoulders. To each his own, I guess...

"Hello?"

No movement.

"Hello?" Please, don't be dead. I creep forward until I'm close enough to really see him. He looks completely unharmed. It looks like he's asleep.

Poking my foot forward, I tap his leg. "Hello? Are you alright?"

He still doesn't move.

"Shit. Mister, I'm going to get help, ok? I have a phone somewhere, I'll find it and call an ambulance."

As I run through the field toward my car, I almost step on a snake.

"Holy shit!" I scream. "Why are you like that?"

The snake is coiled up with its head in the air, like it's watching. It didn't move, even when I almost stepped on it.

It's just sitting there, perfectly still, looking in the direction of the man. Does it understand what's going on here? It looks like it. It's unsettling how it's just staring that way.

Creeping past it, I continue toward my car.

A chill runs up my spine. There is another snake here. And beyond it, another.

Where are they coming from?

Turning around, I search for a car or an airplane, or something. Where did this guy come from, and how did he get here?

Maybe the snakes are his. He could have been transporting them and had an accident. And now they're just sitting here watching over him loyally like dogs. Maybe they're his pets. That would explain the tattoos.

I don't know very much about snakes or snake behaviors. They could be very loyal and loving.

I'm grasping at straws, trying to find an explanation that makes sense with what I'm looking at.

Swallowing down the growing fear, I run back to my totaled car. Wading through the muck, I climb back in through the window and try to find my phone. I've looked everywhere. It's not here.

Frustration is about to get the best of me. Whatever the smallest unit of measurement is, that's how close I am to losing my shit.

Falling out of my car again, I cautiously walk back to the man. There are more snakes.

"I can't find my phone. Do you have one in your pocket, maybe?" I bend down and touch his pants. The stiff material is cold and hard against my fingers.

Just as I skim my fingertips over his pocket, his hand grabs my arm roughly.

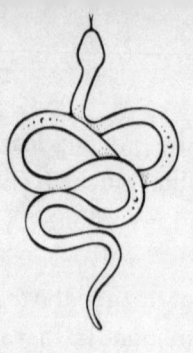

CHAPTER 2

A scream so loud that it scares even me flies out of my mouth. I stumble back, my ass hitting the ground hard as I try to get away.

Scrambling to stand, I turn, face to face with a fucking snake.

Another ear piercing scream, more clambering, more panic. This is straight out of a nightmare.

"What fresh hell is this?" I look at the snakes that have now moved in on us, surrounding us completely. "Shoo!" I wave my hand at one of them, but it doesn't budge.

"Where are we?" His voice is so strange that it stops all of my panicking. It's almost melodic. He has an accent I can't quite place. He's also so incredibly calm that it's unsettling. He just woke up in a field, half naked, surrounded by snakes. He must be in shock.

"W-What?" There is something dark and frightening about him. We aren't close enough to touch, but there is a coldness to him that I can feel from here. Sitting up, awake, and alive, he looks less human.

"Where are we?" He repeats, more slowly this time.

"Um, Wyoming."

He doesn't look like that's registering to him—like he doesn't know where that is.

"America?" I try again with a broader answer.

Still nothing.

He looks up at the sky and points. "I need to be over there, there is too much cloud coverage here."

Now I'm the confused one.

"Take me there." He says very slowly.

"What do you mean? Just in that general direction?" The longer I look at him, the more of a nightmare this is. He has modifications on his teeth. He has to. There is no way those are real. Where his canines should be, he has long fangs. And he's wearing freaky contacts. Yellow colored eyes with vertical pupils... Everything about him is giving me pause.

I need to leave. Even if it means walking home and calling a tow truck tomorrow, This guy is giving me a bad feeling. Each second that passes, I feel more unsafe here.

"Yes. Take me there."

"Um, my car is stuck in that ditch." I point across the field of snakes.

He blinks slowly, a dead, cold expression in his strange yellow eyes. When he stands, all the snakes suddenly move. They lower their heads, almost as if they're bowing. At least fifty snakes are sitting in the dirt crater with us, bowing their heads all at once. Again, I'm no snake expert, but this seems unusual.

"Are - are you seeing this?" I gape at them.

He doesn't respond. When I turn to look at him, he's standing. My body jerks, and my instincts kick into overdrive. I need to get the fuck away from him right now.

My limited options make this mission a failure before it starts, but I do it anyway.

Sprinting as quickly as I can, I make my escape. Dodging snakes really slows me down, though, and I'm barely able to make it out of the dirt before he tackles me to the ground. A full body, all of his weight tackle that lays me out.

"Do not run. You won't make it far." He growls against my ear. There is a slight, almost imperceptible hiss in his voice.

Running was a bad idea. He's angry now, and to make matters worse, the snakes seem agitated.

"I'm sorry, I won't run." Not yet, anyway, not until I have a clear route to escape.

He drags me toward my car. "This is for transportation?" He looks disgusted.

"Yes." I feel defensive of Rhonda. She's thirty years old, give her a break. "I crashed."

"We will find another."

I'm kidnapped and forced to participate in grand theft auto.

Headlights shine in the distance, and relief washes over me. I'm saved!

Down the lonely stretch of road, a semi-truck is driving toward us. The seconds that pass feel eternal. He's still gripping my arm painfully tight, and the snakes have followed us to the roadside.

The driver pulls his truck to a stop on the other side of the street. His brakes hiss, and the engine whirls loudly. "Are you alright?"

"Oh, I-"

In one second flat, with no warning whatsoever, the truck driver is flat on the ground. Screaming, I stumble back watching in slow motion terror as the poor good samaritan is beaten to a bloody pulp.

I'm not sure if he's dead or alive when the monster sets his sights on me.

"Come." He's not out of breath or disheveled at all.

I hesitate. After seeing what he just did with such ease, I know I should just go with him. He was able to take that rather large man down with one hit. I don't want him to turn that on me.

"Come." The hiss is back.

My legs feel like they're about to give out as I walk toward the truck.

"Take me there." He points in the general direction of the sky to the east.

"I don't know how to drive a big rig!" I'm shocked. He expects me to hop behind the wheel of this thing. Under absolute circumstances, I wouldn't be able to drive this truck, but after being kidnapped and watching him beat a man to death, I'm definitely not going to be able to drive this truck.

"You will drive it." He takes a step toward me, and it's enough to have me nod my head in agreement.

"O-Ok, I'll drive it."

I'm not going to give him any reasons to hurt me.

The cab of this truck is huge. There are knobs and switches, radios, buttons, screens, and shifters. I have no idea how to start this.

My hands shake so violently that I can barely turn the key. "Um, I…"

The gear shift is easy enough to spot, but when I move it into 'drive' nothing happens. "Oh, god." I panic. "The break. I don't know how to release the break."

His hand comes to rest on my shoulder, not a comforting touch but threatening. "Figure it out."

"Ok." I can do this. My life depends on it.

My eyes flutter closed, and I take a breath. Searching the dashboard, I find a few options. I'll just try them until something happens.

Three buttons later, a light changes from red to green beside the drive gear.

"I've never driven anything this big before." I creep toward the center of the road. This thing is a beast and having him stand over my shoulder, breathing down my neck, is making it much harder.

The sun is rising in the sky as we drive past my apartment. I would give anything to be inside the safety of those shabby walls right now.

Biting into my lip and blinking excessively, I hope to hold back my tears until I'm somewhere safe.

If I'm ever somewhere safe again.

Maybe it's the fact that I'm unsure about whether or not I'll be around to see this tomorrow, but everything around us is brighter and more vivid.

I've never wanted my life more than I do right now.

CHAPTER 3

The only positive here is that I'm so afraid that adrenaline is coursing through me. Under any other circumstances, I would have fallen asleep at the wheel.

"How old are you?" He asks out of the blue.

"Twenty-six." I peek nervously at him without turning my head.

"And you are female?"

"Yes." Where is he going with this?

"Very good."

My heart rate speeds up. "Why is that very good?"

"I find myself in a precarious situation. You might be able to assist me."

"Assist you, how? I thought I was already assisting you." I can't take my eyes off the road, but I can feel him looking at me. When he lets out a low hiss, I nearly veer into oncoming traffic.

Swerving back into our lane, I look at him, waiting for an answer.

"I believe Riven Adder would like you."

"Who is that, and why?"

"Yes," he hums quietly. "You will do."

Do what?

With a white-knuckled grip on the wheel, I focus my attention on staying in my lane rather than the gnawing anxiety in my stomach.

In the distance, pulled to the side of the road, I see a highway patrol vehicle. He might be running radar on people's speeds. I hope he is.

Gently, I press my foot down on the petal, accelerating slowly.

I'm trying to have the increase be so smooth and gradual that he doesn't notice that I'm doing it. After seeing what he did to the truck driver, I don't know what a police officer would be able to do for me, but it's worth trying.

"You have accelerated, why?" He picked up on the slight change immediately. I moved between sixty and sixty-two, and he felt it.

"S-Sorry. I didn't realize." I ease off of accelerating, my soul dying a little bit. This isn't fast enough to get pulled over.

We whiz past the officer, and my lip trembles—the only show of emotion I will allow. Looking in the large side mirrors, I watch him fade as we continue down the road. Any hope that we will get pulled over shrivels up.

Someone has to have found the truck driver now. There should be people looking for this truck. Where the fuck is everyone? We should be surrounded by a swat team right now. No one is going to save me.

"Is the sky clear enough here?" Desperation is sinking in. My heart rate won't slow down, and my pulse is pounding in my ears.

"No."

He doesn't offer anything else, so I continue driving.

There is a fledgling sprout of hope in my chest that he will let me go when we get to whatever destination he deems right. I've been agreeable, I have done what he asked. He has no reason not to let me go.

"You know, I can tell the police that you had blonde hair and blue eyes. I'll tell them that you had a rose tattooed on your arm. I'll lie for you to throw them off your trail." I wonder if everyone in this situation says this. Obvious lies.

When he starts to laugh, I feel sick to my stomach.

"Your authorities will not be able to reach me where I'm going." He is so sure, it makes me believe him.

"I really need to go to the bathroom." I squirm in my seat, both from the actual need for a restroom and from the fear that he will see this as an attempt to run. "There is a rest stop coming up; can I pull over?"

"You may."

My tiny bud of hope grows slightly. If I can signal to someone at the rest stop that I'm in trouble, that might be my only chance.

My hands tremble as I pull off the highway. There are a few cars and other big rigs here.

"I'll be right back."

He smiles, a sinister spine-chilling chuckle rumbling in his chest. "Do you take me for a fool? I will accompany you."

"Oh, right." Of course.

Slipping out of the truck, my eyes scan the area. Please, someone notice me.

Each step toward the bathroom feels like a missed opportunity.

The bathrooms are one concrete building divided in two. The doorway to each is nestled inside a small, walled-off area. Once I walk in, unless there is someone already inside, I'll be alone.

As we reach the door, my mind still reeling with the possible ways this might play out, he shoves me inside.

He slams me into the wall, paying no attention to whether or not the bathroom is occupied. I press myself into the tile, trying to create space when there isn't any. I hate the feeling of his body against mine.

When he leans in, I freeze. My mind instantly starts to withdraw. Protective instincts are taking over to help me get through this.

He nestles his face into the crook of my neck and inhales.

"The King will be very pleased with you." His voice makes my skin crawl. His breath hits my skin, and I want to disintegrate. "Do what you need to do." He releases me. "Hurry. We are close now."

For the moment, I will focus my attention on how grateful I am that that didn't go where I thought it was going to go. Whatever he meant by the king will be pleased with you, I have to push that out of my mind.

In the stall by myself, I take a few deep breaths. I have to keep myself calm. If I'm too panicked, I might miss the only opportunity to get away from him.

The window has bars on it. I can't climb out.

Then an idea hits me. When we get to the truck, if he lets me walk to my side alone, I will run the length of the truck. When I reach the back, I can decide what direction will be best. It might not happen, but if it does, I'm seizing the chance.

Outside of the bathroom, there is a small crowd gathered around the bathrooms, staring at the ground.

"It's the damnedest thing." One of the older men laughs. "They just came right up here, all three of them together!"

"I've never seen anything like it!" Another one laughs.

Snakes. Three of them sitting perfectly still on the ground with their heads in the air.

"I'll kill all of them." He whispers into my ear. "Don't try anything."

In the small gathering, there is a woman with two small children. Shit.

Nodding, I follow him past the group toward the truck. My heart breaks when he walks me, ever the gentleman apparently, to my side. Opening the driver's door, he smiles, waiting for me to climb inside.

The next hour is a blur of frantic thoughts. We're going to have to stop at a gas station soon. No matter what, I cannot get back in this truck once I get out.

"Pull off of the road here, drive over to that hill." He points to a hill in the middle of a field.

"That's where we're going?"

"Yes. It's perfect."

Can he read my mind? Every time I have a thought or an idea, he seems to intercept the plan before I'm able to even put any of the steps in motion. There is no time to think of another plan. I'm going to have to take any opportunities as they come. It might be for the best.

Driving the truck off the road is a bumpy experience. First gravel, then long grass. I push until we're stuck.

"We'll walk the rest of the way." He opens his door. "Hurry."

Alone in the truck, I pause. The wheels are well and truly stuck in this field, but I decide to do the only thing I can think of. Jumping over into the passenger seat, I pull his open door closed and hit the lock.

If he can't get into the truck eventually, he'll give up, right?

Grabbing the handheld radio, I start pushing buttons, trying to figure out how to call for help.

A voice comes through the radio, another driver is calling for a warning about a speed trap. "Hello?" I hold down the button and frantically yell. "Please, help me!"

The next voice is just someone thanking the first driver for the warning. They can't hear me.

There's a sound outside of the door, like the handle being pulled. I breathe a very short-lived sigh of relief when the door doesn't open.

With the next breath, the door is wrenched from the hinges, the metal bending and cracking before giving way completely. He tosses the door aside and climbs up. "Defy me, and you'll regret it."

Sliding out of the cab behind him, I'm numb. He just ripped the door off with his bare hands.

"What are you?" I whimper, staring at the gathering of snakes in the field.

CHAPTER 4

"The general will be here soon. A distress call is met with utmost seriousness. We will not have to wait long." He looks skyward.

"What are you?" The volume of my voice grows slightly as my frustration starts to become unmanageable.

"I am a Fen Warden." His chest puffs with pride. "We are the best of the Ophidian races."

None of that made sense to me.

"I- I don't know what any of that means."

"Ah," he smiles softly. "You will."

That sounds like a threat. Before I can ask any more questions, a whooshing sound stops me.

A sleek silver pod comes down from the sky. I can hear myself screaming, but it's not registering that it's me. I turn to run, but he grabs my arm. Fighting is useless, but I do it anyway. I pull and yank, but his grip is like a vice around me.

He drags me into the pod, and I drop to the floor. I'm on my hands and knees with my neck bent downward. I can't lift my head. The force of pressure holds me down, like someone is pressing me into the floor. The dizzying vertigo sensation of shooting straight up makes me lightheaded.

Slowly, the grinding force eases up enough for me to sit upright.

There are two of them now. The new one has a shirt on to match his pants. From his collar, I can see tattoos on his skin as well, fading into his scalp. They are scales too, but they are the most vivid turquoise color. They look more like body paint.

He turns around, and his eyes mesmerize me. Hypnotic blue, so light they're almost clear against his tan skin. The blue scales wrap around his head at his temples, then fade into white hair.

If I thought the first one was scary, there aren't words to describe him. I'm so deeply unsettled that I feel my stomach tightening, and I'm sure I'm going to be sick.

"Who is this?" He stands, an oily smile stretching across his lips. He has the same long fangs. The hiss is more prominent in his voice.

"You know, I never caught her name." He laughs.

He moves toward me, his movements are so graceful, he glides over the ground. "What is your name?" He takes my face in his hand.

I can't respond. The word, my name, is on the tip of my tongue, but I can't say it. His crystal eyes are making me dizzy.

"I'm General Hydriss. Welcome aboard our humble cruiser." There is a hiss in his voice that makes me feel very small and afraid.

"I brought her for Riven Adder." My captor growls.

The general laughs, but his jaw clicks. "Why would you give away such a pretty treasure?"

"I need favor. I escaped a prison transport. He isn't going to pardon my crimes for nothing. Maybe she will sweeten him up."

"You murdered six of his guards. You think a gift is going to make him more lenient on you?"

"It is worth it to try. I could keep her until he inevitably finds me, then I will offer her as leverage." He looks like he's considering his options.

"You could give her to your general as a way to apologize for being caught on your last mission." The general sniffs me, the same way he did. "He won't forgive your transgressions so easily, but I will."

He takes my wrist, wrapping his hand around it. With one yank of his arm, I'm standing flush against his body. "I want her."

"General, I need her. She very well could be the only bargaining chip I ever get." They talk about me like I'm an object, not a living woman sitting right here listening to all of this.

"Give her to me." He tucks his head into my neck, and his fangs scrape my skin. "We can get you another one for Adder."

"I want to give him that one."

They sound like children fighting over a toy. I don't know anything about this Riven Adder, but here and now, standing with the general, I think I'll take my chances. He can't be worse.

"Adder won't appreciate you the way I will." He whispers to me.

Turning my head to escape him, I catch a glimpse of what is happening outside of this pod I'm in. We're flying through space like we've been shot out of a cannon, hard and fast. We're far beyond anything I recognize. Outer space.

For a moment, just a split second, I consider finding a way to throw myself out of this thing. Surely, falling through the vast emptiness of the atmosphere would be better than staying with them.

I catch my captor looking over his shoulder at us, a hard, angry look on his face.

"She is for Adder." He stands slowly. When he turns, I know what's about to happen, like a premonition, I can see the whole thing. Scrunching up my face, I brace for impact.

He grabs the general, who loosens his grip on me too late. I fly across the room with them. I hit the ground so hard that it knocks the wind out of me, and I can't catch a breath. Choking and gasping, I crawl out of the way of their brawling.

Clutching my chest, I sit beneath the control panel, watching madness unfold. The pod rocks from side to side as they wrestle on the floor.

This is it. This is how I die.

They fight forever, wrapping their bodies around each other. Squeezing and strangling. It's brutal.

The general is coiled around him so tightly that his eyes bulge. A sick feeling rises in my throat.

He's dying. Right in front of me, I sit motionless and watch it happen.

The general's mouth opens, his jaw unhinging unnaturally to open much wider than it should be able to. His fangs grow—at least an inch—and he plunges them into his neck. I didn't have any love for him—I hate him in fact—but the look on his face— the terror and pain—is burned into my memory forever. His eyes flood red, all of the blood vessels bursting at once. He gives one final moment of struggle, one last effort, grabbing the generals arms and trying to yank them from around him. Then the light goes out. I see it leave him.

His body goes limp, and the general releases him, dropping him to the floor like discarded trash.

"Now, where were we?" He smiles, licking his bloody lips.

CHAPTER 5

O n the floor behind us, my captor is starting to melt. His body, or what once was, is now a puddle on the ground.

I can't stop looking at it. It's so disgusting and horrifying, I can't stop turning around to see if it's actually there.

It started with his eyes, slowly, they started to ooze. Things only got worse from there. Now, there isn't really any part of him that is identifiable.

"That's just my venom." The general looks over his shoulder to see what I'm staring at.

"Venom?" I watch a bit of liquified person roll across the floor.

"You know, you never did tell me your name." He ignores my disgust.

"It's Demi." I swallow down the urge to gag. How did I get here?

He hums, "That's lovely. It suits you."

I don't thank him for the compliment. I've never hated my name until right now.

In front of us, the darkness starts to fade from black to blue.

On the horizon, we're approaching a strange, swirling current in the sky.

"Almost home." He points to a screen with several holograms of planets on it. "Welcome to the belt."

The transition into the current is rough. The pod shakes violently as we burst through, and then the air around us is instantly calming.

Holding onto my seat, I fight the urge to scream. Every time I think that I'm at the bottom of this hellhole and that there is no possible way for things to get worse than they are, they get worse!

There are three planets, almost in a straight line, one after the other. They are very different, at least from this distance. The first is a beautiful blue, like crystal clear water. There are lush green land masses dotted throughout the blue. We fly over it for so long that I wonder if we will ever reach our destination.

At some point, despite my fear, I fall asleep. My body just gives out. So much adrenaline for such a long time has left me drained. I've felt the maximum possible quota of fear and anxiety. Now, I just feel numb.

When I wake up, we're still flying. The ground below us is mountainous and green. It's beautiful. Like a rainforest. But I can't look at it.

Hunger gnaws in my stomach, and my head spins. I don't remember the last time I had water. Closing my eyes, I try to make the dizziness stop.

"I- I need something to drink." I hear myself talking, but it sounds muffled, and I'm not sure if I'm actually saying words. "Help."

I feel a sharp pain, and I realize that I'm now horizontal. Forcing my eyes open, I'm face-to-face with the melted goo that used to be a snake monster man.

Groaning, I try to sit up, but my body isn't cooperating. I don't know how much time passes like this, lying here on the floor.

When I'm lifted off the ground, I almost start to laugh. My life—my real, awake reality—is a nightmare.

Two more of the men, with the same scally tattoos and hypnotic eyes, are carrying me out. The humid air hits me immediately, and I feel nauseous all over again.

We're under a canopy of mossy trees, and as they walk, the sloshing sound of water moves around us. My arm, too heavy to hold, falls down, hanging. It brushes against wet grass and water.

Everything here is too warm. I hate it.

I'm set down too roughly on hard ground. At least there aren't the remnants of a dead person all over this one, so I guess it could be worse.

"Perk her up." I recognize the general's voice. "What fun is a toy when it's unconscious?"

"Let me die." I groan.

"See!" He barks out a laugh. "She is going to bring so much amusement to us here!"

Letting my head rest on the ground, I breathe in the sticky air. My lungs feel fuzzy, like there is cotton in my mouth each time I inhale.

"Here, drink." A voice cuts into my consciousness. As much as I want to spit the water back at them, my body won't let me. Survival instincts are kicking in.

I gulp down the lukewarm water. I don't even care that it tastes odd, and there are grainy particles of sand that grit against my teeth as I drink. I'll be grossed out by that later. I drink until I think I might not be able to keep any more of it down.

"Tie her up in my hut." The general orders before walking out the door.

I'm lifted up again, thrown over someone's shoulder, and carried out the same door. This time, I'm able to open my eyes enough to look at the thick, soupy, swamp we're in. As far as the eye can see, it's just marshland and trees.

"Welcome to the Fen." The man holding me like a sack of potatoes adjusts, bumping me so that my body bounces.

We had to go to the swamp? The other planets we passed, the beautiful ones, what was wrong with those?

He walks toward a small, raised hut with a thatched roof. It's overgrown with moss and falling apart.

The inside isn't much better.

"Get on your knees." He drops me on the ground.

"What?"

"Knees. In the corner." His eyes flicker.

"Wait, listen." I put my hands up. "I-"

The feeling of his open hand making sharp contact with my cheek shuts me right up.

"Get in the corner."

Dropping to my knees, I let him manhandle me into position. He ties my wrists together, then loops that knot through a chain hanging from the ceiling. There are worn areas and scratches on the flood, and the chain was already here.

I'm struck with the horrifying realization that I'm not the first person he's tied up here.

No matter what happens, I'm getting out of here. This hot, horrible swamp is not going to be where I die.

I will get out of here. The general can't kill my spirit; I won't let him.

CHAPTER 6

Yanking against the chain, I struggle to slip my hands out of the restraints. Holding my hand as tightly closed as I can, I try to pull it through the ropes. I almost have one hand free.

The door to the hut slams open, and the general staggers in. He looks drunk.

"There she is." The hiss in his voice is more prominent now.

He starts to strip his clothes off. I don't mean to look, but the turquoise scales cover his whole back. I'm not sure if they're tattoos or a part of his skin.

He sits on the cot beside where I am tied up. "My little treat." His fingers hook under my chin, forcing my head back. "Why shouldn't I get something for all of my efforts?" He huffs. "I picked him up! I made the journey to retrieve him when he got himself in dire straits! And what do I get? Nothing!" He seems to be getting more worked up. "Riven Adder is the king, but I am the general! I rule over the Fenlands! I train the Fen Wardens! I raised that ungrateful bastard! I taught him everything he knew, and he couldn't think of giving me a gift?"

When he stops ranting, we make eye contact. I don't know

how to play this, but it seems like he is feeling underappreciated. Maybe I can play to that.

"Being a ruler sounds difficult." I fake interest. "How do you train the Fen Wardens?"

"The task is not for the faint of heart; I'll tell you that much!" He leans against the wall. "In twenty years, I have done everything asked of me. Since the great wars, I have stood firm and unwavering. Whenever the Fen Wardens were called upon, we answered! Ready!"

"Twenty years, wow!" I hope that my acting is good enough to fool him.

"Yes! This was once a position of respect! Being a Fen Warden was no small thing. If we had support from other nests, we would have won, and I might have become king! I would have had the backing!"

I have no idea what he's talking about. Wars, nests—any of it —but I smile and nod along.

"Riven Adder." He growls, his eyelids taking longer to reopen each time he blinks. He grumbles, complaining about different people and things, until he finally goes silent.

Frozen, I sit, unmoving, watching him breathe.

When I'm sure that he's asleep, as carefully and quietly as I can, I pull my hand out of the rope. It takes a layer of skin off with it, but I hardly notice.

As soon as my other hand is free, I crawl across the floor, looking over my shoulder at him, until I reach the door.

He hasn't moved.

It looks like he's dead, but I don't think I'm that lucky.

My whole body is shaking, coursing with equal parts fear and adrenaline as I slowly open the door. It creaks loudly, like a squeaky front porch screen door that is more rust than anything else.

Holding my breath, I open it just enough to slip out. My heart thunders in my chest.

Without looking back, I run as fast as my legs will carry me. If it kills me, I'm going to get the fuck away from here.

The soupy swamp water sloshes around my ankles, getting deeper until I'm up to my knees. Sinking down so that I'm chest-deep in the thick, slimy water, I hide behind a clump of tall grass. I don't see or hear anything from his hut. I think he's still asleep.

In the distance, there are lights flickering over a splintered wooden dock. It's old and crumbling, but there are several pods on it.

From here, I can see at least five men loading things into one pod, directly in the center of everything.

Moving slowly and quietly, I try not to let the mucky water make sounds as I wade out into the marsh. I can climb up, I hope.

As I get closer, I can hear them talking. I know immediately what they're talking about. Me. And my liquified captor.

"He killed him?"

"Ever since we lost rank, he's been on edge."

"He should have known better than to bring a gift for Adder. Hydriss is obviously going to see that as a slight."

"The girl might have been worth it, though."

"I hope he lets us have a bit of fun when he's done with her."

My stomach rolls.

Pulling myself up onto the wooden posts below the dock, I wait. It's probably not a good idea, but I don't see any other way. I'm going to sneak into that pod.

At this point, I couldn't care less where it's going, as long as it takes me away from here.

Slowly peaking my head up, I plan my next move.

"That's everything." One of the men, with brown scales and yellow eyes, closes the bottom hatch. "We need to get out of here. If we're late, the buyer will leave."

"Hydriss will kill us if we mess up this deal." Another one agrees.

It's now or never.

Crawling onto the dock, I crouch behind a pod, waiting for him to turn around long enough to run inside.

"Maybe you'll find a female to bring back with you!" Another one laughs.

When they start to laugh and joke, I use their loud noise and distractions to run inside. This pod is slightly smaller, but I can still squeeze under the control panel and hide inside the cramped area between the back of the console and the wall of the pod.

The sound of footsteps inside the pod nearly has my heart stopping. I'm afraid he's going to hear my heartbeat. It's so loud in my ears.

Two of them are seated at the controls. I could reach out and touch them.

His legs stretch out beneath the console as it begins to buzz. The whirring sound is much louder under the controls.

The same horrible, dizzy vertigo sensation takes over my senses. We're airborne.

Closing my eyes, I count in my head, trying desperately to hold on for a few more seconds, then a few more.

When the feeling starts to fade, I focus all of my attention on just surviving this. I'll worry about everything else later.

CHAPTER 7

T ime is standing still.

I don't know how long we've been flying, but it feels like days. It hasn't been—likely only a few hours—but sitting here waiting for whatever comes next is unbearable.

We started in the dark; at some point the sun rose, and we're still traveling.

I'm stuck in limbo. I can't do anything, and I don't know what's coming next.

The men I'm with, from what I can gather, are on their way to an illegal, unsanctioned weapons deal that will have major consequences for not only the two of them but all of the Fen Wardens if they are discovered.

What wrong choices have I made in life to wind up here? What horrible atrocities could I have possibly committed in this life or any other to deserve such a cosmically large, karmic bitch slap?

As I contemplate the fact that nothing in the universe is the way that I thought it was just one day ago and how even if by some miracle I make it home, my life will never be the same again, I'm hit with that horrible sense of vertigo.

We're moving downward.

My heart is in my throat. This is it. All the waiting is over. Whatever is about to happen is happening now.

The whirring comes to a slow stop, and all movement ceases. We're on the ground somewhere.

"Let's unload before he gets here. I want to minimize the amount of time we're around his guy." One of them says.

"He's weird, right?" The other one chimes in.

Their voices fade, then return, then fade again as they pull cases of weapons out of the pod.

After several minutes of silence, I stretch my legs out beneath the console. I can't see anything aside from a patch of green grass beyond the open door.

Crawling out from my hiding place, I listen for any indication that they are nearby. Complete silence—not a sound anywhere. Then, suddenly, chaos.

From every direction there is screaming, whirling, shouting, and gunfire.

The pod rocks, a pinging sound echoing through it as tiny holes poke through one side. Beams if light spread across the floor, entering in through the newly formed openings.

Crouching behind the console, I cover my head with my arms. Not that it will do much good, but it's the only thing I can think to do.

One of the men runs into the pod, huffing and puffing and shouting every expletive I've ever heard and some I haven't.

The door isn't even closed as we start to lift off the ground.

From where I'm seated, I can see the trail of blood on the floor.

"Fuck!" He shouts. "Fucking close!"

There is damage to the door. It won't close.

He yells again, and the pod shakes and leans hard to the left. More holes come through the side, and I'm left with no choice. I have to move. At this point, I don't think it really matters if he knows that I'm stowing away here.

Jumping up, we make immediate eye contact. He screams,

and we start to spiral out of control. We're not very high off the ground, so it only takes a second to impact.

This is the worst day of my life.

Sitting in the wreckage, I look around and wonder how the fuck I'm still alive.

The pod held up surprisingly well. It almost doesn't seem like it just slammed into the ground from the air.

"What the fuck are you doing in here?" The man sits up, lunging at me.

Jumping up, my ankle and knee hurt, I think they might be sprained. It doesn't matter. I run. As fast and hard as I can, I run out the half-open door into the grass.

There are several men approaching the pod as I hit the ground.

The sight of me startles them enough to give me a time to run into the dense treeline. We aren't in the marshes anymore. This place is beautiful. If I had a second to stop and look around, I'm sure I would actually like this place. It's stunning. Lush green grass covers the ground, blue, cloudless skies stretch across the horizon, and mountains in the distance look like something from a postcard.

My thighs and lungs burn, but I push myself further. Only when I physically can't take another step do I finally slow down. A trickling stream cuts through the trees—this seems like the best place to stop if there is one.

I haven't seen or heard anyone.

I can only assume that they deemed me unimportant enough to let go. I don't believe for a minute that I outran them.

Sitting down on the rocky waters edge, I run my fingers over the smooth stones. The water is cold and shallow all the way across.

Washing my face and taking a drink, I close my eyes and try to calm my breathing.

Everything hurts, probably a mixture of being thrown around

in the crash and running at full speed for much longer than I've run in years.

Pulling my shoes and socks off, I examine the blisters on my heels.

"Fuck." I put my feet in the water, the cold instantly helping. I wash my severely bruised and scraped wrists too, hoping for anything to soothe them.

A throat clears behind me, and I stumble to my feet, slipping on the mossy stones beneath the water.

The man behind me puts his hands up. "I'm not here to hurt you."

"Please, just leave me alone." I don't even try to get up from the water. I'm too exhausted.

"What's your name?"

"Demi." I sigh.

"Are you injured?"

This question surprises me. When I look up at him, really looking at him for the first time, I'm taken aback.

He looks different than the others I've seen. Very obviously serpentine but different. His copper skin gleams in a lone ray of sunshine, cutting through the canopy of trees. His tattoos are much more subtle than the others. The scales on his bare chest fan up over his shoulders, and I can see them on the sides of his neck.

He has fangs, but he isn't being creepy with them—they aren't pressing into his lip; he's not licking them—they're just there.

"I'm fine."

"Are you sure?" He looks at me like he knows I'm lying.

"I'm fine." I straighten my shoulders. Maybe he's just trying to suss out if I'm injured enough to be an easy kill. Don't snakes eat things whole? The thought makes me feel sick.

"How did you get here?" His voice is so... nice. It's low and raspy but soft.

"I was kidnapped."

"By the Fen Wardens in that transporter?"

"No. Not them." I'm not sure what is happening. Maybe it's his voice or the genuine concern in his face, but I break. "I was just driving home from work and I saw him. I thought it was an accident or something. I tried to help him! So much for being a good samaritan! He forced me to drive him, and then he made me get into his pod! He wanted to give me to Riven Adder because he killed someone and he wanted favor! Then the general—Hydro—or something like that decided that he wants me instead! And he killed the other guy. He melted! He chained me up in his hut, but I escaped. I snuck onto that pod, transporter, whatever, and then it crashed because, of course, it would crash!" By the end of my rant, I'm pacing and sobbing. "I just want to go home!"

I didn't realize he was coming closer until we're standing toe to toe.

"He was going to give you to Riven Adder?" He takes my hand gently, turning it to look at my wrist.

"Yes."

"Come with me. Let me see if I can help you."

"Are you going to hurt me?"

"No."

For some reason, maybe it's just the inability to fight anymore, I follow him.

CHAPTER 8

F ollowing him through the forest, all of the events of my life that could have led me to this moment come into my mind. It doesn't add up. What wrong turn did I make?

This place, the forest, might be the most beautiful thing I've ever seen. The trees are tall and wide, they look older than time.

Every so often, he looks back over his shoulder at me, probably to make sure I'm still following him.

I shouldn't be. This is insane. But I don't know what else to do.

He's different from the others. Still completely terrifying but not creepy. He doesn't make my skin crawl.

He's a different kind of scary. There is a kindness in his eyes, but there is cunning behind it. Where everyone has seemed so open about their thoughts—about the things they wanted to do to me—he hasn't expressed any of that. I'm not sure how to interpret it. Is he not saying vile things because he's not thinking them, or is he hiding his intentions? It's impossible to tell.

This might be the reason that he scares me most of all.

I can't trust him.

Whenever a ray of sunlight comes through the canopy of

trees and lands on him, his skin glows. An iridescent shimmer ripples in his copper colored tattoos.

He walks through the forest with ease, an unusual grace in his movements.

My steps are loud, leaves and twigs crunch beneath my bare feet. He doesn't make a sound. Every move is fluid and silent, he never trips or stumbles.

"Do you need help?" He watches me struggle.

"No." Every part of me hurts but I don't want his help. The distance we have between us is working just fine for me.

"Are you sure? It looks like you're in pain."

"I'm positive." I wipe the sweat from my brow. "I can make it."

"If you change your mind..."

I let out a relieved breath when he turns around. I don't like looking at his face.

Each step is a victory. If we don't get to wherever we're going —and fast—I won't make it. After several minutes, we're barely moving. The time between steps is growing. My stride isn't just slow but unnatural—step, pause, step, pause. It's become so excruciating I'm barely containing a sob with each step.

"Demi." The velvety timber of his voice sets me on edge. He's too smooth. I can't let him disarm me. "Let me help you. I can see that you are struggling. You're injured."

"How much further?" I would rather walk on two broken feet than get closer to him than I already am.

"You ran a long way. We still have a way to go."

My chest heaves, and I crumble. I was keeping myself going by telling the lie that our destination is only a few steps away. Now that I know that we're not close at all, I can't continue.

He scoops me up in his arms. I want to protest, but I can't muster up the strength. Resting my head against his shoulder, I feel myself drifting in and out of consciousness as he walks. His skin feels strange, not like mine at all. Cool to the touch and firm, I can feel the tattoos, slighting raised, as if the ink is an outline. I find myself tracing them with the tip of my finger absent-mindedly.

It feels like something I might recognize, but I don't know from what. I'm not even sure if I'm actually awake, if this is a dream, or if I'm hallucinating all of this. My eyes are so heavy, the pain and exhaustion robbing me of the shrewdness I need most.

"Here we are." The slightly raspy quality to his voice and the hiss at the end have me scrambling out of his arms.

"Wait, what is that?" I gape at the pod sitting on the ground in front of us.

"We are not far from the capitol. If you would rather I walk you there, I can, but—"

"No, I just wasn't expecting to have to get into another one of those." I swallow down the panic that's rising up in the form of bile in my throat.

As we enter the large pod, the three men already inside stand from their seats.

"Bring us back to the capitol." He nods to them. I take the opportunity to quickly move toward the small set of empty seats.

All around me, everyone jumps right to work.

"Here." He offers me a very heavy crystal oval.

My hand trembles as I hold it.

"You drink it." He explains, and I catch sight of his fangs again.

"Oh, right."

This is a solid. I don't know how to drink it, so I just continue to hold it.

"Bring it up to your mouth like this." He guides it upward to my mouth. The tip creates an opening as soon as my lips touch it.

"Oh." I gulp down the cold, refreshing water. It's much better than the sandy river water from before.

Over the end of the bottle, I see a city on the horizon. It's built into the trees like the most incredible stained glass tree houses ever built.

Abandoning the water, I step toward the window to look as we approach. It's futuristic and modern, but there are elements of nature incorporated into everything. The platform we land gently down on is made of a slab of wood so large I can't imagine what the tree looked like.

"I will bring you to the infirmary. They can treat your feet." He reaches for me.

"I'll walk." I recoil from his touch. My body instantly rages against that decision, but I don't care.

He nods, taking a step back.

Every person we pass looks like him. Serpentine and slightly inhuman. Their strange eyes follow me as I follow him.

"Why are you helping me?" I pluck up the courage to ask him.

"It's my fault you're here. It's the least I can do."

"I don't understand." We enter into a pristine white room.

"I am Riven Adder. The King over all Ophidians."

CHAPTER 9

don't know if this is his fault. Did he ask for gifts? The history and culture here are completely unknown to me. It could be that they go around abducting people for him all of the time - I could be one of many.

Whatever fear I felt before has been turned up tenfold. It might be everything added together to create this overwhelming, paralyzing sensation, but I feel myself starting to shut down.

"Are you really going to help me?" I force myself to look into his eyes, hoping for a clue. I need something solid to stand on.

"I am."

He's not human. I can't read him at all. Is he lying? Maybe. None of the cues I would normally see are present on his face—he's holding eye contact, not fidgeting or nervous. That doesn't mean he's being truthful, though—maybe he's just an excellent liar.

He tries to help me onto an exam table, but I brush past him and climb up on my own.

A woman—a snake, alien, monster woman—comes to stand in front of me. "I am the kings Physic. I will bandage your injuries. I can see your feet and ankles need attention, and your face is bruised. Do you have any more injuries?"

Where to start? Everything hurts.

"My ribs hurt." I whisper. I wish he would leave. My eyes are trained down to the floor, but I can feel him watching me, and it's making me more nervous.

Too many thoughts are racing through my mind.

With a surprisingly gentle touch, she cleans and bandages my face and feet. I hardly notice it—I know she's touching me and standing over me—but I can't focus on anything. When she starts to wrap a bandage around my waist, everything is amplified.

I can't seem to slow my breath. The room is warm, but I'm trembling. A heavy weight has settled in my chest, and I feel lightheaded.

"Are you alright?" Her voice sounds muffled and far away.

Dropping down off the table, I stumble away from her blindly. My vision is blurry, and my stomach churns.

She grabs me, her hand wrapping tightly around my arm. Thrashing my body, I try to escape from her grip.

"Let her go." His voice is like a beacon in the dark.

"She'll hurt herself."

"Demi?" His voice surrounds me. It's hard to hear him. The tone of his voice is being drowned out by the sound of blood rushing in my ears.

I feel myself falling, but I never hit the ground.

"What's happening to me?"

Pinching my eyes closed, I try to make everything stop spinning. Instead, the room continues around and a round, but now I get the added bonus of terrifying images in my head. My captores eyes bulge before blood starts to pour from his open mouth. The general's teeth embedded in his neck. Liquified remains roll across the floor, creating puddles.

Covering my ears with my hands, I try to escape it, but I can't.

Every breath gets harder to take. I struggle, gasping to fill my lungs, but the weight in my chest is growing. It's so heavy now it feels like it's breaking my ribs.

Hands on my shoulders shake me, but I don't open my eyes.

"Demi!" My name sounds far away and unfamiliar—I hardly recognize it. "Open your eyes!"

"No!" I scream. "No. No. No."

This can't be real. All of the horrible, painful, vile things I've seen aren't real. The truck driver's lifeless body on the ground. The snakes. So many snakes.

There is a sharp sting in my neck, and I kick my legs, fighting against whoever is holding me. "Don't kill me! Don't bite me, please!" I wait for the venom, for the pain.

"Open your eyes."

"I'm scared." I sob, clinging to something silky in both hands.

"I know, but you're safe. Open your eyes." The gentle voice coaxes.

Peeking them open, I lose track of everything. All I see is copper colored light, I feel it, like the sun's rays on my skin.

"You're alright, Demi." A voice cuts through my frantic, racing mind. For a moment there is calm—my body stops fighting—and I float, drifting away.

"I'm alright." I hear my own voice saying before I start to feel loose and relaxed, like my body is wrapped in something soft and warm.

"You're alright." The voice is soothing.

It's hypnotic.

One by one, from my tense shoulders down to my toes, my muscles turn to jelly. My fingers release whatever I had clenched in my hands.

"There you go. You're safe, Demi."

"I'm safe." I hum, my eyelids fluttering. I feel safe.

Copper swirls around me, like a kaleidoscope of warmth. I'm awake; I know I am, but this feels like a dream.

"Where am I?"

"This is my home."

"What planet is this?" I giggle. "I've never had to ask anyone that before." Can dehydration present as drunkenness? I haven't had anything, but I feel the telltale lightheadedness of too much alcohol.

"The planet actually doesn't have a name. This is the royal court." He explains.

"I want to go home." I whimper, sadness creeping to this strange state of nothingness I feel.

"Where is your home?"

"I'm from Wyoming."

"I'll find it." There is a promise in his voice, an earnestness that I believe suddenly.

"Ok." I let my eyes close.

What an unusual feeling. I'm still awake, but it's as if I'm caught—stuck—in the soft, hazy moment before sleep. I'm just there, in limbo. It feels nice.

Spreading my hand out, I run my fingers over the smooth surface I'm lying on.

"Rest. We will figure everything out when you're feeling better." His hand skims over my cheek.

"Ok." I let myself stretch out. In the back of my mind, it occurs to me that something is wrong. Where did the fear go? This peace I suddenly feel is all wrong, but I can't stop it from settling into my chest.

CHAPTER 10

was drugged. There is no other explanation for this.

Why am I so calm? Why can't I stand up? I'm awake, but I'm in a dreamlike stupor. Enough clarity has come back to me for my brain to put that much together. The longer I lie here, the more clear it becomes.

"What did you do to me?" My voice sounds comically small and weird to my ears.

"We only calmed you down. Your heart rate was dangerously high." His voice is distorted too. "You couldn't catch a breath."

"I don't like this." I struggle to move my heavy limbs.

"While you are lucid but still under the effects of the sedative, I would like to ask you some questions. I do not know your species. What are you?"

"What am I?" Maybe it's hubris, but I can't believe he doesn't know what humans are!

"Yes, I have never come across your kind before." His voice is clearer now.

"I'm human. What are you?"

"Ophidian."

Someone has said that before. Ophidian. My mind is scattered like ash blown in the wind. It seems like I'll never be able to recollect all of the pieces.

The natural capacity of my brain to bring information together is not functioning. The pieces I am desperately holding onto in my mind are floating around, not connecting to form a larger picture.

He is Riven Adder, the king. The king of what and who? I feel like I should know this.

"I'm confused about everything." I stare at the nothingness behind my closed eyelids.

"I know." His voice is reassuring to me now—like a tether that keeps me from floating away completely. It's odd to be so fully and deeply afraid of someone but also comforted by his presence. "It will get better."

I have doubts.

There is no rhyme or reason here, no time. Has it been a minute? An hour? A day?

Taking a breath, I think about things that I know are real. Things that I'm completely sure of.

My mom's name is Beth. I graduated from Glenrock High School. My boss' name is Marcy. I have three unpaid parking tickets.

Before I was sucked out of my life and brought here, I existed.

As my senses come back to me slowly, I know that I have to keep my guard up. If he's not really going to help me—if this nice guy routine is just an act—I can't fall for it. Whether I ever make it home or not depends on it.

"You said before that General Hydriss wanted to claim you for himself?"

Just hearing his name sends a shiver down my spine.

"Yes." My mind goes to a place I would rather forget. Chained on my knees in his hut.

Through this horrible ordeal, I've considered myself extremely unlucky, but in this one case there might have still been a little bit of luck on my side. I don't even want to allow myself to consider all of the horrible things he might have done to me if he hadn't fallen asleep instead.

I can't focus on it for too long because it starts to pull me down into an unending spiral of frightening scenarios.

My eyes blink open finally, my body functioning in sync with my brain again.

Copper colored hair and concentrating eyes. He's sitting beside me, his fingers swiping over a screen in his hand.

He looks up at me over the top of the device. "Oh, you're awake."

"Was I asleep?" It never felt like it.

"You were." His brows furrow. "Does your species have another name? I can't find human anywhere in any database."

"What?"

"I cannot find anything about you in any system. Human and Wyoming are not coming up anywhere." He looks annoyed. "Are you a new species? Or a slave race from the outer rim of the ecliptic planes that would not have much information ?"

"I'm from Earth." I don't remember telling him that I'm from Wyoming. Everything since the crash feels hard to remember—like it happened a long time ago and I'm trying to recall it. "I don't know what the ecliptic plane is. I'm from the Milky Way." I know that is right. We are taught that in school, but for some reason, saying it right now feels stupid and wrong.

"I see." He starts to furiously type something against the screen of his device.

He sets the screen down on his lap and rubs his hand over his face before letting out an irritated sigh.

"There are no results for that either. Can you tell me anything about your planet? I will pull up a map of the known systems. Maybe you will see it." He taps the screen again, and the wall beside my bed illuminates with a map of space. It looks like a video, but not. It's moving past me, as if I were standing in the center of it.

I wish I had paid more attention during earth and space science. Planet after planet whiz past and I don't recognize anything.

"Um, Jupiter." I blurt out with no context. My brain is still sluggish.

"Jupiter?"

"It has rings around it. It's a planet near earth that I would recognize." I stumble through an explanation.

He hums and begins to search through his databases again.

"This?" A planet appears on the screen before me.

"Um, no. That's not it. Also, try Saturn." I cringe. "Saturn is the planet with the rings around it." I'm going to go ahead and chalk this up to all of the trauma.

"Saturn." He nods, no judgment in his expression or voice. "Is this it?"

"No." The pit in my stomach is growing. The big, brilliant blue planet surrounded by reddish rings is not one I recognize."

"The Fen Warden Viris was being transported to a prison planet for crimes against my guard. General Hydriss is allowing his wardens to run amok. They are causing chaos and committing crimes in several galaxies. Viris killed his transporters and stole the cruiser. I can only assume it is on your planet, but we cannot get any tracker readings. I do not believe it would be a smart idea to ask Hydriss for assistance in this matter." He looks tired suddenly.

Viris. So that was his name. It suits him—cold and sterile.

"We will find your home." He cranes his neck to catch my gaze. "We will."

CHAPTER 11

"**D**o you feel well enough to walk?"

When I don't answer, he looks up from the screen. We've been studying for hours and haven't found anything even remotely like earth.

"Until we are successful in locating your home planet, we will give you a room here. Unless you would rather stay in the medical wing."

Every option feels like the wrong one. He hasn't been creepy even once, but I can't shake my fear. None of the kind or reassuring things he has done are helping.

Wiggling my toes, I check to see if my body will cooperate.

"I think I can walk." I drop my legs down over the side of the bed.

The room was bright white and sterile, but just outside the door, it's warm, rich, and beautiful. The wooden paneled walls and the soft sunlight give a much different feeling.

As I follow him out of the hallway and outside, hobbling slightly on my bandaged feet, I stop, awestruck. In pain and afraid for my life, I forgot about this.

This place.

Each step seems to be taking me further from reality. We are at ground level, standing just beside a massive tree trunk—that we exited from. The medical unit was tucked inside of it. I've never seen such a large tree. Above us, the branches grow for miles, holding up several buildings that wrap around the entirety of the tree or that seem to grow out of it. A staircase wraps around a tree trunk leading up as far as I can see. Several buildings cling to the sides, built right into the tree, connected by stairs and bridges that lead to more trees and buildings.

My mouth hangs open as I take it all in. Every direction has something incredible to see.

The cobblestone streets are quaint, lined with planets and businesses. It looks like a fairytale version of a bustling city. Except instead of cute fairytale creatures—bunny rabbits and elves—there are snake people with frightening eyes and scales.

"This is my home," he leads me toward a crystal glass building twisting around the trunk of another huge tree. The staircase that leads to the carved double doors have guards standing watch. It looks like fifty people could live there with room to spare. "You will be staying here." He directs me toward a cluster of buildings further up the street.

"Riven!" A woman's voice purrs. "Where have you been?"

"Phaedra." He opens his arms to her, and she gladly nestles herself between them.

Phaedra is stunning. Long and lean with a mass of white hair gathered on top of her head. Her rich onyx skin contrasts so deeply with her hair that she is almost hypnotizing to look like.

"I've been looking for you." The hiss in her voice is more pronounced than in his.

"Sorry, love. I lost track of time." His arm is wrapped around her waist, holding her close to him. His gaze moves to where I'm standing uncomfortably.

"Oh," she gasps. "Is this it?"

"Yes, her name is Demi." He makes the unnecessary introduction. She doesn't care what my name is. I've spent all of thirty seconds with her, and I can see that. She called me 'it.'

"Oh, how strange." She untangles herself from him and steps in front of me. She takes a limp piece of my hair in her hand, studying it. "Does it speak or?" She tilts her head. "Look how small it is!"

"She speaks." His lips tug upward slightly, but he doesn't let himself smile fully.

Indignation blooms in my chest, growing roots rapidly. I hate them. How condescending and demeaning.

She hums, taking my face in her hands. "I understand why Viris wanted to give her to you. She makes an excellent gift."

"I am returning her to her home planet." He gently takes her hand and pulls her away from me.

"A pity." She pouts her lower lip, her fangs pressing into it.

I can't put my finger on it, but she reminds me of something —someone. Not her looks—I've never seen anyone as beautiful as her, ever. But there is something in her voice and attitude that I recognize.

"I have her set up in the guest suites." He starts to walk, leading her in the direction he pointed to before.

"A suite?" She sounds shocked.

Where should I stay? A jail cell? I roll my lips into my mouth to keep quiet. She could kill me—likely with little to no effort.

Crossing my arms over my chest, I feel small. I was stolen from my home, chained up, threatened with abuse, I saw a man murdered, and I lived through a space shuttle crash. Today has been, without a doubt, the worst day of my life.

As I walk behind them, I notice for the first time how everyone here is watching us. I'm trying to convince myself that they are staring at them, not me.

But I know they're looking at me. I can tell by the curiosity on their faces. I'm a spectacle.

Breathing a sigh of relief to be out of everyone's view, I follow them through a door carved into the tree.

"I had this room prepared for you." He opens a door at the end of a long hallway.

The room is beyond what I was expecting. Small, but clean and minimal. It's not outwardly fancy but there is something luxurious about it. Quality is in every detail.

Doubts creep into my head again. The others have been so vile, it doesn't seem possible that he is decent. And yet.

"Thank you." My voice wavers and cracks.

"I have one more possible lead in tracking down your planet. I will reach out to my contact and see if we are able to find it." He gives me a reassuring nod before leading Phaedra out of the room.

"I think you should reconsider, Riven! She might be worth something! A unique creature like that would fetch a high price at auction! Collectors would give everything they have for something like her!" She whines, completely unconcerned about the fact that I can hear her.

"Phaedra, I will find a way to send her home." His voice sounds so stern, I almost want to believe him.

"Fine. What a waste." She grumbles.

As soon as I'm alone, I search for a place to hide. It's only a matter of time before she wears him down with her asking and whining. Eventually he's going to give in.

CHAPTER 12

n the midst of all of this turmoil, I sit in the small, cozy bedroom, staring out at the bridge just outside of my window.

It's made of sleek silver metal that has been almost completely grown over with vines. It almost looks like it's made out of plants. It's beautiful. Everything is. The architecture, the trees, the sky. The blue is so bright and clear.

My mind is reeling, running between a million different thoughts, overlapping, melding together, it's chaos. I can't think of anything clearly. As one thought pops into my head, I can't even work it out before another is there. But I'm just sitting here. My body is too tired to move. From the outside, no one would know that my insides are a mess.

A deep and inescapable hopelessness washes over me like tsunami-sized waves. I'm under the water being held down—there is no escape.

How am I ever going to get home? They can't even find it. I described earth to him, and he still couldn't find it. I'm feeling pretty small and insignificant right now.

In my little corner, curled up against the window, I watch the sun set in the distance. Or, is it the sun? It's obviously not our sun. I'm so far from home I'm not even in the same galaxy.

My head feels heavy on my shoulders, like it weighs a hundred pounds. Leaning it against the wall, I watch the snake people outside. They aren't so different from us, not really. They are all tall and slim with long, lean muscles. The similarities stop there, though. Each has a very distinct and unique color and pattern to their scales. I can't be sure, but I believe they're real—not tattooed on.

They are living their lives, walking, talking, and going about their days. I watch pods like the ones I've been on, land and take off. Strange hovering motorcycles zoom back and forth over the bridges.

All this time, I didn't really believe in life outside of humans and earth. I didn't really care about it. Maybe there are 'aliens', maybe not—it's none of my business.

Now, it's very much my business in the worst possible way.

Across the room, the door swings open and a man walks in. My instincts kick in, and I jump up, taking a step toward the table. I'm not sure how much damage I could do with one of the heavy, crystal water bottles, but I'll try.

Phaedra steps into the room behind him. "Here it is." She announces excitedly.

"Remarkable!" He strides toward me. "I've never seen anything like it!"

I grab the bottle, holding it, ready to hit him if he steps any closer.

"A feisty little thing!" He laughs, wide-eyed excitement on his face.

"Riven wants to send it home!"

"What?" His eyes go wide, and he looks panicked. "You can't do that! It's extraordinary!"

"She." I clear my throat. "I'm not an 'it.' I'm a woman." My voice shakes, but I have to say it. If they call me 'it' one more time, I'm going to do absolutely nothing about it because there isn't anything I can do. But I still had to speak up. If they start to see me as something living and real, maybe they will feel guilt about harming me.

A big smile spread across his face. I'm not sure what his meaning is or if his intention is to be creepy, but that is all I'm getting.

"Phaedra! Murious!" Riven comes into the room. He looks surprised to see them here. "I was not informed of your arrival. What-"

"Riven! I came as soon as you called. I have never heard of a human, and in my travels, I have never seen a planet like the one you described. I will give you anything you ask for her. I want her." He says it very calmly.

What is wrong with them?

"Murious, I will find her home and release her."

Release me, like a captured animal.

That's what I am to them. A novelty. An exotic animal to own or collect.

It's as if I'm suddenly struck by lightning. The realization hits me so fast and hard, it sends me to my knees.

My stomach tightens into a ball, cramping and bringing up the water I've been drinking since arriving here. Unceremoniously, right in the middle of the floor, I heave until I'm empty.

Normally, I would be embarrassed about this, but I can't find it in me to care right now. In fact, I hope they're grossed out. Maybe they will leave me alone.

I can't ever go home.

If they find out where earth is, everyone will be in danger.

What's to stop them from coming to collect more people? All of the people? The thought of my mom and friends being chained up in the general's hut makes me feel sick again.

"What's wrong with it?" Phaedra looks disgusted.

Good.

"Call the medic." Riven moves her toward the door. She

leaves without fighting, and I feel relieved that she's not watching me anymore. "Murious, please go."

He starts to whine, but Riven turns with a flat expression, his tall posture imposing his irritation without the need for words.

"Fine." He grumbles. "I am not underestimating what I would give you for her. Anything, name it and it's yours. She would be the crown jewel of my collection."

Collection of what? I shiver involuntarily.

"Go, Murious." He hisses.

When we're alone, he pulls a silky silver blanket from the untouched bed and drapes it over my shoulders.

"Are you ill?"

"Please, you have to stop telling people about me. I know you called him to see if he could help me get home, but we have to stop the search. If anyone finds earth..." I sit up on my knees, begging him. "No one will be safe."

He takes a step back, a strange look on his face. His head tilts slightly to one side, and a line forms between his brows.

This might be the best view I've had of his face.

There is something snake-like about his bone structure. His eyes are stunning—not just in their beauty, but I actually feel stunned as I look at them. Hypnotized.

"What are you doing to me?" I whimper. "Why can't I look away?"

"I am calming you." His soothing voice is warm and soft.

"Stop. Please." The words come out but they sound more like 'yes, please.'

"I will make sure that you aren't harmed. You are safe."

CHAPTER 13

linking my eyes open, I slowly sit up. I'm in a bed, wrapped in a blanket that feels both soft and alien against my skin. Time seems to have slipped away from me again—vanished, gone.

What did he do to me? The question pulses through my mind. I feel strangely well-rested, but there's a lingering fog in my head—the slight dizziness of a mild hangover.

I sit up fully, glancing around the room. It's clean and comfortable but very sterile. There isn't anything warm or welcoming. A bright light streams across the floor, coming from an open window. It's not the harsh light of the sun, but it's not the gentle glow of the moon. It's something in between, casting everything in a bluish light.

Crawling out from under the blanket, I climb out of bed and creep toward the window. I peek out cautiously, half-expecting to see something terrifying. Instead, I find myself staring in awe at the night sky. Two huge moons hang there, suspended above the trees. The closer one is so near that it almost feels like I could reach out and touch it if I just stretched a little farther. The other moon, slightly more distant, glows faint blue.

"Wow," I whisper, my breath catching in my throat. The

moons are perfectly round and full. It's like something out of a dream, too perfect to be real, yet here I am, staring at it with my own eyes.

A thought crosses my mind suddenly, out of nowhere, just popping up. What if I just left? Could I do that? Could I walk away from this place, this nightmare.

With a deep breath, I tiptoe toward the door and reach out for the handle. To my surprise, the door isn't locked. It swings open silently, revealing a dimly lit hallway.

I pause, listening to the voices that I can hear just down the hallway.

"It's not about wanting to keep her for himself," a female voice hisses, sharp and frustrated. It might be Phaedra, but I can't tell. "You know Riven. He has that over convoluted sense of integrity. He told it that he would make sure it got back to whatever primitive planet it was snatched from. Now, he won't back down." She sighs. "He tries my patience. Why should we lose sleep over finding a planet that is such a blip no one has even bothered to study it?"

My heart skips a beat at her words, the implications sending a chill down my spine.

Then, a voice that makes my blood run cold answers her, slithering and creepy. "I will take her with me when I leave."

That's got to be the other guy—Murious.

My breath catches, and I press myself against the wall, every instinct screaming at me to stay hidden. I don't know much about this place or Riven, but so far, he seems to be the best of them. I would rather be here with him than anyone else.

"Apparently there are wardens coming from the outer sector to see it," she continues, her tone full of disdain.

At this point, it feels like it might actually kill Phaedra to acknowledge me as anything other than a curiosity, an "it" that she doesn't want to deal with. I've corrected her before, and so has Riven, but it's never a mistake on her part. It's deliberate.

More aliens are coming to see me, to gawk at me.

I don't know what to do. Maybe running really would be the best option. Slip into the jungle and disappear.

It would be better to try than to stay here, waiting for Phaedra to 'accidentally' kill me.

Pulling the door closed softly, I pace around, walking through the moonlight on the floor, over and over again.

As I look around the room, my eyes dart frantically over every surface, desperate to find something, anything, that could help me escape.

Water. That's all I have here. A single glass bottle is sitting on the table.

Looking down at my feet, I remember, I don't even have shoes.

But there's no time to worry about supplies. I know that if I don't leave right now, at this very moment, I might never get the chance again. Who knows what wonderful things Murious has planned for me once he adds me to his collection.

I don't want to find out.

My heart pounds, adrenaline pumping through my veins as I take one last, desperate look around. Taking a deep breath, I clutch the water bottle to my chest and make my decision.

I'm doing this. It's now or never.

With a silent prayer, I take my first step toward the window. It opens easily, swinging out like a door, wide and clear.

Slipping down to the ground, I crouch, my bare feet in the dirt. Peeking through the flowering bushes, I hold my breath and watch for any signs of life. Minutes pass while I sit, frozen, too afraid to move.

The street that was so busy earlier is completely quiet now, eerily so.

With my heart pounding in my throat, I run out from my hiding place, crossing the street to hide behind a row of neatly trimmed shrubs. Each step brings me closer to my goal. I pass by tree after tree, the biggest trees I've ever seen—big enough to hold houses and buildings in their branches.

Eventually, the buildings begin to be fewer and farther between. The trees are just trees, and the cobblestone street is the only evidence of life.

With nowhere in particular to go, I walk along the edge of the road. Hopefully something will present itself to me—the perfect place.

With each step, I feel clearer. Fear is still rooted into the base of my neck, keeping me on edge, but the further I go, the easier it is to breathe.

In the distance, the end of the forest becomes visible. The trees on both sides of the road grow more and more sparse before they stop all together. The road dips down slightly, a downward incline.

The valley below stretches as far as I can see. Another city sprawls in all directions.

There must be hundreds of thousands of snake people living there.

My shoulders slump and my eyes fill with tears. I'm not giving up; this is just a setback.

CHAPTER 14

"Demi?"

The sound of my name, spoken in that smooth, unsettling voice, freezes me in place. My breath catches in my throat. I'm caught. I'm like a deer caught in the headlights—stunned and defenseless.

I didn't even hear him coming. Of course, I didn't.

He steps into view, circling around me. I brace myself for anger. But when his eyes meet mine, it's not fury that I find—it's amusement. The corners of his lips pull upward into a slight smile, and his eyes hold no fury.

"This is not the way to run." His voice is a mixture of kindness and authority. He gestures to the sprawling city in the valley. "You will not be safe there."

"I'm not safe anywhere." I struggle to keep my voice steady. The truth of those words settles heavily in my chest, and I have to fight the urge to let my shoulders slump in defeat. Should I tell him what I overheard? It was obvious from what I heard that he isn't a part of her plans. Could I trust him? Would he even believe me? If he did believe me, would he help me?

He studies me for a moment, his gaze penetrating as if he's trying to read my thoughts. There's a sincerity in his eyes, a quiet conviction that makes my breath hitch. "You are safe in my court, I assure you," he seems so genuine—he really believes that.

Rolling my lips into my mouth I choose not to say anything. I can't risk it.

A soft laugh escapes him, drawing my attention back to his face. The sound is light, almost pleasant, but the sharp glint of his fanged teeth turns it into something far more ominous. I can't help but flinch, jerking my head up to meet his gaze.

"Your scent led me straight to you," he shakes his head.

"My…" Heat spreads across my cheeks. "My scent?"

I'm too flustered to respond.

"You should not be walking on your injured feet." He touches my elbow gently. "Come back with me."

He's not asking, but there is a softness in his tone. It's not like I have a choice here. I'm alone, defenseless, and my body aches. It's not just my injured feet. It's my entire body. Every single muscle feels worn out and overworked.

I nod. "Alright."

As I walk behind him, I sniff my shirt discreetly. Do I smell?

Deeply humiliated, my mind fixates on his words. He could smell me? Somehow so strongly that he was able to find me. It's horrifying. I can't smell anything.

He didn't say that it was a bad smell.

It doesn't matter. Following my scent is so personal and intimate. I have to force the thoughts out of my head. Obsessing over it isn't going to do me any good.

"What is going to happen to me?" There isn't any harm in asking. Maybe he'll even be honest with me.

He sighs, his posture stiffening. "I have been going over it. We will have to find your home in secret. Then, I will personally return you without a crew. That way, I am the only one that knows the location of your planet."

"Hydriss knows. He picked us up there." Panic grips my throat like a vice. "He's going to go back!"

"Don't worry about him." There is a finality in his voice that both soothes and frightens me. He obviously has plans for General Hydriss.

I follow him silently down the center of the street I so quietly crept down just a few moments ago.

"I brought this for you." He walks ahead of me to where one of the hovering motorcycles is stopped on the side of the road.

"Um." I hesitate until I realize he didn't mean the bike but the contents of a small silver box. "Thank you." I open it carefully to find food inside.

I'm hungry, but I don't want to eat this. I've never understood a hunger strike until this moment. I have no control over anything, but I can refuse to eat. Putting this food in my mouth or not is one small power I still have—one thing I can choose.

Closing the box, I watch a line form between his brows as he quickly understands that I'm not going to eat.

"You are too weak as it is! You need to eat. You must be starved!" A hint of anger is mixed with the surprise in his voice.

This only makes me want to dig my heels in more.

He gapes at the willful expression on my face. "You are being stubborn to your own detriment! Eat!"

"No." I don't raise my voice, only my brow.

"Eat!" He takes a step toward me, his low, slithering voice sending a chill down my spine.

I don't know him. This kind of obstinate disobedience might anger him enough to cause him to lash out violently. He might choose to send me with one of the other men. He's been decent so far, but maybe this is his limit. No power—especially in this small measure—is worth being killed over.

Cowering back, I slip the lid of the box and take a piece of the food inside. My fingers tremble as I bring it up to my lips. "I'm sorry."

The rage slips from his face, and he opens his clenched fists. "Wait. I'm not going to hurt you."

I shove another piece of fruit in my mouth, looking down at his feet.

"Demi, stop." He steps forward. "I'm not going to hurt you. You need to eat for your health. I am concerned for your well-being. That's all. Don't be afraid of me."

I nod, taking another bite. I'm too afraid to look at him or to stop eating.

"Look at me," he urges.

Peeking up, our eyes meet, and I physically feel the fear leaving me. It's like a weight being lifted off of my chest. It's almost soothing.

"Wait!" I step back, breaking the intense eye contact. My heart hammers in my chest as I slap my hands over my eyes to cover them. "What are you doing to me? Stop!"

"Look at me! I'm helping you!" His tone is earnest, and his hands gently settle on my shoulders, grounding me.

"Helping me how? What are you doing to me? Why do I feel like I'm not in control of myself?" I jerk away from his grasp, panic clawing its way back into my mind.

"I am using my transfiction to help you calm down," he explains calmly.

"Transfiction? What the hell is that?" I close my eyes tighter, determined not to let him manipulate me any further. The idea of him tampering with my mind and twisting my emotions makes me hysterical.

"I am only controlling your panic. You—"

"No! Stay out of my head!" I scream, my voice trembling with a mix of fear and anger. My fists clench by my sides, and my nails bite into my palms. "Don't try to shrink my emotions down!"

He steps closer, but I flinch away.

"I didn't think it would upset you."

"Well, it does! I don't want you in my mind, controlling how I'm feeling! If I can't even control my own thoughts and feelings, what else do I have here? You can't take that away from me!" I need to make him understand.

For a moment, he says nothing. The silence stretches between us, heavy and oppressive, until he finally speaks, his tone softer, almost regretful. "I wasn't trying to take that away from you."

My harsh panting breaths hand in the air between us. He can manipulate my emotions? How many times has he done this to me?

"What is transfiction?" I try to stop the way my voice shakes.

"It's a gift. I can soothe away panic and fear."

"Please, don't do it again."

"I won't."

I don't know if I can trust him.

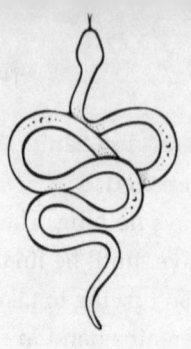

CHAPTER 15

Things are tense as we ride on his motorcycle back to my prison.

I would rather fly off the back of this thing than hold onto him, so I sit rigidly with my thighs as tight around the seat as I can make them. We're moving so slowly that it takes almost the same amount of time to ride back as it did for me to walk.

My aching feet are grateful for the seat, at least.

The road is busy now. People are awake and out living.

I've never been to Paris, but I imagine this is what it would look like if it were woven into the towering branches of colossal trees. It doesn't quite look real.

Everyone here is breathtakingly beautiful, yet their beauty is alien, almost too perfect with a touch of something not human.

They wear clothes that seem to defy gravity—draping fabrics that shimmer with iridescence, adorned with patterns that shift and change as they move. Their hairstyles are wild. Some of them have huge manes of curls, while others have sculpted their hair into shapes. And then there are their scales—glistening, vibrant patches of color. They range from black and copper to teal and red.

They are incredible.

A part of me is filled with awe at their elegance and grace, but there's also a simmering fear. Fear that is holding me at the base of my neck, squeezing.

They are not human—this is clear in every subtle movement. Yet, from a distance, they are human enough to be mesmerizing.

But up close, all of their features are just slightly off. Eyes too big and with vertical slits that make them equal measures terrifying and fascinating.

"Riven!" A sharp yell comes from somewhere above us as he stops the motorcycle beside the window I snuck out from. "We need you on the security platform, right now!" Phaedra screams down from an open panoramic window on the building across the street.

A man in a black military type uniform steps forward, his shoulders back and his body straight as an arrow. "Sir, Hydriss has sent a message. It's urgent that you hear it."

"Hydriss?" I accidentally blurt out. I know he wasn't talking to me, but I heard him anyway.

"Come with me." Riven gestures for me to walk across the street.

The guard narrows his eyes but doesn't speak. As I walk across the street, he's right behind me, stepping in time to stay just beyond the point of comfort, he's too close.

We walk in at ground level, through glass sliding doors built into a tree. Inside, it looks like any reception lobby in any tech building—it's sleek and minimalist with modern design. Two white stone benches are the only furniture in the huge room.

How did they make the inside of a tree look like this?

I follow him to a hidden door, an opening in the pristine white walls that leads us to a small glass room. An elevator?

We move upward, the floor disappearing from beneath the glass as we move higher and higher until it stops.

The door opens, and we're inside the room with Phaedra and several other uniformed snake soldiers.

I want to run and hide.

"Riven!" Phaedra jumps up in a panic. "Hydriss is coming! He wants his human back, and he's willing to fight you to get it!" She flings herself dramatically into his arms.

You would think that Hydriss was coming to hurt her with her theatrics.

"He wouldn't dare. If he comes here intent on fighting, he will find that I will not only rise to the occasion but that his disrespect will be the end of him." The hiss that I've heard in so many voices is now fully present in his. He's angry.

"See reason!" Phaedra looks horrified and on the verge of tears. "Send her back with him! We do not need war on our doorstep!" She snaps at him, peeling herself out of his arms. "This is foolish! Why would you-"

"I am the king!"

His voice booms over the room, silencing everyone.

"I am the king. I will not send her back to him because I said that I would not! He is disrespecting me, my authority, my crown! I will not stand by and allow it. Sending her back would be cowering to him, and I would rather my head roll from my shoulders than to allow General Hydriss to think, even for the briefest moment, that I fear him or that he has any power here. He can demand all he wants, but I will *never* give in to him. I beat him so badly in the civil wars that he should still be hiding somewhere, licking his wounds. The fact that he has so quickly forgotten his place tells me all I need to know. This time, I won't allow him to keep his life."

The room is so quiet I can hear him breathing—slightly labored.

Peeking up, I scan everyone. Phaedra is the only one looking directly at him. The soldiers are staring at the ground like they're afraid not to.

"Call a council." He snaps. "Play the message."

One of the men quickly leaves the room while another taps on buttons on a tablet.

Hydriss' face comes up beside me on the wall, a full-life-size image that nearly scares the life right out of me.

I jump out of my skin, and Riven grabs my arm, moving me behind him slightly.

"Start the message." He nods to the soldier.

Cowering behind him, I peek out enough to see his unhinged face up close to the camera. He looks even more terrifying now —completely unglued and hanging onto sanity by a very thin thread.

"That human is mine. I want her back." He hisses, ripping at his hair. "Give her to me or you will suffer the consequences. You think you can just do whatever you want." His voice is a sick, low rumble. "I will show you that you are not above me. You will learn it."

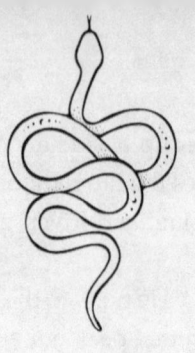

CHAPTER 16

The room is uncomfortably quiet.

After seeing that unhinged message, seeing the wild look in Hydriss' eyes, and hearing the feral snarl in his voice, it's no wonder they are afraid.

I can't blame them. If I were them, I would want to send me back too.

If they are afraid of him, I don't stand a chance. The only hope I can cling to is that Riven really is a man of his word and that the disrespect Hydriss has shown is wounding his ego enough to cause him to stand against him.

The smartest option, the way of least resistance, seems to be sending me back into his waiting arms.

The thought makes nausea coil in my stomach. I'm hanging on by the thinnest thread.

Riven has been silent. He hasn't uttered a single word in several minutes. His thoughts might be mysteries, but his anger is not. His jaw and his fists are clenched tight as his fiery eyes dart around the room, not looking at anything in particular.

The panoramic window collapses into the wall, allowing the room to be an open air gallery with sweeping views of the city. I've been staring out, watching the bridge in the distance. I can't go home - it would endanger everyone. They are probably already in danger; once Hydriss gets over the obsession with being slighted, he will go back and find someone else. I can't help but feel like I can't stay here either. I'm a danger to all of them.

I'm not sure why I care, but I do. Some of them might not be horrible.

"Is the council gathered?" His voice finally breaks the tense silence—low and simmering with barely restrained rage.

"Yes, sir."

Phaedra stands from the chair she's been pouting in. Her movements are sharp and agitated. She shoves past him, her shoulder brushing his as she storms out of the room ahead of everyone.

He watches her go, his expression unreadable. But there's a dangerous edge to his silence.

"Let's go." He reaches for me, tugging my arm.

The guards fall into step behind us. His long strides are fast and steady, unlike my clumsy, stumbling steps with wobbly legs.

We walk down long wooden hallways; the smell of the wood wafts through the air—the soft scent of oak.

We move in silence, down a level, and into a room that is identical to the one we just left. Only in this room, there are thirteen people seated in the high-backed chairs around the table.

Each of them has the same reaction when they see me, only the expressions vary a bit. Shock.

Some of their mouths drop open. Brows furrow. Heads tilt. Some of them audibly gasp.

"Riven," one of the women speaks softly, not hiding the shock in her voice. "What is this?"

I have never felt less wanted anywhere before.

"This is Demi. I-"

"I mean, why is she here? Son, this person should not be allowed to listen in on meetings with your inner sanctum." Her voice grows more stern with each word.

Now that she has mentioned it, their resemblance is clear. He looks like her.

"This involves her directly. Her life and safety are at stake." He shoots her a look that would have me cowering back.

She doesn't run for cover though, not at all.

"Her life and safety should be secondary to everyone else here." The biting edge in her voice is razor sharp.

Ouch. Hard to hear but not unexpected.

"The lives and safety of everyone here are my number one priority. She was taken from her home under the misguided notion that I would want her as a gift. If not for that, she would not be here at our court because of the role that I indirectly played in her abduction. I am choosing to ensure her safety."

All eyes in the room are on me, and with the exception of two of them, their disdain is clear in the way that they glare. I feel small.

"From this moment on, no one is to speak of her, except in the presence of the present company. We will not be reaching out to anyone to try to find her origins or home planet. From this moment forward everything will be done in house, and she will not be mentioned again."

Phaedra sighs loudly. "But, Riven, she…"

"No!" The calm chill in his voice shuts her mouth. "The more people that know about her, the more unsafe this becomes, not just for her but for everyone. If Hydriss really is stupid enough to try to attack, we will be ready for him. We don't want other fragile alliances ripped apart by curiosity; if word starts to spread about her, others may come to have a look for themselves and decide that they want her. We can fight Hydriss and win. We can fight several factions, but I do not want to deplete the resources or put our people in harm's way doing so."

Her jaw clenches, and she looks at me as if I am the one that snapped at her.

Wonderful. Another enemy.

She didn't care for me before; that much was clear, but now

the loathing in her eyes is palpable—violent, almost. It's as though something dark and primal has awakened in her, a hatred that simmers visibly in her eyes.

"We need to turn our full attention to Hydriss." His voice is cold and commanding, effectively ending the conversation about me. "I want him captured and imprisoned before he has the chance to strike again or return to her home planet to abduct more innocents. Once it's safe, I will personally see to it that she is returned home. Until then, she remains here, under our protection—as our guest."

They start to plan his capture, which should be very interesting to me, but the conversation is muffled and distant. It's hard to focus on their plans with Phaedra's gaze locked onto me, unblinking, as if she's trying to burn holes into my skin from across the table.

CHAPTER 17

A fter I was escorted back to my room last night, exhaustion hit me like a wave. I slipped under the covers on the bed, and sleep washed over me almost immediately. It was deep and dreamless, like falling into the abyss.

When I finally wake up, the room is bathed in the soft blue glow of twilight.

I think I slept for a full night and the next day.

Disoriented and thirsty, I roll out of bed. For the first time in days, I feel a sense of clarity. I'm more like myself.

Stumbling into the bathroom, curious, I investigate it. I haven't had the strength or interest up until this point to look around.

"Oh, my god." The bathroom is a masterpiece of natural elegance. The bedroom is minimal, but this is a sanctuary.

One entire wall is covered in a lush, living, vibrant green moss. It's soft to the touch and releases a delicate scent through the room. It's magical. Squishing my fingertips into it—it seems to breathe with me.

The shower is a gentle cascade from the ceiling like a summer rain, cool and refreshing. I fumble with the controls, trying to figure out how to make the water warmer, but after a few minutes I give up. This is fine.

The cool rain is washing away all of the tension I've felt in my muscles.

The floor is made of smooth, polished stones that my feet sink into. It's like walking in a river.

If I could just stay here forever, everything would be alright. I feel safe here, like I'm in a secret garden where nothing can hurt me.

By the time I finally force myself out, the sun has set and the double moons are hanging outside of my windows. There aren't any towels.

Letting myself air dry, I comb my fingers through my tangled hair.

Stepping out of the bathroom, I feel brand new.

"Demi." Riven's voice makes me scream. Unsure of where to cover, I spin in a circle before running back into the bathroom.

"What are you doing here?" I search for something to cover myself.

"I have been coming to check in on you. I assumed after such a long sleep, you would be hungry." He calls. "There are clothes here as well."

I stare down at my old clothes, soaking wet on the bathroom floor.

"Can you toss the clothes in here?" I squeak.

An emerald colored piece of fabric flies through the air, the soft, sheer material floating down into my hands. It's silky and cool to the touch. Slipping it on, I feel like I'm wearing a very fancy nightgown.

I hate it instantly.

Everyone here wears these beautiful, vibrant things, but I feel like I'm still naked. I feel like a child playing dress up.

Staring at myself in the mirror, I try to produce a scrape of confidence.

"Is everything alright?" He calls.

Gathering the extra fabric up, I walk out, my cheeks burning as I half expect him to laugh at how ridiculous I look.

"I thought you might have escaped again." He smiles. "Here, let me help you."

"With what?"

He takes two pieces of the fabric and ties them behind my back. His fingers touch my bare skin, skimming up my spine as he makes the dress less loose.

"Thank you."

"I thought this color would suit you." He moves effortlessly across the room. "Come, join me."

"Oh, you're eating too?" I fumble awkwardly toward the open seat.

"If you don't mind."

Truthfully, I would rather he leave. "S-Sure, of course."

We eat in silence until he sets his heavy marble utensil down. "What do you do on earth?"

"I'm a waitress. Temporarily. I'm saving up."

"A waitress." He nods. "What are you waiting for?"

"Um, I take food orders and bring people the food at a little diner." I'm guessing that isn't a job here.

He hums. "Do you enjoy this work?"

A hideous snort bubbles up in my nose. "No."

We get lost in shockingly easy conversation. I tell him about my job, my overnight shift and he tells me about being King. Our jobs couldn't be more different. Talking to him feels easy.

"And your family? Do humans have families? Forgive me, I usually research and prepare before meeting someone."

I don't mean to laugh, but the question is so strange. "Yes, we have families. I'm not super close with mine though.' I regret that more than anything now.

He nods thoughtfully and quickly changes the subject. "And your population and planet? Are they very small?"

"I'm not sure what you consider small, but there are about

eight billion people on earth." And out of all of them, somehow I end up here.

"That is not small by any means!" He looks shocked. "How have we not discovered one another until now?"

My knowledge of space and our exploration of it is limited, but I tell him what I know.

Slowly, I start to feel myself relaxing—not fully, but some. He seems genuinely decent. The more we talk, the more I can see it.

He isn't anything like the general. There is something regal about him. He's the king, sure, but it's more than that. It's him. He's captivating in a way that makes me wonder if he's still hypnotizing me.

My guard is still up, the high walls firmly in place, but I am enjoying talking to him. He's free and open with information about his people—the Ophidians.

"I am sorry that the council was so unkind. I should have known they would be and spared you that."

"Oh." I'm surprised by his earnestness. "Honestly, I get it. I'm bringing danger to their homes. I would probably say the same things they did."

"You are more understanding than you should be." His expression is confusing. He looks almost sad. "I will not allow Hydriss or anyone else to take you from here. I was under the illusion that you would be able to live safely here, but there is more danger surrounding you than I thought."

A bubble of nervous energy rises in my chest. A lump of anxiety that makes my throat feel tight. "Um, about that…"

Am I really doing this? I'm on the edge, looking over, but the ground is nowhere in sight. Do I trust him? Can I believe him?

Taking a deep breath, I steady my trembling hands. "That guy, Murrious, I overheard him. He's going to try to take me with him when he leaves."

For a moment, there is no reaction. I question if he heard me or not. But then he stands.

"I'll take care of this." His demeanor has completely changed. With confident, quick strides, he's gone.

Well, at least he believed me.

CHAPTER 18

can't be sure, but it feels like it's the middle of the night. My eyes sting, and my limbs feel heavy and tired. I slept for a whole day, but I'm ready for more.

Just as I slide into my bed again, snuggling in and finding the perfect spot, the door flies open.

Phaedra stalks into the room. She moves with a dangerous grace, her steps measured, shoulders tensed upward. She looks like a predator, ready to pounce. The frown etched into her features is deep, carved with a permanent rage that makes my heart rate shoot up.

I barely have time to react, a sharp gasp is all I can manage. I try to sit up, but she's faster than me. So much faster. In a blink, she's on me, her hands gripping my shoulders to pin me to the bed. The weight of her body presses down, trapping me beneath her.

Her eyes are wild. I brace myself, expecting the worst—a slap, a punch, something violent to match the fury in her gaze. But she doesn't strike. She doesn't even speak.

Instead, she leans down, her face so close that I can feel the heat of her breath on my skin. She never breaks eye contact as she lowers her head, closer and closer.

I'm sure she's about to bite me. To sink her teeth into my neck and fill me with venom like Hydriss did.

I'm about to be melted goo. This is the end. I brace myself, pinching my eyes closed tight, and I try to picture something beautiful. I don't want the hatred in her face to be the last thing I ever see.

But she doesn't bite me.

She sniffs me.

It's slow and deliberate, her nose brushing against my skin, inhaling deeply as if she's searching for something. The sensation sends a shockwave of revulsion through me. The memories I've fought to bury come crashing back. The general, his cold, calculating eyes as he pressed his nose into the curve of my neck, breathing me in. The thought of it makes my stomach turn.

"What was he doing in here?" She sits back enough to let her piercing gaze meet mine again. "I don't smell him on your skin."

"What?" I can barely sputter. She thinks she's going to be able to smell Riven on me? "Oh god, no, no, no! He never touched me!" As soon as the words leave my mouth, I remember that isn't exactly true. His finger skimmed my back as he helped me with the ties on the dress. She won't be able to smell that, will she?

"He's mine." The words slither out of her mouth with a thick, snake-like growl in her voice that chills me down to the bone.

"Ok." I nod quickly, my heart hammering against my chest.

Her eyes narrow. "What was he doing in here with you for so long?"

"We were just talking!" My voice wobbles.

"Talking?" Her lips curl and her fangs elongate. "Talking?" The word drips with disbelief.

"Yes, just—" I try to explain, but the words die in my throat when she moves her hand. It slides from my shoulder to my jaw, clamping down. The pressure is immediate, the pain sharp as her nails dig into my jaw, breaking the skin.

When I whimper, she smiles, a slick, sadistic grin as she presses harder. She's thoroughly enjoying this.

"What were you talking about for so long?" Her voice is low, almost a purr, but there's nothing gentle in it.

"He wanted information about Earth," I manage to choke out, I choose to leave out the other details. Something tells me she won't be pleased to hear about our heart to heart.

Long tendrils of her stark white hair fall forward, touching my face. Even they feel threatening, like they're reaching for me.

"You will not take him from me, you treacherous little beast." She growls.

"I won't. He doesn't want me!" I hope she believes me.

Her head tilts to one side, her eyes never leaving mine as she studies my face curiously. "What have you done to him?" Her voice is softer now, but no less menacing. "He is willing to risk upsetting his people to keep you safe. Why? What can you do?"

I don't understand what she means.

The nails on her fingers are fully embedded in my face. I feel the trickle of blood as it drips down onto my neck.

"Do you have some kind of gift? A talent or skill that he finds valuable? What are you good for?" She presses her nails harder, my jaw aching under the pressure.

"I don't." I force the words out. I can't take much more of her grip on my face. "I'm not valuable."

"So he's doing it for nothing?" She leans down, releasing my face and moving in to sniff me again. "He didn't even fuck you! He is truly getting nothing out of it?" Her eyes are wide and full of disgust. "This is worse than I thought!" She swings her leg up and over, climbing off of me. "He is throwing everything away for no reason!"

With one last look of disdain, she leaves the room, in a whirlwind, just like she arrived.

For a moment, I don't breathe. I just sit, bleeding, waiting for her to come back and finish. When she doesn't, I jump out of bed and run to the bathroom. Blood is running down my face, a little trail of drops hitting the ground.

Perfect little crescent shaped cuts in my cheeks, four on the right cheek and one on the left. The skin around each wound is tender and sore.

Feeling jittery, I manage to make it back to bed. Just because she didn't kill me this time doesn't mean I'm safe. She can come back at any moment.

As I slip into it, covering myself again, there is a tap on the door.

"What?" I practically cry. Please, no more for tonight.

CHAPTER 19

"It's me." Riven opens the door gently—slowly—as if trying not to startle me. He steps into the room with another tray in his hands. "I brought you this." He carefully sets it on the table. I think he thinks that this cautious approach will make me feel better—safer. But it doesn't.

Phaedra is probably watching, her terrifying eyes trained on me from somewhere in the shadows. She's going to come in here and kill me.

"There will be a guard in front of your room. His name is Verrin. I trust him with my life; he will protect you." His tone is resolute, as if the matter is already settled. "Murrious has been sent away on a research mission in the outer rim. He'll be preoccupied, out of the way. You are—" His voice stops dead. "What happened to your face? Who did that?"

I flinch at the sharpness in his voice. The tone switched dizzyingly fast. "Thank you for bringing Verrin. I appreciate it," I tread lightly.

His eyes narrow, and a low, dangerous hiss passes through his lips, sending a shiver up my spine. He steps closer, the concern in his gaze morphing into something darker, angrier. "Demi, what happened to your face?" he demands.

"I don't want to talk about it," my voice trembles despite my efforts to keep calm. I stare at the blanket over my lap, his gaze burns.

"Who?" He growls. "Tell me."

He must know. Who else would do it?

For a moment, the room is silent except for the faint sound of our breathing.

Shaking my head, I don't dare look up. "Please, let it go."

"You're bruised and bleeding. You were not in this state when I left you. Who did it?" He isn't going to let it go.

Peeking up at him, I'm met with his clenched jaw. He rolls his head before letting out a sharp exhale. "I am the king, and I am giving you an order. Who was it?" Each word of his question is punctuated with authority. It's not the volume of his voice that scares me; it's the tone - deadly.

He's giving me an order?

Despite my fear, I feel a sudden streak of defiance. I know that he could kill me very quickly and very easily. I should just give him the answer he's looking for, but I don't want to give it to him. He's been so kind, so insistent that I am safe with him, but at the first sign of noncompliance, he starts barking orders.

I'm glad I didn't believe him—I didn't trust him. I kept my guard up.

When I don't speak, he clenches his fists and storms out of the room. The door hangs open for a moment, and I catch a glimpse of a man in uniform standing outside in the hallway. Our eyes meet for a brief moment before the door swings closed.

He is head and shoulders taller than anyone I've seen here so far and absolutely massive. Red, green, and black colored scales in perfect vertical lines pattern his neck.

If that is Verrin, I don't doubt that he could keep me safe if he wanted to. Nothing is getting through him.

Sitting in the bed, I run my fingers over the fabric of the blankets. I feel so vulnerable again. Not that I ever felt secure, but at least he was on my side.

Phaedra is going to be his wife. I can't go around accusing her of things, not even if it's the truth. This feels very much like a rock and a hard place.

Alone in the room, I sit in the bed and stare out the window. Not very long ago, just a few short days ago, my life was boring. I wished for excitement, for something new. I would give anything to go back now.

I took it all for granted. It might not have been a thrilling life, but it was safe. I struggled to pay my rent some months, but I never worried about someone injecting me with venom from their teeth and killing me! I didn't realize that simple wasn't bad until nothing was simple. I should have called my mom more. I should have eaten more cheesecake. I should have gone on more road trips and told the whole town that Justin cheated on me. I tiptoed around, never making waves. I never did anything with the life I had.

The angry look on his face keeps coming into my mind. Sighing, I curl up in the bed and try to ignore the desperate, clawing, gnawing feeling in my chest. I want to go home so badly it makes me feel nauseous. The hopelessness is swirling around, twisting me in knots.

Another tap at my door turns my already anxious stomach over on itself, turning the dial on my fear up a few notches.

The door opens, and Riven steps inside. His shoulders are slumped down, defeated.

"Demi," he walks toward the bed, his usually proud strides nowhere to be seen. "I'm sorry. You are a guest here and not one of my subjects. I should not have spoken to you that way. Please, tell me who did that to your face."

He already knows. I can tell. He just wants me to say it.

"I think you already know who it was." I whisper, still too afraid to speak her name out loud.

He nods his head heavily.

"She was upset that you were spending so much time here. I think she thought something else was going on." Heat floods my cheeks. I shouldn't have even said anything. As soon as the words leave my mouth, I wish I could take them back.

"I should have seen this coming." His voice is soft as he reaches out to gently touch my cheek. He grazes my broken skin so softly I hardly feel it. "I apologize for this. It seems I am unable to keep my word regarding your safety. At every turn, I am failing you."

"What?" I don't understand why he's taking this so hard. "Wait, you didn't-"

Abruptly he stands, his purposeful steps carrying him toward the door. "I'll fix this."

CHAPTER 20

Fix it? Fix it, how?

My unease is so intense it's palpable. A crushing weight in my chest and a pit in my stomach. I can't escape it.

Something bad is coming.

Time passes, minutes ticking by into hours, but I can't sleep. I'm frozen here, lost in my thoughts.

For some reason, a conversation that I had with mom years ago keeps coming into my brain. I haven't thought about it in years, but tonight, it's heavy on my mind. I was six when my parents divorced. I hardly remember anything before that. I never really cared about the specifics, the how's and why's—they broke up, that was that. But one night, right after my thirteenth birthday, I asked her about it.

I remember the look on her face as she told me about it—why she finally left him.

It wasn't really sadness. To this day, I can't place it. She just always seems resigned to her life. It is what it is, and she doesn't do anything to change it. She only did something about it once.

"He never apologized." She actually laughed as she said it. "There were a lot of things wrong in that relationship, but it ended up being that. I just couldn't take it. He was unable to say sorry when he was wrong—it was like the words wouldn't come out. I knew that he wouldn't change. He would never take responsibility for the things he did. I had to leave."

After that night, we went on with our lives, years passed, it was pretty inconsequential in my life. But for some reason, tonight, I can't stop thinking about it.

Riven apologized.

In a weird way, it makes me feel safe—like I can trust him. My own father couldn't apologize.

A commotion out in the street rips through the silence. Someone is really unhappy.

I shouldn't, it's none of my business, but I creep toward the window to look out. As I sneak toward it, I recognize the screeching voice. It's Phaedra.

Abandoning the notion that I need to stay hidden, I run toward the window and look out, not trying to cover myself at all.

Riven and a group of three others are trying to calm Phaedra down. It looks like they are trying to coax her back into the building, but she is obviously refusing. I guess she wants to cause a public scene.

People are starting to gather. Despite the late hour, there are people peeking out from windows and doorways, watching just like me. She's screaming at the top of her lungs now, calling him names that I would never dare repeat.

Then, suddenly, she goes quiet. Whatever she's saying to him now, she doesn't want anyone else to hear it. His tense posture tells me it isn't good.

As she turns to walk away from him, he reaches for her arm, but she snatches it away.

I can't help but wonder if whatever they're arguing about has something to do with him 'fixing' the situation.

Phaedra holds her head high, her long strides like a model on the runway as she leaves him behind. Her eyes flick toward me.

I'm not sure if she knew I was here or if she just wanted to sneer in my direction, but we make eye contact.

Yikes.

Ducking down, I hit the floor as fast as my body will move.

She is definitely going to kill me.

The way her eyes locked onto me then flickered—I might be the thing she hates most.

"Demi?" A low, raspy voice from behind me makes me scream.

Spinning around, still crouched on the floor by the window, I'm met with the confused face of the mountain.

"Oh, hello." I clear my throat and stand on wobbly legs.

"I have been instructed to move you." His huge body takes up the whole doorway.

"Move me?"

"Yes, please come with me." He gestures his hand, waiting for me to come out into the hallway.

"You're Verrin, right?" I try to smile. Just when I was starting to get used to these snake people, he shows up.

If I saw a snake like him in the wild, there would be immediate alarm bells. The bright red and green in his scales seem to scream danger—poison and venom.

"I am." He nods curtly. Not very chatty, this one.

"Nice to meet you." I walk pressed against the wall, giving him as much space as I can possibly create between us.

He nods again but doesn't say anything.

As we step outside, he reaches for me, taking my hand and wrapping his body around mine, shielding me. Wordlessly, he moves me across the cobblestone street and into another building.

Inside, we're in a lobby with several other uniformed guards. They look like Verrin, large and imposing - stoic. I didn't expect them to welcome me warmly, but they're so intimidating.

One of them steps toward me aggressively, reaching for me, but Verrin stops him. "She is not to be searched."

"What? No one comes in without being searched, it's protocol. She could be concealing anything in-"

"By order of Adder. She is not to be searched, touched, or otherwise bothered in any way. Let us pass and leave her alone." He growls before pressing forward, his shoulder checking the other guard roughly.

He leads me through the group, everyone now staring at me with narrowed eyes.

I'm making friends everywhere.

We move up a spiraling staircase made of honey colored wood. The spindles in the banister are snakes, carved with such meticulous details they look alive. I have to move quickly to keep up with Verrin, but my eyes linger on everything as long as they can. It's beautiful.

"You will stay here." He opens a door to a small sitting room. "I will be right outside."

I turn to thank him, but he's already closing the door, leaving me alone.

Collapsing onto one of the chairs, I lean back, letting my heavy eyes drift closed. I don't know what's going to happen next, but I'm not excited to find out. Things keep happening to me—things I have zero control over. I just have to ride with it. I have no other choice.

CHAPTER 21

t's such a strange and uncomfortable feeling to be so far away from home.

I've been awake for hours, just sitting here in this room. I slept hunched over in a chair for the night, and my body feels it. My neck and back are tight, and the dull ache of too little sleep sits right behind my eyes.

Can I leave the room? Do I ask Verrin for food? I'm caught in a loop of uncertainty.

Verrin has been tasked with watching me, but I don't know what that really means. Did he volunteer for the job? Will I be bothering him if I open the door and make a request?

Instead of doing anything about my hunger and thirst, I sit here silently.

This room is starting to feel smaller by the hour. It's nice enough. The two oversized chairs are soft and comfortable. Not so much for sleeping, but for sitting, they're nice. There's nothing else here. Just four windowless walls.

Slouching against the back of the seat, I stare up at the ceiling.

A noise from outside the door catches my attention instantly.

Talking.

Leaning forward, I strain to listen to the low voices.

It's Riven.

I never expected to feel relieved to know he was near.

A light tap on the door is like a calming wave rolling over me. I know it's him by the knock.

"Demi?" He cracks the door open. "I have your new room prepared."

Something is off. He's upset.

Quickly following him, we walk down the hallway in silence with Verrin right behind us.

I want to ask him if he's alright but I don't know if I should. His shoulders are tense and a deep frown tugs his lips down. Even his walk is different, usually light steps have been replaced by fast stomping.

"You will stay here." He leads me into a room. When I gasp loudly, he turns to face me. I notice the unreadable look on his face, but I can't think about that right now.

"This is-" There aren't words. My mouth gapes open as I take in the details. It's like the bathroom from the previous room only on a grander scale. The beauty is so unexpected, I feel like the air has been knocked out of my lungs.

The walls are covered in lush moss that makes the whole room feel like I'm not inside of a room at all but wandering in a secluded cove. The air is crisp and clean, with sunlight shining in on all of the greenery. The smooth stone floor is soothing to my feet. All of the aches and pains, the stress, melt away.

In the far corner of the room, there is a large, round bed surrounded by a gauzy curtain. It looks like it belongs to a woodland fairy princess. Layers of cream and green fabrics are draped over the bed; they look soft and inviting, like sinking into a cloud.

"You like it, then?" He's still watching me closely.

"It's incredible." The faint smell of flowers and fresh air waft around me. "It's gorgeous."

"Good." He nods. "My room is just across the hallway. If you need anything, day or night, please, feel free to open the door. Verrin will still be there, standing watch, but you are free here, safe. You can leave the room if you wish to."

"Your room?" Everything he said after that was lost. "Is this your house?"

"It is."

Now I'm at a loss for words for a different reason.

"You will be safer here." His deep frown somehow deepens.

"Did something happen?" The threat from Hydriss was pretty bad, but he didn't move me. Something worse than that must be looming over me.

"No." He nods, but I think he's lying. "I have matters that require my immediate attention. I will be back to check on you shortly."

Admittedly, I don't know him at all. I can say with confidence that this is strange. He's never rushed away so quickly except after Phaedra hurt my face.

Pushing my hunger aside, I explore the room. It's the most enchanted place I've ever seen. Everything is soft and smooth, but completely natural. Above the bed, a skylight is open to the canopy of leaves above.

It's an indescribable feeling. It's not like being inside of a forest but inside of a plant itself.

It starts in my toes and moves upward. A wave, growing each second until I'm totally consumed by it crashes on me.

A painful sob rips from my chest, and my body crumbles to the ground, unable to withstand the weight for another second. All of the feelings I've been battling with and trying to hold in pour out—a dam splintering apart.

"Demi?" Riven's soft, concerned voice only makes everything hurt more. "Why are you crying?"

"I don't know." I cover my face in my hands. I don't want him to see it.

His arms wrap around my body, holding me against his chest. He sits quietly, comforting me until I have no tears left.

His chest rises and falls steadily beneath my cheek, the rhythm of his breath. This feels intimate—like something we should not be doing, but I won't stop it.

His presence is a quiet assurance, a fortress surrounding me and protecting me from everyone else.

"Do you know why I'm so intent on ensuring your safety?" His voice is low, barely above a whisper. His hand rubs gentle circles over my back. "It's your strength despite your vulnerability. You're alone, taken from your home against your will, and yet you still think of others. It's rare to find that kind of selflessness in a world that values only power."

I lean back slightly, I look at him—really allowing myself to see him. I don't cower back or let fear in.

He's beautiful.

In the way that nature is beautiful—in the way a snake is beautiful.

For the first time, I feel like somehow things might be okay.

CHAPTER 22

"Are you sure that it's alright that I'm here?" I ask again. Staying in his house is so personal.

"I believe it is the best way to protect you." He looks at me over the rim of his glass while he drinks.

"I just don't want to be in the way. Your home is-"

"My home is here for you to use as long as you would like to." He shuts me down, again.

"This room is incredible. I've never stayed anywhere this nice." Incredible doesn't even cover it. I can't think of words to tell him how much I like it.

"I'm glad." He nods, but his eyes wander toward the door. That's the third time in five minutes.

"Do you have somewhere you need to be?" I feel guilty for taking up so much of his time with my breakdown.

"If I leave, will you be alright?" He looks skeptical.

Oh, god. I'm embarrassed.

"I'll be fine. I'm so sorry. I didn't mean to keep you from anything." My voice is shaky and nasal from my congested nose.

"Don't apologize." A slight hiss of irritation is suddenly present in his voice that makes me flinch.

"Ok." I've done something to upset him somehow.

"Verrin will show you around. You don't have to hide here. Walk freely, no one will harm you in my house." He stands, pausing for a moment. "Are you sure you'll be alright if I leave you?"

"I promise," I try to force my voice to sound convincing. The truth is, I don't know if I'll be alright. The tidal wave of emotions that hit me came out of nowhere. I can't guarantee it won't happen again. I didn't expect this.

He doesn't move, he stands there watching me with an unreadable expression for what feels like several minutes. His gaze feels heavy, too intimate and personal, as his eyes roam over me. "Go with Verrin." He finally turns toward the door, but he still doesn't actually go through it. He lingers there, "I would like you to have dinner with me tonight."

"Oh, ok." I don't know what to say. He wasn't asking—that was a statement. I don't know if I have a choice here.

"I will see you then." He finally leaves, closing the door softly behind him.

I sit on the floor, staring up at the sky, and the branches of trees through the skylight, trying to process everything that just happened.

That was weird.

He comforted me.

I feel drained—not just tired but empty—like all of my emotions poured out with my tears.

"Are you prepared to tour the house?" Verrin pokes his head in the door.

"Yes," I smooth out my hair. I can feel that my face is swollen from crying. It's probably red and blotchy too. I can only guess what he's thinking right now. I'm sure it's not his first choice to give the weepy, emotionally unstable woman a house tour.

"We will start here and work downward." He waits for me at the door.

"Sounds great!" I smile. If I act normal, maybe he will forget about all of the wailing that I'm sure he could hear through the door.

"Here," he points to the door directly across the hall from mine, "is King Adders' room."

I haven't heard anyone call him that yet. It's weird. I know he's the king. I'm staying in the house of a serpentine alien king. Any of those things by themselves would be hard to wrap my brain around, but all of them together somehow I keep forgetting pieces of it. I'm barely hanging on with the fact that he's an alien.. He's also the king.

I am grateful when we walk past his room without going inside. I didn't think the tour would include a stop inside of the king's bedroom, but I'm still relieved to know for sure that it doesn't.

"This is King Adders personal collection of ophidian history." He pushes open a set of large double doors at the end of the hallway to reveal A room that seems like a mixture between a museum and a library.

"It's bea-" before I can compliment the beauty of the room. He is slamming the door closed and marching down the hallway. "Right." I jog after him.

Passing our bedrooms again, we walk down a grand spiraling staircase that leads to a warm, sunny foyer. Just like everything else, it's a mixture of wood and marble everywhere.

There are four sets of double doors, one in each corner of the room.

"These doors lead to King Adders working wing. His offices, meeting rooms, and security headquarters are here." Again, he walks past those doors without opening them, and we move into the doors on the opposite side of the hallway.

"The kitchen, dining hall, reception hall, and pantries are located here. I've been instructed to inform you that you may come here at all hours for food. There is always staff on site." His voice doesn't hold an ounce of warmth.

We walk quickly through the hallway, stopping to look inside the rooms.

Stunning.

The kitchen and dining hall specifically are like something out of a dream.

Both natural and modern, old and new, it's as if he built the rooms in the middle of an ancient secret garden. The rooms are so full of plants they feel alive.

"Here we have the gardens." He leads me across the foyer through another set of doors.

"Oh my god." My jaw drops open. The humid air clings to my skin as we walk into a jungle right in the middle of his house.

"And this way," he starts to usher me out.

"Wait, please," I can't leave yet. I have to look just a minute longer. "Is there a waterfall here?" I can't see it but the sound fills the air.

"There is." He points. "Follow this path through the trees."

"Wow." My heart skips. I will definitely be coming here to look around.

I hate to go, but I tear myself away. I don't want to make him wait.

"And lastly, this hallway contains the royal hall of records. It is similar to kind adders private collections, but guests are allowed to view this." He opens the doors and moves to let me walk inside.

It's much larger than the one upstairs but very similar. A warm library with artifacts and artwork on display. It's missing the coziness of his personal space. This feels more sterile and formal.

"If you are satisfied with the tour, we should return to your room. His Majesty's seamstress is waiting to take your measurements." Verrin stands straight, waiting for my response.

"His what?" I heard him, but what he said was so surreal that it needs to be repeated.

"A seamstress is waiting to measure you for clothing." His head tilts slightly, confusion over my reaction, I'm guessing.

"Ok, let's go." I roll my shoulders back and try to appear confident.

CHAPTER 23

"I've never seen anything like you." She walks around me, studying me. For fifteen minutes she's fawned over me. Mostly harmless, a few times she tried to look under my dress.

"What environment do you hail from? You don't really look suited to any I recognize." She looks puzzled. "You wouldn't really camouflage well anywhere."

"We don't really do that." I don't know what to say.

"Fascinating." She lifts the loose, limp strands of hair hanging by my face. "Riveting."

"I suppose I should begin. I've delayed long enough. I just can't believe it. Just when you think all of the species out there have been discovered, another one pops up!" She waves her hand and laughs.

Sidra, the seamstress, starts rushing around the room, gathering things and muttering to herself.

Every so often, she comes back to where I'm awkwardly standing, unsure of what to do with myself. She measures something or holds a small piece of fabric against my skin or hair. Then she mumbles more and scurries away.

This is a strange experience. She doesn't seem disgusted by

me, which is a pleasant surprise, but everything she does is so odd. I can only liken it to someone dealing with an animal that they're slightly nervous around. She doesn't seem afraid, but she keeps looking over her shoulder at me.

I guess we're both unsure of each other still.

"Dark purples and greens will work best with your eyes." She brings several small squares of fabric over. "I'll be working within this palate. Are there any pieces you want specifically?"

"Um, whatever you think is best." I've never had a custom made wardrobe. I don't know what to ask for.

She smiles, her prominent fangs on full display. "Wonderful! Now, if you'll strip down, I am going to alter a piece to fit you for tonight."

"Tonight?"

"You're dining with the King. You need something more suitable than this!" She gestures to my dress.

"Oh, right."

I almost forgot about that.

"I'm thinking purple, it really makes your eyes stand out." She brings a dress out of her seemingly endless bag of supplies. "I'll just have to hem up the bottom and bring it in around your waist."

"Alright," I nod in agreement. I don't have anything to add.

"Off, off!" She tugs gently at my dress. "I'm thinking maybe a dramatic neckline!"

"Oh, well," I cringe, slipping my arms free as she hastily unties the secure strings that Riven tied around me earlier. "Um, I guess we could try that."

I step into the new dress and immediately hate it. The color is beautiful, but it's so sheer.

"Is there more to this?" I stare down at my completely visible body beneath the fabric.

"What do you mean?" She looks up. "More?" Her face falls, and I know instantly that I've offended her somehow.

"It's so beautiful, really. But another layer maybe?" I gesture over my chest.

"Why would you want to cover this? It's lovely!" She stares openly at me.

Even though I'm uncomfortable, her stare isn't malicious or perverse. It's appreciative. She's not staring at any specific place for too long, she's not looking at me sexually.

"I made this design for my most recent line and couldn't keep it in stock. Everyone wanted one. This is the prototype." She smiles proudly at it.

"I'm honored to wear it." I swallow down my fears. This isn't home.

She works quickly, pinning and tucking the fabric in different places. The quiet spreads around us, each second feeling heavier than the last. With nothing to say, I'm left alone with my thoughts. That's a dangerous place to be.

Nerves start creeping in from every direction.

This is just dinner. Not a big deal. A meal. Simple.

But he's an alien. And the king.

And I'm wearing a see-through gown.

I try to convince myself that this is just their way. A strange custom from a strange land. At home, this is not the kind of dress you wear to a simple dinner, let alone a meal with royalty.

"Finished!" She clasps her hands together. "You are a vision!"

"Thank you, Sidra." I really mean it. She might think I'm a bit strange, but she hasn't looked at me like I'm a creature to own—not once.

"Have fun tonight!" When she leaves the room, I stare at my reflection in the rippling water feature on the wall. It might be the slightly distorted image, but I think I look good. I would never, ever pick this dress, but it doesn't look horrible on me. Aside from the marks on my face, I look nice.

With no tools, I attempt to fix my hair. I have water and my fingers to comb through it but I'll do what I can.

Minutes tick by as I try desperately to make myself more

presentable. Over and over again, I run my fingers through, wetting parts, braiding it, tying it up, a bun, half up, I try it all.

"The King is ready for you." Verrin's stoic voice stops me in my tracks. He never knocks!

Looking at my reflection, my shoulders slump. My hair is hanging down, slightly neater than before but only barely. It's hardly the hairstyle for dinner with royalty, but I don't even have a comb, this is as good as it gets.

As I follow Verrin, it dawns on me that I'm acting like this is a dinner date. It's just dinner.

My cheeks heat, embarrassment coursing through me at my own ridiculousness. This isn't a date.

We walk down the staircase into the foyer again. The double doors that lead to the dining hall are open. We're almost inside, so close, when the doors to his working wing open. Four men, agitated men speaking loudly about the human issue, walk out into the foyer with us.

"Is that her?" One of them growls.

There is an eruption of snarling, growling, snappy talking. Most of it centered around how unworthy I am of this level of protection.

I stare at the floor until Riven's voice cuts through all of theirs. "Don't you have work to do elsewhere? All of you, you're dismissed. Leave now."

CHAPTER 24

apologize for their comments." He takes my arm in his. "I should have made sure that you didn't encounter them."

"It's fine." It's not, but I don't know what else to say.

The dining hall is lit with little flicking lights. They look like candle flames, but there is no candle, just the flame, and they are everywhere. The doors are open on one end, letting the outside in. The table is carved into a tree outside; it's still alive and growing, covered in little blue flowers. The huge table could easily seat twenty and sprawls into the room, with uneven edges and notches in the wood.

At one end, two places are set.

This looks very intimate. All of the twinkling lights and the two seats, right beside each other.

"You look lovely." He stands beside his chair as I sit. "How was your appointment with Sidra?"

"Oh, it was fine. She was nice." I subtly move my chair to the side while I pull it forward. We're so close together; our arms are touching.

There is a moment of silence, thick and awkward. I open my mouth to try to say something, likely something stupid, but I'm saved by three people entering the room with rolling carts.

"I have prepared a meal of our largest export. The waterways here are filled with delicacies. They are what the royal court is most known for throughout this galaxy. The food harvested from here is sent to the outer rim and highly sought after." He looks proud as the people set down trays of brightly colored fish.

They look too pretty to eat.

Pinks and purple scales with iridescent shimmer cover the table. Different plates, in every possible shade, make up a spread for at least ten people.

A rich, meaty smell fills the air, and I suddenly feel famished.

"Thank you for doing this." I hold myself back. I don't know the rules. I wish I would have asked Sidra.

"It's my pleasure. Please, take as much as you like." He looks almost eager, watching me.

Shaking off my nerves, I start to fill my plate.

As we start to eat, I'm shocked at how wonderful everything is. Each bite is better than the last.

It's like nothing I've ever tasted before. I can't even compare it to anything. The textures, the flavors, the smells. It's all incredible and completely new.

The feeling of fear is gone as I focus on the buffet in front of me.

As it's happening, it's not lost on me that this is a truly unique experience. Even on earth, I never got to enjoy traditionally fine dining. Money was too tight.

This is beyond my wildest dreams. A food experience that I couldn't have even imagined.

"Are you enjoying it?"

"So much." My eyes water slightly, and I feel emotional at how extraordinary this is.

This is a lot for an ordinary woman from a small, nothing town, but for the first time in my life, I don't feel like that.

"Tell me about foods from earth. What do you enjoy?"

I suddenly feel ridiculous. My favorite food at home is pizza from a small local restaurant two towns over.

"Well," I forced back a laugh. "It's nothing like this, but there's a pizza place that I love. They make the sauce homemade everyday. It's the best pizza sauce in the world, in my very humble opinion."

His smiles --warm and genuine as he asks questions and listens to me describe what pizza is, how it's made, and the memories I have associated with it, ranging all the way back to my fifth birthday party.

It's not fancy or special, but he doesn't treat it like it's worthless.

We work our way through the different trays, tasting and talking about everything. He tells me the names they're grown and harvested, how it's prepared, and which are his favorites.

We talk about different foods on earth, customs, and celebrations. I explained to him what a birthday party is, apparently that isn't a customary Ophidian tradition.

The conversation flows with ease. He is warm and invested the entire time. I never feel ashamed by the truly limited scope of my existence.

He teaches me. Explains. Shares.

We talk about his travels. Not just here on this planet but around the galaxy and beyond it. Planets made of ice, water, or sand. Places with living plants that attack and defend their own.

I hang on his every word.

He is endlessly fascinating.

But the part I can't wrap my head around is that he seems to think that about me.

He leans in, he listens, and he asks at least as many questions as I do.

I've never had a conversation like this with anyone.

By the time the final tray is brought out, the large moons are hanging in the sky, filling the room with blue light.

The tray is full of small translucent domes of different colors. It looks like Jell-O.

"This looks like something we have on earth."

As soon as I pick one up, I know that it's not, it doesn't jiggle, it feels firm.

The taste is so soft and subtle—a hint of sweetness, a slightly floral fruit flavor—but just barely.

"This one is my favorite." He picks up one of the green tinted ones and hands it to me.

I blush as he watches me eat it, a small, satisfied smile on his face when he can tell that I like it too.

"It's delicious." My cheeks are so warm.

He looks at me, and I feel like he knows me. He sees all of me —the parts I like and the things I don't. The depth in his eyes is almost frightening. He can see through me down to the things I try to hide.

I don't feel the same way about him. He's a mystery.

He can read me like an open book, but all of his pieces feel just out of my grasp.

By the time we stand to leave, I couldn't possibly eat another bite.

We walk, side by side, slowly to my door.

It's funny how much can change in a single night. I was so frightened before but now I find myself wanting to linger a little bit longer.

Standing outside of my door, it might just be my imagination, but it seems like he's hesitating too.

"I really enjoyed tonight. Thank you."

"My presence is required at a meeting with the interplanetary allies and the heads of state. I will return the day after tomorrow."

I'm not sure why my chest falls. The thought of being here without him, even just for a day, is scary.

"Verrin will be here the whole time. He will not leave you." His tone is soft and reassuring.

"I'll be alright." I nod confidently, even though that's not how I feel. "Have a safe trip."

His head tilts to the side, and the corners of his lips tilt up. "Thank you, Demi."

CHAPTER 25

A rough knock wakes me while it's still dark. Shooting upright, fear wraps around my chest.

"Hello?" I call out, my croaky, tired voice echoing.

"Demi." It's Riven.

Sighing, relieved, I open the door. He's in full uniform, standing tall and proud behind my door.

"I have decided that you will accompany me to the council meeting. I apologize for the short notice and the early hour." He holds his arm up; I recognize the garment bags. "Sidra has prepared two outfits. The rest of your things will be here when we return."

"Oh, ok." I feel disoriented. "When are we leaving?"

"Now."

"Oh!" I turn frantically, unsure of what I should do.

"Do not rush. I will be in my office when you are ready." His calm voice and presence make the panic gripping me ease.

I'm still going to rush, but at least I know he's not going to be impatiently waiting on me.

As soon as I'm alone, I run into the bathroom. I don't have time to get lost in the beauty of it today. I have to actively remind myself to clean up and leave. Each second, my attention is pulled toward a small flower or the scent in the air. This place could trap me for an eternity if I let it.

In a blur, I dress in my newly sewn jumpsuit that looks slightly military yet very chic. Sidra is very talented. This looks elegant but also very structured at the same time. It's flattering and surprisingly comfortable. I like it immediately.

With my few belongings packed, I run out the door and straight into Verrin's back.

"Oh, sorry!" I didn't see him this morning when Riven came to the door. "I didn't know you were here!"

"I'm always here." He gestures for me to walk ahead of him. "He is waiting for us downstairs."

The double moons are starting to fade outside, the blue tint changing to the orange-pink of the rising sun. Light filters in through the windows. It's beautiful and peaceful. I find myself quietly appreciating this place. It reminds me of early mornings at home. It's different, the view isn't the same—not even close —but there is something similar about it. Right at sunrise, when the air is still cold, steam rises out of the field, the grass is dewy, and everything looks fresh—almost well rested. It's beautiful.

Verrin opens a door, and I step inside. Riven looks up from his place behind a large desk. Just like the dining room, his office is missing a wall. His desk is made from the roots of a tree that are coming up out of the floor. It's incredible.

"You're ready?" He seems surprised.

"I am." I tuck a loose hair behind my ear. We always seem to shift between awkward and comfortable. It's a constant back and forth. Just when I think we're good, it feels strange again.

"Let's go." He stands, and I sidestep out of the doorway so he can pass by just as he holds his hand out for me to go.

Eventually, we make it outside where a ship—pod thing—is waiting.

The inside is spacious, but Verrin is so large that it doesn't really feel that way. His presence is menacing.

Riven takes one of two available seats and then stares at me. "Aren't you going to sit?"

"Oh, that's okay. Verrin can have it."

"I will not sit while I am working." His voice is stern. I think I offended him. "You sit."

They're both looking at me like I've said something truly unhinged. "Alright, thank you." I take the seat beside Riven and knot my fingers together.

"After I left you last night, I couldn't stop thinking about all of the things that could happen if I left you." His admission surprises me. It seems to surprise him too. He jerks his gaze up to Verrin. "Not that I don't trust you. I didn't want to risk anyone attempting something because they know I'm not at home."

Verrin nods, his expression unchanging.

"I thought the best course of action would be to have you accompany me." He explains.

I don't know what to say. I'm not sure anyone has ever cared this much about my safety. I know he promised to take care of me, but this is above and beyond.

"Thank you. I appreciate it."

Last night we were so open. We talked freely, comfortably. Maybe it's the fact that Verrin is here, stoic and stern, listening to every word. The casual nature of last night's meal is gone.

"When we arrive, I will be checking into a stay-room. This conference is usually held in my court, but I had it moved this year. Having fewer visitors seemed appropriate given the current situation." He continues. "Elapidia is an aquatic planet— salt water. We will be staying in the general's home. His staff is small, and no one else will know of your presence."

He's thought of everything, apparently.

Before long, the planet comes into view. Deep, endless blue. It's serene in a way. There is no land anywhere, just water as far as the eye can see.

Leaning forward, I watch with unhidable curiosity as the

ship lands on the open water, seemingly in the middle of nowhere. Then there is a whirring sound, and the ship shudders.

It feels like we're in an elevator, moving downward as water spills up over the sides of the ship. It only takes a moment, and we're fully submerged.

I almost panic, but Riven is so calm, I'm reassured that this is supposed to be happening.

We move down, deeper and deeper.

Gasping, I can't contain myself anymore. Jumping up, I press my hands to the window and watch as we approach a glowing city beneath the surface of the water. It's incredible. The glow of the lights, thousands of them, like skyscrapers—illuminates the water.

"Oh my god." I whisper, watching as we enter a building. We are stopped, then moved upward, coming out of the water.

There are several people standing, waiting.

"Paleous!" Riven opens his arms to the man in front. He looks at me with surprise but quickly hugs him back.

"Your majesty! Welcome to Elapidia. It's been too long. Thank you for allowing me the honor of hosting this meeting!" His voice is low but warm and friendly. "Who is this?" He turns his attention and curiosity to me.

"She is my guest." He gives no other details.

I can't hear what Paleous says to him, but Riven seems unbothered. "That is fine, my friend."

No one here looks disgusted by me, but they all seem surprised by my presence.

"Let me show you to your room." He leads us through his large home. Everything is made of glass, looking out at the water surrounding us. Tall stalks of seaweed grow all around, shielding parts of the house from view.

"You will stay here tonight." He stops outside of a room. "If you need anything, please, let Ossa know. She is the head of my household team and can get anything you need at any hour."

"Thank you," we both nod and enter the room.

With wide eyes and an open mouth, I take in the room. It's glorious. An underwater oasis. The glass ceiling gives a view of the water. Another wall made of dark stone has water running down it into a pool.

"Wow." I whisper, stepping forward. "This is–"

The words stop in my throat as I notice it. There is only one bed.

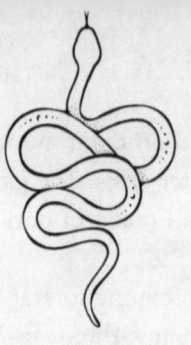

CHAPTER 26

"Demi?" He looks at me —full of concern.

"Oh, yeah, everything is great. This place is just so cool." I choke out.

I don't want him to know that my mind immediately starts to panic at the thought of sharing a bed with him. I'm an adult.

Hell, he hasn't even offered me the bed! He might want me to sleep on the chair! I shouldn't just assume. I calm myself down. There's no use in getting myself frazzled right now. We just got here.

He looks at me like he doesn't believe me, but he lets it go.

"Verrin is bringing us lunch here. I thought you would be more comfortable away from the prying eyes and questioning." He sits on one of the chairs that appear to be made of glass.

"Oh, thank you. If you want to eat with them, I understand. They seem so happy to have you here. I don't want you to stay hidden here for my sake." I feel guilty. The people here welcomed him with open arms – thrilled by his presence, and he's planning to eat in the room with me? It seems rude. "Will they be upset if you stay here?"

His head tilts in that way; it always seems to when I speak.

"They might be. But they will survive it." He seems confused.

"I'm sure they will." I laugh. "But I don't want to keep you from your duties. I'll be fine here."

"I brought you here with me so that I can ensure your safety. It would be counter to the point to leave you here alone while I socialize."

"I wouldn't be alone. My trusty bodyguard is here." I smile anxiously under the weight of his gaze. His piercing eyes are glued to me. It makes me self-conscious of everything—I'm nervous to move under his scrutiny.

"Would you like to come with me?"

"To dinner?" I choke. "With everybody?"

I want to point out that the previously mentioned prying eyes and intrusive questioning will still be a problem.

"Yes," his lips tip upward at the corners.

"Um, sure. I can do that." I nod. I'm going for casual, but I think I sound nervous.

"I want to show you something before we eat. There is a place here that is very special." He opens the door and waits for me.

As we walk down the tubular glass hallways, I try to keep my composure, but this place is too amazing. It's like walking through a carved-out tunnel in an aquarium where they've put you beneath the tanks. I keep my eyes peeled, looking for fish, but so far there are only plants. incredible plants, brightly colored and iridescent, they glow in the dark water.

We walked for a long time, passing people who bow their heads to him and sneak curious glances at me.

No one speaks to me, which is fine, but I can feel their eyes on me and see the confusion on their faces.

It's still so strange to me that no one knows what a human is and no one has seen us before. It's funny that I must look as alien to them as they look to me.

It's just here. He brings me down into a large dome like we're sitting in the middle of a snow globe. Only the waters on the outside.

The lights are dimmed, glowing just enough to see the breathtaking blue that is completely surrounding us.

"Watch." The hushed whisper of his voice makes my shoulders slightly. I don't know what's going to happen, but it feels like it's important.

We stand in silence for about thirty seconds, and I wonder if whatever I'm supposed to be seeing is happening already and I'm missing it.

But then it happens.

From below us, a million tiny bubbles come up around us. We're surrounded. They wrap around the dome, rising to the surface.

"Wow." My mouth hangs open. "This is–"

He smiles, looking up. There is something almost childlike wonder in his face.

We stand quietly, watching until all of the bubbles are gone. "It will happen again in four minutes. Do you want to stay and watch one more?"

"Yes!" I answer too quickly.

This seems to make him happy. "I'm glad you liked it."

An excited giggle bursts from my chest when the bubbling starts again. It's magic.

"Thank you for showing me this." I feel breathless as it starts for a third time. I never want to leave.

"I thought you would like it. I don't come here often, but when I do, I stop here, even to see it once. There is a geyser below us, it forces the water up and creates the bubbles." He explains as we slowly walk out of the room.

"I knew there had to be an explanation for it." I bite into my cheek. The snake king might be more kind and thoughtful than my last three boyfriends.

This place feels more alien than his court—all glass and metal, it feels futuristic.

The dining room is breathtaking. I know we're inside, but the glass isn't visible. It looks like we're in an air bubble floating.

Several eyes go wide as I sit down beside him at the table. The hum of their whispers circles the room. Sinking into my chair, I lean toward Riven, hiding myself beside him.

"Do not hide." He whispers, a slight growl in his voice.

"Sorry." I stare down at my hands.

A sound. A deep rumble in his chest makes me want to apologize again.

The meal passes slowly and crawls like torture. They talk on and on about people, places, and things I don't know or understand. That wouldn't be so bad except that there is one woman in particular that won't stop staring at me. What's worse—she looks like she wants to knock my head off of my shoulders. I don't know what I did to her, but she hates my guts.

"So," someone clears their throat, and I instantly know this is going to be about me. "Who is this, your majesty?"

"This is Demi."

That's it. That's all he says. No explanations, no details. Just Demi.

The tension gets so awkward and thick that I almost laugh. The squeaky, embarrassed, inappropriate laugh that comes when I'm so nervous my body malfunctions, and laughter is the only response.

"Forgive me, Your Majesty, but what is—"

"No." His voice booms, not loud but final. "We will not discuss her. Leave the subject alone."

The rest of the dinner is quiet. It makes me miss the chatter. I wasn't a part of it, but at least it was happening. Now everyone is uncomfortable.

The woman is still staring, rage emanating from her pores.

Trays of delicious food are spread across the table, but I can't even taste it anymore. My stomach is tied in a knot. Damn, my good manners. I wish I had just accepted his invitation to eat in the room. Who cares if they feel disappointed? This is awful.

Finally, when everyone has had enough, poor Paleous rises,

giving a small speech about how honored he is to host this meeting.

"We will meet in the conference room in—" he goes over the schedule, but his voice fades into the background as I make eye contact with the woman again.

A wicked smile pulls at the corners of her mouth as she pins me to the seat with her gaze.

I think she's going to try to kill me.

CHAPTER 27

"The Fenlands have been extensively searched. Most of the Fen Wardens are not on his side. They're growing tired of his antics. They paid dearly, with the lives of their friends and loved ones and with the loss of titles last time they followed him. His circle is small."

Riven sits back, listening to the report.

"There is footage of him departing at the southernmost point. He is beyond the outer rim." The man continues. Behind him, crystal-clear video plays of a pod hurtling through space. A picture populates in the corner of the screen—a close-up of the pilot.

A shiver runs down my spine as I see him. General Hydriss. It's obviously him—the snarl on his face is unmistakable.

"Set up patrols on the edge of our system. I want him apprehended immediately if he tries to reenter. I am sending three patrols into the outer rim and authorizing full-force tactics. Bring him in—dead or alive."

The room is quiet.

"No one has anything to add?" His brow quirks up.

Silence.

He hums, "If no one has anything to say, we can close that matter and move on. There is a-"

"Your majesty!" The woman from dinner interjects. Her voice sounds frustrated. "Sir, with all due respect, I simply must state the obvious here! You're sending three patrols—that's twelve of our highly trained assets into the outer rim after him to keep her safe?"

The disgust emphasized in her voice when she says 'her' isn't missed on anyone.

He turns to her, not speaking a word. The confidence in her face and squared shoulders falters. The longer the pause grows, the more uncomfortable the room gets. Without a single word, he has commanded the room. Each second is unbearable.

"Does anyone have anything useful to add on this subject or shall we move on?" He grits through his teeth after an excruciatingly long pause.

The rest of the meeting passes without further emotional outbursts. They talk about imports, exports, leadership, promotions, infrastructure, building plans, and new planet acquisition —things that seem so surprisingly normal for a governing body.

As I sit, listening, I'm able to piece together who the different players are.

I don't know what their exact titles are, but it seems they have something similar to our structure at home—mayors, governors, senators, then Riven above them all. Each planet has a local government structured like that of an individual state, but they all fall below him.

I keep my eyes glued to him the whole time. The woman has been watching me, seething, since he put her in her place.

When the meeting is finally over, I follow him silently back to the room. He's angry.

It's everywhere. The way he's walking. The tension in his jaw and shoulders. The way his mouth is pressed into a thin line. It's oppressive. The air around us feels palpably heavy and warm. Suddenly, being far below the surface of the water—far away from fresh air—feels different than it did just a few hours ago.

"Riven," I jog behind him.

"Demi," the way he growls my name, makes me shut my mouth. "If you're about to say something about not wanting to cause trouble or all of this being unnecessary, don't."

Rolling my lips into my mouth, I follow him into the room.

"We will have our meal delivered to the room. I am not subjecting either of us to hours sitting with them." He rolls his neck.

"Alright." This time I don't dare argue.

"If you need anything, just call me." He disappears into the bathroom.

Sitting at the small table, I stare up at the water through the openings in the ceiling. I don't know how much time passes, but when he comes out, he's wearing only pants, and his hair is wet.

My eyes immediately jerk to look at the floor.

"Would you like to use the whirlpools?" He asks. Either he's oblivious to the way I'm trying not to look at him or he just doesn't care.

"Sure." That sounds wonderful.

"Touch the red light twice, then the green light once."

As soon as I'm alone in the bathroom, I see what he meant. The panel on the wall doesn't have buttons, just glowing lights.

Red twice. Green once.

A swirling sound starts, and a large tub fills with water from the bottom, rising like a river. It bubbles and moves. The temperature is perfect, and the current is just strong enough to feel like a massage against my body.

I don't want to rush it, but I also don't want to keep him waiting. After sitting through that tense meeting, this is nice—not just the water but a moment alone. Being watched that closely, every movement scrutinized, makes me tense.

Here, completely alone, I can relax.

Deep down, in the quiet parts of my mind that I don't let

myself focus on, I hope they find Hydriss and kill him. Then maybe I can go home.

I can't let myself think about that for too long. I can't let myself have hope.

Climbing out of the whirlpool, I pull out the dress Sidra made. The purple fabric is an intricate lace with shimmering beads up the bodice. It looks too fancy for any occasion that I'll ever have, but I slip it on anyway.

The material is so soft, like buttery silk that feels cool to the touch. On both sides of the skirt, high slits open all the way up to my hips.

Feeling slightly ridiculous, I step out into the room. Riven and Verrin are at the table, looking over several screens.

"Are you-" He looks up, and his mouth snaps closed.

"I-I know it's fancy. This is the only other thing I have to wear." I should have just put the jumpsuit back on. "I'll go change. I-"

"It's lovely." He clears his throat. "We are just finishing up here. Come, sit. Our food will arrive any minute." He gestures to the seat across from him. "Please."

"Okay." I gather up the material in my hands and quickly take the seat.

"Actually, we will finish this later, Verrin. You're dismissed." Riven hands him the screen.

We sit silently for a moment, an uncomfortable tension in the air.

"We will leave first thing in the morning." He blurts out.

"Oh, alright." I answer too quickly.

Maybe it's the way his eyes are all over me, or the sheerness of this dress, but I feel almost naked. Too vulnerable. Too exposed.

Someone knocks at the door, and he leaps up before it's even finished. "That will be the food!"

"Great." I rub my nervous hands over my thighs.

Trays are set on the table between us. Just like our meal at his house, he tells me about everything—what it's called, where it comes from. The tension starts to break. The comfort returns.

"Is the outer rim a dangerous place?" I finally pluck up enough courage to ask.

"It can be. It's not owned or governed. People go there to avoid the rule of law and order. It doesn't have to be dangerous —not everyone there is inherently bad. Some just want to live free. Others, like Hydriss, are there to evade the consequences of their actions." He watches me intently as he speaks.

"Will they find him?"

"I won't stop until they do." There is a promise in his tone. "Until then though, I will keep you safe."

The trays are soon empty, picked over, and enjoyed.

I don't mean to yawn, but I do. And he sees it.

"You're tired."

"A little bit. I'm fine."

I've been avoiding this subject all day.

"Rest."

"I'll take the chairs over there." I point across the room to the small seating area.

"Why would you sleep there?"

"There's only one bed. I didn't want to assume-"

"Demi, the bed is big enough for both of us." With that tone, he might as well be saying, 'Don't be stupid.'

"Oh, alright." My legs feel shaky as I walk to the bed and lie down.

"See." He gets in on the other side.

"I didn't want to assume." I repeat myself nervously.

"I appreciate your considerate nature, but there is room for both of us to be comfortable."

As I close my eyes, I listen to the sound of his breathing. Knowing that he's close is oddly comforting as I drift to sleep.

CHAPTER 28

Sometimes you wake up and it happens slowly, it's like you're still groggy. Sleep is clinging to you. You don't really remember where you are. The world is sort of hazy and dreamlike—like it's in the distance.

Then other times it's not like that at all.

There are moments when you wake sharply, like being doused in cold water, snapping you to the present as soon as your eyes are opened.

This is one of those times.

My eyes open, and I'm immediately conscious of every detail around me. The weight of the blankets, the softness of the sheets, the dim morning light filtering through the room—everything comes into sharp focus. There's no lingering haze, no confusion.

I know exactly where I am. And I know exactly who is lying beside me.

My face is pressed into his warm chest—a slow, rhythmic thump against my ear.

His breath is calm, shallow, and steady—the quiet rhythm of sleep.

I try to move, but I can't. His arms are wrapped around me too tightly; he's holding onto me for dear life.

I'm warm. Completely surrounded by him. I don't know what to do. Should I wake him?

I decide not to. Sitting, patient and motionless, letting him rest. I don't know much about his mental state, but being king must be stressful. More sleep probably couldn't hurt.

The soft thump of his heartbeat makes me feel calm, like it's pulling me back to sleep.

Being wrapped up in his arms, held close —it's kind of nice.

The thought feels strange even as I think it. I'm in bed, in the arms of an alien king. It's never lost on me that my life has become something out of a movie script.

I'm almost drifting back to sleep when he moves, it's subtle, just shifting in his sleep. But something happens.

As his hips come forward, so does something else. Something big and hard, pressing into my stomach.

My breath catches in my throat, and he lets out a low, rumbling sound that vibrates in his chest. I feel it.

He moves his hips again, pressing them forward, and I have to roll my lips into my mouth to stop the gasp from escaping. It's pressed flat against his stomach and mine, between us.

Oh my God.

My heart is racing. What do I do?

He pushes his hips forward again, and the sound he makes fills my stomach with butterflies. His grip around me tightens, only for a second.

He gasps and releases me completely, rolling back slightly.

"Demi?"

"Yes?" I squeak.

"I'm sorry!" He backs away further, putting as much space as possible between us.

"Oh, it's fine." I wave my hand, but my heart is about to beat out of my chest. I don't sound convincing at all. I'm breathless and blushing.

"I–" He stops, clearing his throat. "I'm sorry." He repeats again.

"Don't apologize, Riven. It's really ok. You know, biology and stuff. It's just a natural reaction." Shut up, Demi. I'm rambling about biology. Why? What is wrong with me?

He drops his legs out of the bed, moving to stand, and for some reason, completely out of my control, I look.

It's massive. Standing up between his legs.

I don't mean to gasp, but I can't stop it. He has copper-colored scales around his hips, they move up from inside of his pants, fading into his sides. It's like an arrow, drawing my eyes right to *it*.

We lock eyes. He knows I was looking. I know he knows.

Now here we sit, both knowing, wide-eyed and frozen.

Without breaking eye contact, his neck tenses, and he clenches his jaw. His posture and the look in his eyes might be mistaken for anger, but I know it's not. He's not angry. It's something equally frightening.

I catch his hands, flexing and clenching by his sides before he turns and quickly walks into the bathroom.

Of all of the thoughts swirling around in my head, the only one that sticks—the one I cling to—is the idea that he's in there taking care of it. My insides clench at the images that flood my brain.

Sitting up on my knees, I lean forward, listening.

I feel like a voyeur. I'm invading his privacy. I just have to know. The thought that he might be in there right now, just behind that door—doing *that*. An overwhelming warmth spreads from my stomach outward.

"Riven?" I don't know why I call out to him. I hear my voice as it happens, like it's not coming from me but from someone else.

There is a pause. A moment that passes where I can only panic. Why did I call him? I ruined everything.

Tangled up in my dress, I climb out of the bed. Taking one step toward the bathroom, the door opens. I freeze again.

"Come here." He moves, stepping back slightly.

Everything courses through me at once. There is fear there, but it's buried beneath curiosity, and right now, that's winning. Deep down, I know he isn't going to hurt me. The realization of the trust I have in him spurs my feet forward.

I'm not really sure what I'm walking toward.

I half expect him to grab me and pin me to the wall. Last night, it never would have occurred to me that we might be in this position. But now that it's staring me in the face, I'm consumed by it.

He takes my hand gently—definitely not with the intention of ravishing me.

I let him lead me into the bathroom, all the way back to the whirlpool.

He starts the water before taking a piece of the moss from the wall. Using it like a sponge, he washes my neck, my shoulders, and my arms.

Nervous about these feelings, I don't want to make eye contact with him. Instead, I watch the muscles in his chest move beneath his skin. He moves like water, a graceful fluidity, almost a ripple.

An equally bad place to look. Nowhere is safe.

"My scent is all over you." The gruff, desperate sound is almost pleading. "I can't stand it."

When he swipes over my collarbone, the cool water, his touch, the rasp in his voice, the fire in his eyes—all of it hit me hard. A shiver runs down my spine, and a sound—a whimper from the back of my throat accidentally escapes.

His other hand grabs my arm, holding it tightly.

This has to stop now. We can't do this –whatever this is.

"Demi."

He's said my name before. Plenty of times. But this time it sounds like sex on his tongue. That's how he would say it if we gave in to this strange and sudden yearning.

A loud banging sound from outside breaks the tension.

He rolls his neck and lets out an angry huff before leaving me alone with my half melted brain.

Stripping out of the dress, I wade into the whirlpool. I can't smell him on my skin, but knowing that he's there is going to distract me all day.

CHAPTER 29

As I scrub my skin, I can't help but overhear the conversation happening just outside of the door.

It's impossible to ignore.

"Phaedra is brokenhearted, Riven! You have made your choice! A worthless outsider over your own Queen!" A woman's voice yells so loudly it's as if she is standing in front of me. It's the woman with the death glare. There is a sharpness in her voice that is unmistakable.

Whatever he says in response, I can't hear it. His voice is just a low rumble, calm and measured.

"You did!" She screams back. "You chose her the moment you kicked Phaedra out! The woman that was to be your wife told you to get rid of her. There should have been no more conversations! You should have shown enough respect for her to at least consider it!"

"You have forgotten your place, Kimora. Leave. Now." His voice is louder now but still held back, restrained by his unshakable calm.

He kicked Phaedra out? A pit forms in my stomach, replacing the fluttering feeling that was just there.

"You are blinded by lust! How could you degrade yourself?

How could you do that to Phaedra! She was the most sought-after Ophidian, and she chose you." Her seething voice makes me cower back even with a wall separating us.

"Lust? What lies has Phaedra fed you?" He laughs. "She was the most sought-after. That is true, but do not act like you know what it is to be entangled with her. My concern for the human is only the tip of the spear. I'm honestly surprised she even noticed we have a guest at all. None of this has anything to do with you, even if it were all true. Being related to Phaedra has emboldened you in the worst way. She can't protect you, and what's worse, she wouldn't try to. Don't attempt to come to her defense by disrespecting me."

The human? Ouch.

Quickly climbing out of the water, I have no choice but to put the same dress back on. The dress that he rubbed himself all over.

"Everyone else is too afraid to question you to your face, but there is chatter, Riven." Her voice is still bitter and sharp, but the volume has gone down significantly. I have to strain to hear it now.

"Next time you hear 'chatter' tell them to come to me directly and I'll address it." He growls.

"You need to prepare yourself for backlash. People are questioning your ability to rule. You think you're untouchable. If everyone rises up, you won't survive it." She sounds pleased by this. I can just imagine the smile on her face. It's not hurting her one bit to be the one to tell him this.

I wish I hadn't heard any of that.

It doesn't make sense why he is willing to risk so much for me.

The door opens, and he steps inside, his eyes finding mine immediately. "How much of that did you hear?"

"Just the important bits." I can't hold eye contact. I'm freaking out.

Awful conversation aside, my mind is reeling. What the hell just happened?

He was hard as a rick and grinding against me. I didn't imagine that. Now that he isn't physically pressing into my body, I can think more clearly about it. The shock, though still very present, is less intense than in the moment.

It must have been a product of a multitude of factors that came together all at once to create the perfect storm. Friction and sensation have very little to do with attraction. I was pressed against it, and the feeling made him hard. That's all.

"Don't worry about her. Kimora's all bark and no bite." He takes two long strides, and we're face to face.

"Are you sure?"

"Never rattle before you strike, Demi. She's on my radar. If she tries anything, she'll be stopped. She likes to speak to hear the sound of her own voice." He seems so sure.

"But," I gulp. "What about everyone else? If they rise up?"

"They won't." His lips twitch upward into a smile. "Don't worry about that. I have more friends than enemies. Phaedra's sister holds no sway over the people. They can be as angry as they want to be. It doesn't matter to me."

Her anger and hatred toward me make more sense now. Phaedra's sister.

"I would really like to leave. Are you ready?" His eyes sweep down over my body in a way that feels physical. His gaze touches my skin, a feather-light graze that makes goosebumps roll up my arms.

"Ready." I croak.

I guess we aren't going to talk about what happened earlier. That's probably for the best.

Hearing him say that it was nothing more than an involuntary response would sting.

Again, what is wrong with me?

The time, I thought I was panicking, that my reaction to his touch was fear, but looking back, that wasn't it at all.

I wasn't afraid. Just surprised.

This is bad.

I think there is a name for this syndrome. He isn't my kidnapper, but I'm here against my will. His kindness is messing with my head.

Walking beside him, I keep my eyes on the floor as we make our way back to the pod. I would rather not see all of the disgruntled faces as we pass them.

"Hold your head up," he whispers, his voice low, but there's an unmistakable authority in it. His hand presses gently against my lower back, guiding me. "Look them in the eyes."

A small, involuntary shiver runs through me at the contact. I hate that my body responds at all, but I force myself to comply, jerking my head up and straightening my spine, like I'm on autopilot. I meet his gaze briefly, but I don't dare linger there.

"Sorry." I jerk my head up and straighten my spine.

"Don't apologize." His voice is softer now.

We walk in heavy silence, we speak to no one, and no one speaks to us until we reach the platform.

"It was my pleasure to host you." Paleous bows his head. "It would be my honor, any time you feel the inclination."

"Thank you." Riven nods before stepping into the pod.

"Thank you." I don't know if I should speak, but I can't in good conscience leave without saying a single word.

"You are most welcome." He bows his head again.

CHAPTER 30

The air in this pod is stifling. The wonder of our arrival here is gone, and the journey up to the surface of the water feels eternal.

Riven is visibly tense. Verrin too—but that seems to be his normal state.

With my lips rolled into my mouth, I stare out the windows as the water goes from deep, dark blue, to light as we get closer.

While down below, I never felt suffocated or claustrophobic, but as we near the surface, I feel myself relaxing from a stress I didn't know I had.

It's still early, the sky is pink and orange as we lift off of the platform and into the air. It was hard to tell the time down there, the artificially lit day and night made it impossible to tell the actual time.

"How do your days and nights work?" My question slips out into the silence before I realize I'm saying it.

They both look surprised, turning to me with furrowed brows.

"We have thirty-six-hour cycles." Riven looks at me the way he always does, with a curiosity that makes me nervous. "Why do you ask?"

"I was just wondering. Nights feel longer than they do at home, I guess."

He hums, waiting for the rest of my questions that he's obviously anticipating.

"How many planets are in your kingdom?"

"Seven."

"And beyond your rule? That's the outer rim?" I don't know why I ask; knowing changes nothing. There is a shortness in his answers, clipped and quick. He isn't usually like that. But I'm curious, and sometimes listening to him speak makes me feel calm. There is something soothing and rhythmic about his voice. Maybe I'm trying to suss out if he's annoyed with me. He hasn't mentioned anything from earlier. I guess we aren't going to discuss it.

"Yes. The outer rim is the space between this galaxy and the next."

"No man's land." I whisper to myself.

He stands suddenly, abruptly ending our conversation. "We will arrive shortly." He says over his shoulder like an afterthought.

The rest of the journey, I'm alone, listening to Riven and Verrin talking quietly to each other. He's definitely annoyed.

I shrink in my seat. It almost looked like he was going to kiss me, which is crazy. Of course he wasn't about to kiss me.

My head is swimming.

A sinking feeling settles into my chest. Is this why he's being short and distant? He's regretting it.

The longer I think about it, the more muddled my feelings get. I don't think I regret it—whatever it was. We didn't really do anything. But the way he touched me... it was charged. There was something in it. The way his fingers grazed my skin. No one has ever washed me like that.

We need to discuss it at some point because all of the one sided conversations happening in my head are only assumptions. I have no clue what he's actually thinking.

It's more than likely true that it was nothing, and I'm blowing it up, inflating it into something real and meaningful in my head.

The one thought that keeps popping up, keeps circling around, is the one I'm most trying to ignore.

Did I actually want him to kiss me?

The snake-alien king?

I think I did. Heat rushes to my face and chest, a red blush spreading.

When the lush green of the court comes into view on the horizon, I accidentally let out an audible sigh of relief. I need space—just a moment to breathe in some fresh air and gather myself.

It happened so quickly. We went to sleep last night, and it was the farthest thing from my mind.

Then it crept in and took root quickly. I want him to kiss me. I want him to put his hands on me like he did before.

The feelings may be unexpected, but they're strong.

I'll ignore them. I can do that. I have to do that.

Not waiting a second, I'm up, waiting at the door before it opens.

"I have meetings today. Stay away from my office." Riven calls after me, and I freeze. Ouch.

"I'll stay away." I can't turn around. I don't want to see the look on his face; I can only assume it's disgust.

Verrin is behind me, not close but hovering, always there in the background.

Physically, I'm hungry, and I wanted to explore the gardens, but right now my room seems like the best place. I can hide and lick my wounds in private.

In the privacy of my room, I let myself crumble a little bit. Pacing around the luxurious bathroom, I try to remember every detail. Was I overly eager? Did I seem like I was desperate? Maybe it really was just a biological response, and I made him uncomfortable.

Shit.

This is for the best. I nod to myself.

There is a pile of clothes on my bed, laid out to display how beautiful and intricate each piece is.

Stripping down, I stand in the shower, letting myself get lost in the feeling of being out in nature. Another shower and a new outfit will help me feel better.

I don't have the same sense of smell that he does, but knowing that he rubbed against those clothes and that if I could smell him, I would, makes me want to change.

The shower is magic. My stress and worries melt away in the water. It's too calming and peaceful to feel anything but serene. Taking a piece of the moss, like he showed me, I scrub my body clean. It's incredible. I feel fresh and alive. The inner turmoil is on the back burner.

If I could bottle this feeling, I would be a billionaire in seconds. It's like I've been rejuvenated.

Running out to my bedroom with renewed excitement, I look through the clothes that Sidra left. Each piece is gorgeous. I can't believe these clothes were made for me. These are for glamorous women at red-carpet events and gala dinners. Not me.

"Wow." I pick up a deep purple lace dress. The bodice is see-through, but the skirt has fabric beneath the lace. Sliding it up my body, I catch sight of myself in the flowing water feature.

I look like I belong in this dress.

It fits me like a second skin, tailor-made exactly for me.

Something about it makes me feel emotional. Like I'm special. I matter enough to have a dress like this made just for me.

A tap at my door pulls me out of my little bubble of confidence and peace.

"Yes?" I hope it's Verrin.

It's not.

"You look…" He doesn't speak whatever word he was going

to say. Clearing his throat, he squares his shoulders. "I would like to invite you to have an indulgence with me."

"W-What does that mean?"

CHAPTER 31

had my kitchen staff prepare a tray. It is my second favorite. After yesterday's meeting, I think we deserve it." He smiles.

"So, it's like a treat?" I smile despite myself. I think we do deserve a little treat!

"Yes, will you come?" He looks genuine, as if he truly wants me to.

I nod, trying not to seem overeager.

As we walk down the hallway, nerves and doubt swirl around me. He doesn't seem angry at all. Things are back to the way they were before we woke up wrapped in each other's arms. I feel unsteady—like I'm walking on eggshells. I don't know what to do or say. He was very hot, then cold, then even colder. Now he seems to be warming up again.

I don't like not knowing where I stand or if I'm doing something wrong. I don't like feeling nervous all the time.

"Are you alright?" He turns, stopping me at the bottom of the stairs.

"What?" I force myself out of my head to focus on what he's saying.

"I said, are you alright? You seem distressed." His mesmerizing eyes draw me in just enough to make my knees feel wobbly before I look down at the floor. He might be hypnotizing me again.

"I'm fine." I start to lie, then, for some reason, anger rises to the surface. Just a little bubble of pent up frustration that pops and turns into something bigger. Boldness fills my chest. "Actually, I don't know how I should behave. You were mad at me earlier. Now you seem fine. I realize that it might not have had anything to do with me, maybe you're just stressed. But maybe it did have to do with me, you know, after this morning. And I don't know where I stand or what I should be doing. I don't want you to be upset with me, but I can't help that if you don't tell me what I did."

His lips tip upward before very quickly tugging down into a frown. "I was never angry at you. Why would you have thought that?" There is a hardness in his face—not anger, but it's there.

"I mean," I chuckle. "You said 'stay away from my office.' I understand not wanting to be disturbed, but that seemed like more than that."

His face softens. "There was a debrief of the council meeting today. I didn't want you to encounter anyone coming in or out of my office. It wasn't about you. I don't want you to be made to face people that still don't understand. You are welcome in my office any time."

"Oh." My chest relaxes some. "So, you're not mad at me?"

"Not at all." The genuine softness in his voice is all I need to relax completely. "And about this morning," he takes a step closer. "I am not upset about that. Frustrated, yes. But not upset."

"You're frustrated?" As soon as the words leave my lips, I'm hit with understanding. He's *frustrated*. "Oh!"

"Come, indulge with me." He takes my wrist gently and leads me toward the kitchen.

Suddenly, 'indulge' seems like it might also mean something else.

We pass the dining room, and I almost sigh with relief. The kitchen is bustling and full of people. That will give me a chance to calm down and think about this.

As we step through the door, I gasp. It's completely empty. There is a tray on the counter with two large bowls sitting, ready and waiting. Where is everyone?

His hands come down to my waist, lifting me up to sit on the counter. A small, surprised sound comes from the back of my throat and my cheeks heat. I'm not going to be able to think about anything. Well, except maybe one thing.

"Here." He slides one of the bowls toward me. A round, pink ball sits in the center. It almost looks like ice cream, but it's too shiny. "You pour this over it." He demonstrates, pouring white liquid from a little pitcher over the ball.

"What is it?" I pour my pitcher of liquid over the ball. It looks like a thick sauce.

"This is a fruit from an underwater tree, served chilled." He takes a spoonful of the pink ball. "The sauce is warm, it is made from the nectar of another fruit that grows only here, at my court." He brings the spoon up to his mouth, and his eyes seem to close involuntarily.

Tearing my gaze away from his lips, I dig into my own bowl.

This is better than anything I've tried. Not just here, but ever, in my life.

The pink ball is cold but so smooth and rich. The warm sauce is silky and thick with a caramel flavor. Each bite is somehow more delicious than the last. Swinging my feet, I can't contain myself as I eat the whole thing.

"This is my favorite." I slide my spoon through the last of the sauce, making sure to get as much of it as I can. I don't want to waste a drop.

"I'm glad to hear it. They will make it for you whenever you ask. You can eat it every day."

He chuckles, and I jerk my head up to look at him. He's

smiling as he brings his hand up, running his thumb over my lower lip. "You have some here."

"Oh," my heart thunders in my chest. He hasn't stepped away or moved his hand.

We sit like this, frozen. His eyes move down over my face, stopping at my lips and lingering there.

Unsure of what to do or how to invite him to come in if he wants to, I move in. Only a bit, hardly at all.

"I want to taste your skin." The hiss in his voice makes me shudder, goosebumps roll over my skin. "Can I?"

"Yes." I stutter, not at all unsure but so nervous that my body trembles.

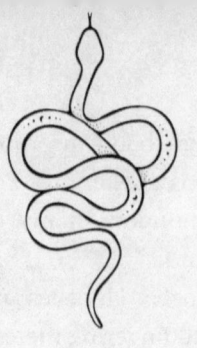

CHAPTER 32

He's so soft and gentle. When our lips finally touch, it's like taking in a breath of fresh air after holding it for so long. My eyes flutter closed, and a galaxy of stars plays in my mind. I'm free, like I'm on a swing at the top of the world.

One hand wraps around my waist while the other comes up to hold the back of my neck. Sitting here, his body nestled between my knees, I feel open and vulnerable.

I'm engulfed in him.

This is more than a kiss. His hands wrap around my upper arms, holding me firmly in place.

My mind is racing and simultaneously blank. Every thought and feeling rushes through me, but I can't focus, I can't hold on to anything but him.

This is exactly what I wanted it to be. It's more, really.

He hums against my lips, the low, vibrating sound sending shivers through my body. It travels from my lips to my core, settling in the pit of my stomach. His need is almost tangible. I can taste it. It's in the sounds, the tension in his body, the rough grip of his hands.

I might be misreading the situation or projecting my own feelings onto him. I hope he feels what I'm feeling.

Pulling back, I force our mouths apart.

I need to see his eyes. Is he feeling the same way that I am? Is the desperation real, or is it my own feelings clouding my mind?

Peeking up, my doubts are burned to ash as soon as I meet his gaze. With his chest heaving and his eyes wide and wild, his grip on my arms tightens almost painfully.

This is all the reassurance I need. I'm not misreading anything.

The intensity of his gaze burns through me, and for a moment, the world stills. In that look, I see everything—the desire, the hunger, the desperation that mirrors my own. There's no mistaking it.

A rough, guttural sound rumbles from deep within his chest, and before I can even catch my breath, his lips are on mine again, more urgent, more frantic. This time, I don't hesitate. Wrapping my arms around his neck, I pull him closer, closing the distance between us completely.

His fangs are there, longer than what I'm used to, but they are surprisingly out of the way. I don't feel them the way I was expecting to.

Feeling confident, I slip my tongue through his lips and let one of his fangs scrape against it.

He lifts me up, the fabric of my dress tangled up in his hands as he grips my thighs.

Just as I wrap my legs around his waist, locking him into place, there is a sound from somewhere in the kitchen.

We break apart and fear courses through me. We just got caught.

Verrin is standing uncomfortably in the doorway, his eyes laser-focused on the floor.

"Sir. I'm sorry to interrupt, but there is an urgent matter that you need to address." He bows his head lower.

My heart sinks. For only a moment, I wonder what is going

on in Riven's head. Is he upset or embarrassed that he was seen in this position with me?

I don't have to wonder for long.

As he sets me back on my feet, he presses his lips to mine. Not hot or passionate, just a quick kiss. He doesn't care that Verrin is here or that he will see it.

A boldness and confidence that I don't usually feel courses through me. He doesn't care if anyone sees him. He doesn't look embarrassed at all.

"Stay here?" He tilts his head down to meet my gaze. "I'll attend to this quickly."

"Ok." My breathless voice barely makes a sound.

"Ok." His lips twitch, pulling up into a smile. "Wait here."

"Ok."

His demeanor changes in an instant; the moment he turns away from me, his posture straightens and his shoulders square up. "What happened?"

Whatever Verrin replies, I can't hear it. They're already half way down the hall.

The tips of my fingers come up to my swollen lips.

He kissed me.

I'm floating on cloud nine. If I close my eyes, I could truly make myself believe that I'm not standing on solid ground but drifting, weightless in the sky. I

But then it hits me. Reality, ever the downer, brings me back to solid ground with a swiftness. Cold and unforgiving, I'm disconnected from my daydreams.

There are so many issues with this.

Most glaringly, he's not even human! His scales, his eyes, the hiss in his voice—he's so absolutely alien. For a second, it hits me that we might not even be compatible—physically. But I felt it. I definitely think it would work...

I'm getting sidetracked.

He's an alien. And he's the king.

What am I going to do with a king? I'm putting the horse

before the cart here, but I can't be queen! He didn't ask me to be. His kiss didn't come with promises or grand declarations. But it came with something. A shift. A ripple in the air between us that I can't take back.

Taking a breath, I feel myself starting to panic. It's like a slow leak that's getting faster and faster until I'm completely underwater.

Whatever that was—whatever we are—he's the king! I can't even wrap my mind around it.

One kiss, and I feel like I'm losing it. I'm a teenage girl all over again, doodling his name in my notebook. One kiss isn't a proposal of marriage. I need to relax.

Phaedra's face, cool and deadly, pops into my head. If she hated me before, she will really hate me now.

Do I have a death wish? What am I doing? I should be laying low, keeping my head down. Instead, I'm making out with kings.

Running out of the kitchen, I zip past Verrin. Shit, Verrin. Of course, he's waiting in the hallway!

I know he's behind me, silent but ever-present as I rush up the stairs.

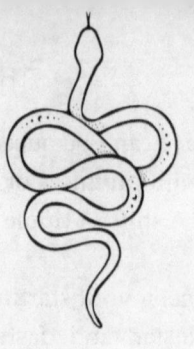

CHAPTER 33

As soon as my hand touches the doorknob, I freeze.

I know Verrin is behind me, watching, waiting. I can't make myself go inside.

Why am I running away? Yes, there are a thousand considerations swirling in my mind—what I might find inside, what I might lose—but I shouldn't be running.

With a deep breath, I spin around, the motion abrupt, taking him by surprise. We awkwardly shuffle around each other so that he's behind me again. I don't think he was expecting me to run again.

Rushing back down the hallway, I reach the stairs just as Riven does. He's at the bottom. I'm at the top.

"I'm sorry."

We move at the same time, colliding in the middle. His hands find me before I can think—rougher this time.

Verrin's presence is forgotten immediately.

"I shouldn't have run." I attempt an apology as his lips ghost over mine.

He doesn't say anything. But he carries me with ease, gracefully bringing us up the stairs and into his bedroom.

Oh, man. We're doing this. We're in his bedroom. My heart races, nervousness, and excitement bubbling up like it has nowhere to go.

I brace myself for instant heat—fire and passion. But when he places me back on my feet, there's no rush, no fevered rush. He steps back, his eyes searching mine.

"What happened?" His voice is impossibly gentle, catching me off guard. I expected hunger, not this.

"I panicked."

"Why?" His tone is so soft, coaxing.

"Well," I hesitate, wondering how to put the mess in my head into delicate words. "You're the king." That pretty much sums it up.

"I am." The corner of his mouth lips into a smile.

"And we're not the same species. Your people don't exactly seem to care much for me. Don't you think they would be really upset by anything that were to happen between us? Hell, they're already upset, and nothing has happened. I don't want to cause you any trouble." I stare at the intricate silver buttons on his uniform. I can't bring myself to look at his face.

"Forget about everything outside of this room, just for a moment." The soft tips of his fingers move down my arm. "If I wasn't the king, what would your reservations be?"

A blazing hot blush spread over my cheeks. He's going to make me say this out loud? I open my mouth, but no words come out.

Inhaling a deep breath, I clench my fists and just blurt it out. I'm an adult. We can have a conversation about this.

"I'm afraid we aren't compatible sexually." There. I said it. I didn't stutter, and my voice didn't shake.

A low, rumbling hum comes from his throat. "I have also wondered about our compatibility. There is only one way to know."

"Right." My breath catches. "That's true."

"I am the king, Demi." His fingers thread through my hair. "I am fair and just. I do not ward over my people with an iron fist. I don't demand their allegiance; I have earned it. For honesty's sake, I won't lie and say that everyone will be fine with you standing beside me. But I can also say, with certainty, that knowledge changes nothing. I won't demand that they bow, but I will not allow their displeasure to run my life."

My mouth hangs open. All of the reasons I had for putting a stop to this feel like excuses now.

Coming up on my toes, I take his face in my hands and kiss him. There is no hesitation in his response. Lifting me up, he sits down so that I'm straddling his lap.

While the kiss is great, too many things are swirling around in my mind. I'm uncomfortably flustered.

"Riven," I feel the need to just get to it. If we're not compatible, I don't want to build it up. "Look at me."

"All I see is you," he moves in to kiss me again.

"No. Really look at me." I pull back. "I want to know."

He looks confused until I slide off of his lap and start to untie my dress. When he realizes what I'm doing, his eyes go wide, and he sits forward.

Dropping my clothes down around my ankles, fully naked before him, I wait.

His eyes dart over my skin, landing between my legs. Leaning in, he reaches his hand out, slipping his fingers into the already wet skin.

The sound that he makes will echo through my dreams forever. Somewhere between pleasure and pain, a tortured, desperate sound crawls up from deep in his stomach. It makes my whole body clench.

"Lie down, I need to see it." His raspy voice takes any hesitation I might have and strangles it.

On wobbly legs, I walk over to his bed and sit on the edge. He's right on my heels, leaning down to kiss me as he gently pushes me back onto the mattress.

His grip on my ankle is firm as he lifts it up and to the side, spreading my legs open. Then he just stares.

For a moment, I can't tell what he's thinking, but as the seconds pass, it becomes more and more clear.

The anticipation gets the better of me, and I can't wait any longer. "Well?"

"It will fit." His jaw clenches.

In my lust-drunk brain, that's as good as a guarantee. Sitting up, I reach for him. He's still very clothed. I plan to remedy that as quickly as possible. My fingers snap the clasps open until he's able to slide out of his shirt.

Grazing the scales on his stomach, I'm surprised by how smooth they are.

His fingers hook the waistband of his pants, and my breath catches. I felt it. But seeing it is going to be very different.

When his pants pool at his ankles, I gasp, and my body instinctively leans away.

Copper colored and covered in the same smooth scales, two stand proudly where one should be.

The base is a single, thick shaft that splits into two near the middle. One of them would fit nicely, both of them together, surely not!

"Riven." I can't take my eyes off of him.

"You smell like acacia flowers and the fruit of a Kneac tree." His eyes flutter closed.

I don't know what that means, but it sounds nice, and it seems like he likes it.

"Let's try." A new kind of determination makes me sit a bit taller.

He wraps his hand around both of them, slowly working it up and down. "I have ached since I woke up pressed against you. I have been unable to concentrate on anything else."

I can only nod my head. No one has ever ached for me before. The thought sends a warmth through me.

"Do humans need time for preparation?" His hand flexes as he lets go of himself.

"Like foreplay? I don't need any right now." I let my desperation forward.

"Why not?"

"Because I'm soaked." I can't stand it. Sitting here, staring at him, I don't know if I'm going to combust or lose my nerve. The anticipation is too strong.

His eyes widen, and he drops to his knees. "Ophidian males produce this lubricant." He runs his fingers through it.

"You do?"

"Yes. I would like to give it to you, even if you don't need it." His voice shakes, whatever restraint he has, it's thinning. "It is a way to mark you with my scent."

"Ok." Suddenly, I must have it, whatever it is.

He wraps his hand around the base again and starts to pump it again. When a clear, iridescent fluid comes from the tip, he takes it in his hand.

"What does it taste like?" I blurt out before I can stop it.

"What?" He looks shocked, but I can tell by the way his chest is heaving, he's interested.

"Do you not do that here?"

"Do what?" His voice is so rough now it's almost angry. The wheels are turning in his mind now.

Instead of answering, I slip off of the bed. I hear his breath catch as I lean in. He whimpers as I lick a strip up the entire length.

"Demi." I hardly recognize his voice.

Sucking one tip into my mouth, I hollow out my cheeks and pull him in.

He sways, leaning forward to brace himself against the mattress. The soft pants and gasps spur me on.

"Wait!" He pulls away; the urgency in his voice makes me stop immediately.

"Did I hurt you?" I panic.

"No, quite the opposite. That was the most pleasant experience of my life." He looks disheveled and confused.

"Why did you stop me?"

"Do your men reciprocate that act?"

"Yes." My heart rises up into my throat. The thought of his face between my legs makes me feel lightheaded.

"Because of our fangs, doing that to a male has never been possible, but I can do it to you." His eyes trail down my body. "I would like to."

I nod too quickly. I desperately want him to. If he does it like he does everything else—with attentiveness and gentleness—I'm in for a treat.

"Stand up." He stays on his knees, helping me up. When he hooks my leg up over his shoulder and presses his face forward, I grab his hair to stabilize myself.

He licks and kisses for a moment before leaning back slightly. "Where is your pleasure?"

"Right here." A shiver runs up my spine as I brush my finger over my clit. I'm going to pass out when he licks it.

He hums and gets right to it. His snake tongue licks and tickles at me until my legs are shaking so that I can hardly stand up.

"Oh god, Riven!" I feel myself crumbling, my muscles spasming and contorting unnaturally as I arch toward him.

With too much adrenaline running through my body, I grab him, dropping down to my knees to be close enough to kiss his face.

I'm floating on top of the world. Nothing can ruin this moment. He presses into my stomach, rubbing against me as we kiss.

"Demi, I-" His throaty, groaning voice is cut off by a knock at the door.

He groans.

"Sir, there is urgent communication from the outer rim."

Clenching his fists, he grabs his shirt from the ground. "I'll be there. Wait in my office."

I feel like crying.

"I will be back the very second I can get away. Please be here, naked, waiting for me. I promise, I will make it worth your while." He kisses my forehead.

"I'll be here."

CHAPTER 34

Being brought up so high, soaring so far above the ground you can't even see it, then having it unexpectedly snatched away is jarring. I'm a jumbled-up mess; all of my emotions are all over the place.

How many urgent calls can one king possibly get?

Pulling his shirt on, I sniff it, his clean scent surrounding me.

Pouting, I walk around his room, taking in all of the little details. This is his space. It's so clean and fresh. One of the walls is open, with a terrace and a large tree branch coming inside. There is a dip in the wood, like a seat has been carved out by years of someone sitting there. The view is incredible. The tops of trees and orange skies as far as I can see. It's like I'm on top of the world.

The memory of his hands…and tongue on my skin makes me feel almost dizzy.

He's gone but I still can't see through the fog. His absence hasn't brought me any clarity. I'm buzzing. My blood is rushing through me, my heart ready to beat right out of my chest.

There was desperation in his touch. It was so intense and real —no one has ever wanted me that way. It's like hunger. It was in his eyes, burning me up as he looked at me.

The knotted up tension in my stomach flutters uncomfortably.

Just as I start to wonder how long he will be gone, the door opens violently.

He looks frantic still, but not the same as before. This isn't the desperate, aching feeling from before. He's panicking.

"Demi!" He has me in his arms, holding me tightly like I'll disappear.

"Riven, what happened?" Fear creeps up my spine.

"All it would take is one bite." His grip on me tightens painfully. "You're too vulnerable!"

"What?" I am missing vital information here.

"Hydriss has made his intentions clear. He knows that if he were ever able to get to you, I would not allow the matter to rest. He can't take you anywhere. So his intention now is just to reach you." His jaw ticks. "One bite is all it would take."

"Venom." I whisper, and the horrific memories of melting skin flood my mind.

He sets me down and paces the floor. Watching him scares me even more.

I take a step toward him, reaching out to stop his pacing when he suddenly turns around. We collide, and he uses the opportunity to lift me up.

"Do you trust me?" He looks deep into my eyes, like he's searching for something.

"Yes."

"I'm going to bite you." His chest heaves against mine.

"Bite me?"

"Yes, little by little, I'm going to build up your tolerance to venom. If he ever gets to you, you won't be completely defenseless." He nods, more for himself than to me.

"Will that work?"

"It will, but it isn't legal. Venom is not allowed to be used against anyone or used as a weapon. I have to, though. It's the only way. The end will justify the means. You will be safe." He carries me to his bed.

My head is swimming. This is a lot to take in. A madman wants to kill me, this I know, but it feels even more serious somehow. He's got a plan. Riven wants to break one of his own laws for me and inject me with venom. I need time that I don't have to think about all of this.

"You will be safe." His voice is stern-full of authority. "I will keep you safe."

"I believe you." I gasp as he slides his hand over my skin. He takes the opportunity to slip his tongue into my mouth.

Very quickly we find the feverish desperation that Verrin interrupted us.

"I can't think straight, Demi." He moans against my mouth. "I have to protect you from him. Everyone wants my attention, but since the moment I saw you, I can't seem to think about anything else."

Bucking my hips forward, I search for the friction I need to calm this throbbing ache between my legs.

"Please!" I beg, gripping his arms.

In a rush of frantic movements, his pants are discarded, and the shirt I'm wearing is yanked away.

I want it. There is no questioning that, but... I still have questions about how this is actually going to work. There is a tiny bit of fear lingering behind my desire. It's small, but it's there.

He wraps his hand around his double headed cock and strokes it. Spreading my legs, I plant my feet into the mattress. If this is going to work, I'm going to have to relax and hold on tight.

As my hands clench the blankets beneath me, he lets out a huffed laugh. "I'll be gentle, Demi. I want your pleasure. I'll slide in so slowly your body will be ready."

Well, then.

I watch anxiously, waiting.

In all of my experiences on earth, I realize now that I never really watched them do this. Maybe I didn't really care to.

Watching him is different. It's so sexy somehow. He's not hunched over, sweating, and grunting, which is, I guess, how I assume a human man looks when he does this.

Riven looks powerful. Watching him is intoxicating.

His body, the lust in his eyes, and the look on his face... It's all so attractive.

If he keeps this up for long, I'm not going to need his lubrication.

When he presses his tips against my skin, I feel the warmth of his release. My whole body relaxes involuntarily.

His fingers gently graze my skin; when they sweep over my clit my body jerks.

"Riven, please!" I can't wait another second. In the back of my mind, the fear that we'll be interrupted again has me feeling frantic. "Do it!" I don't mean to sound so forceful, but if someone knocks at the door right now, I'll die.

The lust-filled haze in his eyes clears as he smiles down at me. "Slow."

I almost protest, but he presses forward, just a little bit, just enough to feel it right where I want it.

"I've never done this position before." He looks down between us.

"Really?" I gasp as he nudges further, finally inside of me.

"We stand because the anatomy is slightly different. Higher." He slides in more. "You're so tight around me." His eyes pinch closed.

Inch by inch, little by little he presses forward until he's rooted so deeply inside of me it feels like he's rearranging my organs.

"Slow," he mumbles again, but I don't think he's talking to me this time.

Wrapping my arms around his neck, I hold him close to me. It's a lot. Too much. But I don't want him to stop.

"Look at me, Demi." He slides out, stopping just before he slips out completely. "You feel so good." His pupils are blown out. "Do I need to stop?"

"No! Don't stop!" I can do this. I can take it.

He slides back in, watching me—studying my face.

A choked sob rips from his chest and vibrates in his throat. "It's so..." Whatever he planned to say, he can't.

Looking down, I watch, he slides in and out slowly, his cocks slippery and wet.

"You take me so well." He groans, watching too.

My mind clears; all of the scrambled thoughts, my worries and fears, the tension it lifts away.

When he kisses me, I can't think of anything but his lips. Our bodies move together, my legs wrapping around his waist and his hips meeting mine.

It's slow, steady—wonderful.

"I'm going to bite your shoulder." He moves back to see my eyes.

I nod, unable to speak.

"I'll be gentle, and I promise you, it will only be a drop." He looks sure and confident.

"I believe you. I trust you." I let my head fall back.

Above me he moves slightly, his lips leaving a trail of warm kisses over my face and neck. When he reaches my collarbone, he stops, leaving little nips across to my shoulder. He kisses it, then scrapes his teeth across it.

There's a pinch, sharp and sudden, then he pulls back, leaving a single drop of his venom beneath my skin. The warmth blooms slowly, spreading outward like ink in water, creeping through every nerve. It feels tingly. It's not pain; it's something softer, sweeter, but so incredibly intense. My skin feels alive, sensitized as if touched by a million tiny sparks.

The warmth thickens, deepening into a white heat that flows through me, intoxicating and heavy. It's not just in my shoulder anymore; it radiates, pulsing in time with my own blood, threading through every part of me.

"Oh god! RIven!" It moves through me until I'm tingling everywhere. "It's…"

It's good.

"Are you–"

He drops his head into my neck as I spasm around him, clenching tight. My orgasm hits me so hard and fast I can't control myself. Sounds spill past my lips, his name mixed with moans. He whimpers, a sound that only adds to my crushing release.

When I finally relax, my limbs fall to the mattress, too heavy to hold up. He pulls back to look at me. When our eyes meet, I can't help but laugh.

"That was the most intense thing I've ever felt." I feel over-whelmed.

"Me too." He's still inside me, planted deep. "I can't pull out."

"Why not?" My laughter stops.

"Well, I came." He looks down between us.

"So did I." My brow furrows as I wait for further explanation.

"I'm hooked in." He says slowly. "We usually go for hours. I'm not used to your wonderfully tight, wet warmth. It's different for us. I didn't realize that I would come so fast. I wasn't prepared. I should have pulled out." He's rambling.

"Riven, what does that mean? What is happening?"

"I'm stuck, only for a little while!" He quickly adds.

CHAPTER 35

Apparently, we have very different definitions of 'a little while.' It has been a great, long while. His body is physically stuck inside of mine for an amount of time that doesn't seem quantifiable. He just keeps saying "it will release!" I'm not reassured.

"So," I clear my throat and stare at the same spot on his shoulder that I've been looking at for several minutes. "This might be a little bit awkward, but I guess now is as good a time as any. What happened with Hydriss?"

I feel so exposed. I have blankets pulled over me so that I'm not completely naked, but he's on top of me and inside of me and stuck like this.

"He reached out to someone he believed would side with him—someone that would be his ally. He was incorrect. As soon as they were able, they reached out to me to inform me of the plans he shared with them. For all of the things Hydriss is, he is not a stupid man. He didn't become a general by playing the short game. If he tried to take you, he would be slowed down and easier to catch. Now, his plan is to just get to you. If he could sink his teeth into you, one bite would be all it would take." His voice dips down, a raspy growl tinged with anger. "It would take me seconds."

"How long do you think it will take me to build up a tolerance to the venom from a real bite?" There are opposing thoughts running through my mind at the same time. On one hand, I want the venom tolerance to come quickly. I don't want to be in the position where he could find me and bite me before I'm ready. But on the other hand, thinking about the venom makes my insides flutter in the best possible way. I wouldn't mind having to train several times.

"I can't say with any kind of certainty. I've never trained someone to build up immunity." He stops short of mentioning the next thing I feel compelled to bring up.

"Because it's not legal," I whisper, barely able to meet his gaze.

"Because it's not legal," he echoes with a nod.

I hesitate, searching for the right way to say what's gnawing at me—a way that won't come off as ungrateful or like I'm questioning his judgment. But no matter how I spin it in my head, I know it will. And he's done so much—far more than I had any right to expect.

I take a breath, the words spilling out before I can second-guess them. "Why are you doing it? Don't get me wrong, I'm grateful. More than you probably know. But..."

His lips curve into a smile—the warm, sweet kind that he sometimes gets. I should have known he would understand. He always seems to.

"I can't risk it," he whispers, his voice rough yet tender. He looks away for the first time, unable to look at me. There's a rawness in his tone, an edge of something restrained. But it's not anger; it's a thousand other emotions layered on top of each other—none of them anger.

"Risk what?"

"Your life, Demi. This is the only option that I have. This is

the only thing I can do that will guarantee that you are truly safe.
If it means breaking the law, I'll do it."

"If someone finds out, will you get in trouble?" The thought
of him in trouble fills me with dread. Not only because it would
be my fault, but because if he were out of the picture, there
wouldn't be anyone to protect me.

"If someone were to find out, I don't foresee it being a
problem unless the person was particularly angry with me." He
smiles like he's thinking of someone specific.

"Like Phaedra or her sister?" I grimace, just speaking her
name out loud.

"Yes. If they found out, they would make sure that it became
a problem." He's still smiling.

"You don't look very worried about it."

"I'm not." He chuckles. "How your shoulder?" He presses a
kiss to the bite mark.

"It's fine, actually." I move it a little bit. There is a hint of
pain, like scratched skin being stretched by movement, but it's
hardly noticeable.

"Next time I'll give you two drops."

Next time. The thought of next time sends a shiver of excitement and anticipation down my spine. Even with this time still
technically underway, given that he's still inside of me, I'm
already looking forward to next time.

Heat creeps over my cheeks as I think about it.

"I wanted to ask you something." He clears his throat. He
actually looks nervous, his eyes moving over my face but not
meeting my gaze.

"Sure," I wait. What could be more awkward than this?

"The new solstice is approaching. It is a celebrated tradition
of my people. The weather will change soon, the days will grow
shorter and colder. Ophidians don't like the cold, so this celebration is a goodbye to the warm weather and to remember the
days in the sun. It is a multi day event with different obser-

vances. The last night is a gala. It is a beautiful meal and performance that brings everything to a close."

He stops, hesitating for a second. "I would be honored if you
would accompany me. Obviously you are invited to enjoy all of
the activities, but for the gala specifically, I would like you to sit
beside me."

"Oh," I've never been to a gala before. I didn't even go to my
own senior prom! "That sounds great." I hear myself answering
before my mind has a chance to think of a reason to decline.

He smiles, and a strange feeling shocks me. It's obvious that
he wasn't expecting it either.

His body is releasing me, finally slipping out from between
my legs.

"Oh my god," I whimper. This is so weird. So distinctly not
human.

"I want to bathe you, can I?" His sincerity is so endearing. I
couldn't say no if I wanted to. Not to that face.

CHAPTER 36

He didn't tell me to rush or get back to my room, but I can't help it. I'm afraid of what will happen if Sidra comes and I'm still in his bedroom.

I'd rather not open myself up to that.

Sitting on my bed, I only have to wait for a minute, and she's at the door.

"I have so many plans!" She cheers immediately. "I'm thinking green! It's so lovely on you, and it works perfectly for the occasion!" She's talking a mile a minute. It's obvious that she already put a lot of effort into the design.

"I trust you." I can't help but smile. Whatever share makes will be perfect.

"I want to try something new. Something bold and elegant. I'm thinking sheer lace!" She rattles on, pulling things out of a bag.

"Can you tell me about this gala? He mentioned food and performances." I ask, hoping to gather intel.

Her whole face lights up. 'Oh! It's just the best time! Every year is better than the last. It is a celebration of warmth. The performances are spectacular. They begin working on them immediately after the gala and spend the year perfecting them!

The food, the dancing—it's my favorite night! I look forward to it more than any other celebration." Her eyes sparkle with a dreamy, faraway look. "Just wait until you see the decorations, his majesty goes all out!"

I nod, trying to piece together a mental image. I still don't know what to expect exactly, but it seems most closely comparable to a New Years Eve party. A fancy New Year's Eve party.

I'm cautiously optimistic. There is a knot in my stomach that I'm trying to ignore—apprehension that I can't seem to shake.

He seems unbothered by how my presence seems to ruffle feathers. I am not so unbothered. I'm pretty bothered.

I don't like people to look at me like they want to squish me.

I can only assume that my attendance at their most beloved holiday will have a few people more than a little bit annoyed.

She rattles on about different performances—an aquatic show from one year, fire from another. It all seems otherworldly, which I suppose fits—since it is.

"You can sit with me, love," she offers with a sweet and sincere smile.

It's not a big deal. But for some reason, this causes me panic. Instead of just politely accepting her invitation and dealing with it later, I freeze. Why am I so awkward?

"Are you alright?" She stands from her kneeling position in front of me.

"I'm going to be sitting with Riven." Saying the word out loud makes me panic even more.

Her eyes go wide, and she seems to freeze too.

"Is he teaching you, Sarrik?"

"I don't think so. I don't know what that is."

"It is the traditional dance of Solstice Eve."

"Oh, I don't think so."

"Demi, you absolutely must learn that dance." She puts her hands on her hips, and her voice gets stern and more serious than I've ever heard it.

THE COILED THRONE   161

"Ok." She isn't leaving any room for argument here. Riven didn't say anything about a dance.

"The Eve of Solstice is one of our most honored and celebrated traditions. It is planned with care and affection, starting the day after the gala dinner. There is an entire team whose soul work revolves around Solstice Eve! If you attend and sit with our king, you have to know the dance!" She's frantic by the end.

"I'll learn it." I tried to reassure her, but she's not having it.

"Yes, you will." She walks towards the door. "Because we are going to teach you."

"What? Who?"

"Verrin, get in here!" She ignores me.

"Wait, Sidra, is this really necessary? I'll talk to Riven and—"

"If Riven planned to bring you to the gala, he should have already begun teaching you! He is being naive. If you're there beside him, every eye will be on you. They will all expect you not to know it and be angry at you when you prove them right. I know the dance spectacularly! There is no one better to show you!" She rubs her hands together.

"Alright." I feel the weight of expectation on my shoulders. "Let's do it."

Verrin looks less than thrilled, but I see him nod in agreement more than once.

"Come here, Verrin!" She commands. "We will show you the whole thing once through, then begin!"

Sitting down, I watch in awe as they move around the room. It's the most incredible dance I've ever seen. I'm mesmerized.

Each movement is graceful yet impossibly intricate, as though their bodies are made of water, flowing seamlessly from one shape into another. There's an energy between them that goes beyond dance—an intensity in their shared rhythm, their breath moving in harmony with the music. There is something so fragile about it all.

Their steps follow a pattern I can barely track, pivoting, sweeping low, then stretching high with a fluidity I could never dream of matching. They twist and fold, shifting weight so effortlessly that they seem untethered by gravity. The dance tells a story. It's a celebration of the sun, of warmth. I can feel it on my skin while I watch them. When the sun faces away and they are left in darkness, the movements and music change. The air feels colder. Their bodies speak love and reverence.

As they finish, sinking into a low, synchronized bow, my throat tightens. I barely realize I'm crying until the hot tears slip down my face. Sidra catches my eye and steps forward, her expression soft with concern. She reaches a hand toward me, gently touching my shoulder.

"I'm sorry! I don't mean to cry." I blubber. "It was so beautiful! I don't know why I'm crying. I wasn't expecting it to be that perfect!" She smiles and nods, fully understanding my current emotional state. "I don't think I'm going to be able to do that!"

"Come here." She takes my hand and leads me into the center of the room. "We'll take it slow."

"Do you think we can keep this a secret?" I look at each of them. "I want to surprise him if I'm able to figure it out."

She smiles wide and happy. "Our secret."

CHAPTER 37

Sarrik is difficult. The understatement of the century.

My body physically doesn't move how theirs can. It's like they don't have bones. I definitely have bones, and apparently, two left feet.

"Again." Sidra directs us.

The first few times, I was self conscious and embarrassed dancing with Verrin but now I'm too frustrated with myself to care.

We glide across the floor. Well, he glides, I'm much less graceful.

"Relax your face!" Sidra growls. "Part of the performance is the beauty, and furrowed brows are not beautiful."

Taking a long, slow breath, I close my eyes. I'm doing this for Riven.

Every time I want to give up, I have to remember that.

Keeping this a secret from him is difficult. I think he's starting to grow suspicious of how often Sidra is needing to measure and alter the dress.

"Again!" She calls. "Start from the beginning."

If Verrin is frustrated, he never shows it. He never flinches or even changes his facial expression. He just does what Sidra asks, over and over again without complaint.

We start to dance again, making it further into the choreography than we ever have before. I almost cheer when a knock at my door halts everything.

Verrin steps back quickly, putting distance between us, and Sidra runs toward me with fabric.

The doors swing open, and Riven steps into the room, hopefully none the wiser to what is actually happening in here. His gaze lands on me first, then shifts to Sidra, though I feel the weight of his attention lingering. "Have you decided on a color?" he asks, voice calm but with a hint of expectation.

"I'm not in charge of that." I nod toward Sidra. "She has full control."

Sidra's eyes light up as she holds up two bolts of fabric, one a deep obsidian silk that shimmers like dark water under moonlight. "I've narrowed it down to two options," she says, pressing the dark silk against my skin.

Riven's gaze sharpens. "Is now a bad time to interrupt?" His question is aimed at Sidra, but his eyes don't leave mine. "I have a break in my meeting schedule."

"Please, go ahead." Sidra practically pushes me toward him.

He reaches for me, and his fingers gently wrap around my arm, his touch searing and familiar. For a moment, there's a soft smile on his face, a warmth in his eyes. But as soon as our skin touches, his expression changes—darkening. His brow furrows, the warmth replaced by something fierce and dangerous. His grip tightens, but not painfully—just noticeably. He pauses, looking at me as though he's searching for something.

And then, in a blur, he releases me and spins, grabbing Verrin by the throat. His body hits the wall with a loud thud that echoes through the room.

The muscles in his back are tense, and his shoulders are raised. "Why is your scent all over her?" His voice is low.

I've never seen him like this.

I freeze, barely able to process the shift in him. He's usually so composed.

"He carried the fabrics." Sidra is quick on her feet, rushing over to them. Her fingers gently touching Riven's cautiously removing his hand from Verrin's throat. "He carried the fabrics for me, then I pressed them to her skin."

His shoulders relax only slightly.

"I can smell her on him." His voice is almost unrecognizable.

"Your majesty. Can you smell her on my skin? Can you smell my scent on her? We are all together here, in her room. Everything smells like her." Her voice is soft.

At this point, I want to give the whole thing away. Who cares about the surprise? But I'm too afraid to open my mouth. I don't want to tell him we're lying. He seems too wound up. I don't want to make things worse.

His eyes move between the two of them. My heart is in my throat as I wait for him to decide if he believes her.

Without a word, he's taking my hand again and leading me out of the room.

I jog beside him, down the hall, then the stairs, and out into the gardens.

"R-Riven–" I don't know what to say.

He stops under a large tree with yellow flowers that are bigger than my head blooming all over it.

He turns, his eyes searing into my skin. But before I can say anything, he's kissing me. Desperate and crazed, I feel his rage. When he lifts me up into his arms, I don't resist.

"His scent is all over you." He growls.

"I'm sorry." I whimper, holding his shirt tightly in my fists.

"I'm sorry." He groans, rolling his neck. "I have never felt so consumed and possessive. I don't know what came over me. I scared you."

"N-No." I lie. He absolutely scared the shit out of me.

"Don't lie to spare me. I frighten you. That outburst was

unacceptable." His eyes meet mine, and any fear I felt lingering is gone.

"If it makes you feel better, I can't smell him, but if I could, I wouldn't want his scent on me."

His lips tug upward, only slightly, but it's an improvement to the frown.

"Is that so?"

"Yeah, scouts honor."

"What does that mean?" He tilts his head.

"Nevermind." I lean in to kiss him. I don't want to talk anymore. I want to do something about this slightly achy, thumping feeling between my legs. I'm so empty.

"I want to bite you here. Can I?" He kisses my neck. "My venom in your veins..." He shivers.

"Yes." I'm breathless and suddenly incredibly aware of the positions of our bodies. With my legs wrapped around his waist, we're perfectly aligned if only these pesky clothes weren't in the way.

He sets me down in the soft grass, his fingers sweeping over my skin.

Arching my back, I lift to help him as he pulls my pants down and off.

The garden is magical, like Eden. Under the shade of this tree, it feels even more so.

Maybe it's the raw possessiveness in his touch or the way he tossed Verrin around like a ragdoll, but I'm a needy mess.

"It would see that you enjoyed my momentary loss of control." He pushes two of his fingers into me.

"Yes!" I cry out.

He hums, low and almost sinister. "You like my venom in your blood and my cum in your belly, don't you?" He's asking, but it's not a question.

"Yes." I'm panting, grinding against his hand.

With his pants around his thighs, he removes his hand and replaces it with his cocks. It's just what I needed.

Apparently, it's just what he needed too.

When he sinks his teeth into my neck, we both let out a feral sound.

I know he gave me more venom this time. The intensity is so much more.

I can hardly catch my breath. The burn is just to the point of pain. Right on the edge.

He lets loose, fucking into me like his life depends on it. There is nothing tender, not this time.

"Can you take more?" He growls against my skin, leaving wet kisses on my neck.

"Yes! Please!"

He kisses a spot right above my vein before breaking the skin with his fangs. I scream this time. Fire, everywhere.

I feel my body clench, an orgasm knocking my consciousness from my body. He pulls out, a whimper passes his lips as he comes all over my stomach.

He falls onto me, holding me tightly beneath his body.

I feel strange. I'm awake, but my brain is hazy, like I'm asleep or dreaming.

"How do you feel?" He runs the tips of his fingers over the bite marks.

"Weird." My voice sounds far away.

"It will fade."

"I like it." I close my eyes and rest my face against his chest.

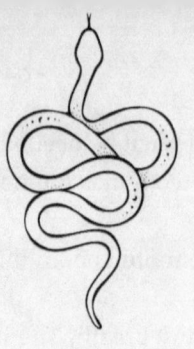

CHAPTER 38

Rushing down the stairs, I try to make it to Riven's office before he comes out looking for me.

Dance practice ran a bit longer than expected. But I'm starting to get it finally. I catch glimpses of Sidra's approval here and there, and I feel desperate for more of them.

I'm not as fluid or graceful as they are, but I'm not completely ruining it either. I have to dance with Sidra now, it's safer that way. Verrin wouldn't touch me with a ten-foot pole at this point.

The hallways are empty and quiet as I run through them. Reaching his door, I pause, smoothing down my dress and tucking loose strands of hair behind my ear, feeling every skipped breath rattling my chest.

"Come in." He calls, his voice muffled through the door. Even from here, I can hear the authority.

The moment I step inside, my steps falter. Riven sits behind his desk, half-shadowed by the dim light. There's no crown, no throne to mark him, yet everything about him radiates power. He looks up, and the weight of his gaze alone makes me stumble. He takes my breath away.

"Are you alright?" He's already standing, concern etched across his face.

I find my voice, clearing a throat that's suddenly dry. "Yes. I'm good. You called for me?"

He nods, gesturing toward the desk as he sinks back into his chair. "Come here."

There's something in the way his eyes track me, slow and steady, as if measuring my every step. The closer I get, the more I feel a nervous thrill in my stomach and a warmth in my chest. The way his eyes follow me is almost predatory.

As soon as I'm within reach, his hand shoots out, firm and decisive, pulling me into his lap. A surprised breath catches in my throat, but he only tightens his hold, anchoring me against him. My pulse skips as his fingers skim over my hip.

"One of the patrols on the outer rim found a base camp," he murmurs, his voice sending a vibration into my back.

"A base camp? You think it's-" His arms wrap around my body, holding my back to his hard chest.

"I know it is."

We don't speak his name, but it hangs in the air above us like a threat.

"He wasn't there anymore, but yes, it was his, and he hadn't been gone long. We're hard and he knows it." His arms wrap around my body, holding my back to his hard chest.

"That's good." I hum, leaning into him. At least it's news. Day after day of nothing, it was starting to feel hopeless.

I feel the tip of his nose on my neck, moving slowly over my skin.

"I am burning from the inside out." His voice drops lower. "When you're near, when we're apart, I can't think straight. I didn't call you down here for this."

"Why waste the opportunity though?" I bite back a moan. Knowing that I make him struggle and that he can't think straight because of me is intoxicating.

"Demi," my name wrapped up in his voice. The slight edge, the ache—it shoots up my spine like an electric jolt.

"Go ahead." I whimper, knowing exactly what he wants to do.

He growls, his fingers digging into my skin as his grip tightens. "I can't. I have a meeting."

"A quickie then." I grind my hips down.

"Demi." His voice is harsh now, angry even. "I…"

"Please, Riven." I press down again, feeling him beneath me.

The whimpering sound that slips up his throat sets my body on fire. He is power and authority, but he's putty in my hands.

"Tell me that you want me." He begs. "Say my name again and tell me how much you want me." He whines.

"I want you, Riven." I moan as his fingers press into my mouth. I let them in and suck them.

"I want to strip you down and lay you out on my desk." He pants.

The air feels charged, like there is electricity pinging off the walls. I can't catch a full breath even though my chest is heaving.

He sweeps my hair over to one side, sucking my skin and scraping his teeth against it.

"Bite me." I reach out, gripping the desk, bracing myself for his fangs to rip through my skin.

He doesn't hesitate, his teeth puncturing my skin, sinking inside. With each pulsating on my vein, he rubs his hips forward.

"Oh, god." The words are lodged in my throat, trapped there.

He releases me, a desperate sound falling from his lips as he thrusts his hips one final time. I feel wetness against my back, a hot spurt hitting my skin and soaking through my clothes.

He shutters, heaving as he drops his forehead onto the back of my shoulder. "I've made a mess everywhere."

I don't mean to, but a bubble of laughter slips out before I can stop it.

"How do you feel? That was six drops." His lips find the bite mark, pressing soft kisses to the tender skin.

"I feel good. The buzz is still there, but it's not as strong as before. It's fading away faster too."

"Next time, I'll do eight." He hums. "You're progressing nicely."

"Good." I square my shoulders, feeling more confident. "I-"

A knock at the door makes us both freeze. "Your majesty?" A voice calls.

"Wait." He booms, standing up with my body still in his lap. "We will go out through the library. I cannot sit through a meeting like this. The smell would likely whip them into a frenzy."

"What does it smell like?" I have to ask because, to my mind, that seems awful.

"My scent is power. Yours is soft, like rain. Mixed together, it smells like nature, like water and grass."

"That doesn't sound so bad."

"It's wonderful." He hums, carrying me through a back hallway I didn't know existed. "But it's strong."

"I wish I could smell it."

He groans. "Don't say things like that."

"Why not?"

"We're already covered in cum. We don't have time for another round."

CHAPTER 39

My throat wobbles as I try to swallow down this sick, churning feeling. I can't remember the last time I was this nervous. Maybe never.

This feels distinctly like a lamb being led to slaughter, which is dramatic on my part. Riven isn't going to let anything happen to me. I trust that.

In the past few weeks, I've also come to trust Verrin and Sidra. They will step in too. But three against everyone else doesn't seem like great odds.

Looking in the mirror, I run my fingers over the delicate fabric. Sidra is a fashion mastermind. The green fabric is so soft, lacey, and sheer but buttery somehow. Simple and understated, it's still the most glamorous thing I have ever seen, let alone actually worn.

The plunging neckline is an illusion, there is actually fabric there, shimmering diamonds and green stones seen directly into the dress.

It fits my body like a second skin, yet I can move. There is nothing restricting or uncomfortable about it. I'll be able to sit, dance, and eat—this gown is as comfortable as my favorite pajamas.

A shimmering powder was spread over my face, and now I glow. I feel beautiful. More than ever before, I feel confident.

If I had scales like they do, they would be highlighted by the cuts of the dress, around my neck and shoulders, and down my back.

I might be frantic inside, but I know I look the part.

"Demi?" Rivens voice outside of my door makes my heart stop.

This is it.

My heart is in my throat as I slowly swing the door open. He looks so handsome. We're matching in the same green, perfectly coordinated. This feels like something out of a fairytale. I'm Cinderella being whisked away to the ball by the prince, but in my case, it's a gala and a king.

"Wow." I whisper, the word slipping out before I can stop it.

"Demi, you look..." He shakes his head; a small smile tugs at his lips.

"You too." I feel myself blushing.

"You will be the most stunning thing in the room. If anyone is able to look at anything else, it will be a miracle." His thumb swipes over my lips, barely. "I won't be looking at anything else."

My stomach flutters. The way he looks at me makes me feel like I'm the most beautiful woman. It's intense and almost vulnerable; it's like he looks into me, not at me. He sees something that he thinks is beautiful and worthy.

He takes my hand, his head high, and his shoulders proud as we walk down the hallway. "Before the festivities begin," he stops, turning to face me. "I want you to know this only because I want you to enjoy yourself and not worry about anything. There are more than triple the normal amount of security personnel on hand tonight. Verrin will be seated to our right, and Sidra will be beside him. You will be surrounded by people that will protect you. That is out of an abundance of caution, however, because there is no way for anyone to sneak in.

Phaedra and Kimora are off planet at the moment. Nothing will interfere with our enjoyment of this night." He sounds so sure, so final.

"I trust you." I hope my smile doesn't give away how nervous I actually am. It's not even Hydriss or Phaedra that I'm so scared of, not tonight. It's everyone else. It's that damn dance. I would have preferred to have another few days, or possibly a year, to perfect it.

Outside, an open-air pod with big, soft seats is waiting to take us. It appears to be self-driving, which would be fascinating if I had any time to admire it. Before we've even taken our seats, the other occupants of the vehicle arrive.

"Oh! Look at you! Verrin, look at her!" Sidra bounces on her toes. "I will not degrade myself to say that I did not give all of my effort to each person that commissioned their wardrobes for tonight from me. But you, my darling, you got the best of me." She takes my hands in hers.

"I've never seen anything so lovely." Riven's voice is soft and it makes me blush again.

We move, the force pinning back to my seat slightly. As we cross the bridge, I can see it—a shimmering half-shell arena built into a tree. One side is completely open, seeming to drop oddly into the air. It's the most incredible architectural feat I've ever seen. It doesn't look possible, yet there it is.

"Wow." I breathe. "That's so…" Lanterns hang in the sky, suspended in the air, glowing soft blue against the darkness. Thousands of them, possibly more. They shimmer and pulsate, like a heartbeat. The closer we get, the more details I'm able to notice, and each one is better than the last.

Past the bridge, we turn onto a narrow road lined with such lush, densely packed greenery that we have to duck and move in our seats to avoid it hitting us as we pass. When it opens into a maze of black stone walls, thick brush, and water features, I can only watch in awe, anticipating what will be beyond the next turn.

The soft hum of music greets us before the last curve. It's strange; I can't quite identify any of the sounds.

As we come around a large tree, the building, the guests, and the large orchestra of alien-looking instruments all come into view. It makes sense now. They have some that look almost human, then others that are very obviously not of earth. One looks like it's made of glass and is both a wind and a string instrument.

With my mouth dropped open, I grab his hand and sit forward. There is too much to see.

Now that we're under the lanterns, I can see that they aren't actually lanterns at all. They look like drops of water suspended in the air. It looks like we're under a sky full of stars, close enough to reach out and touch them.

The orchestra of at least fifty is dressed all in red, each outfit unique, but they flow seamlessly together. The music floats through the air, drifting.

Everyone looks incredible. Like a Hollywood award show, but somehow even better. Each piece is a work of art. Some are more subtle, like mine, the details are impeccable but understated. Then others are showstoppers, big, bold, and in your face. One couple is dressed in vibrate blue that has running water that somehow isn't wetting the floor. It pools around them but stays with them when they walk and the ground isn't wet.

"Demi," Riven laughs, taking my arm to gently pull me out of the pod.

"Oh, sorry. I got distracted."

"Remember, hold your head up. Don't bow down to them." He whispers roughly as we walk, our arms linked toward the grand entrance.

Inside, there are tables to one side, a stage, and a large dance floor.

I can feel everyone watching me as we walk in. At least there isn't a dramatic flight of stairs to walk down. I don't know if my nervous knees could handle it.

Our table is at the front of the room, but luckily, we aren't facing the crowd. The stage is before us, dim lights glowing all around it.

Keeping my head up, I don't let myself look down, no matter how much I want to. He must notice because he squeezes my hand. The gesture gives me what I need to make it all the way to the table.

Once we're seated, the music starts again, and there is a low hum of chatter behind us.

The meal is mostly foods I recognize, like the delicious spread that Riven and I ate together. As long as I keep my eyes forward, I can almost forget that there are hundreds of people behind us.

He leans over all night, whispering to me, never letting me feel like I'm alone here. I can't focus on everyone else because he's so attentive.

"I've never seen anything like this. Not even close. The amount of work that must have gone into this, every little detail... My voice goes quiet as the stage lights dim.

"Your majesty," A woman steps out, her sparkling pink gown catches the light so that it looks like she's covered in diamonds. "Esteemed guests. May I introduce to you, Imelda On Fire."

Around us, everything darkens, then a lone spark flits across the stage. Slowly, more and more fall until it looks like raindrops of fire.

Then a woman steps out. She is stunning. Her red and orange scales would be eye-catching enough already, but her dress—I can't peel my eyes away.

Her dress is made of flames. They sweep down around her ankles and spread across the stage.

As she dances, the flames moving with her, the story starts to take shape.

It's haunting and sad. A woman, all alone, searching for something she can't seem to find. At one point, her fire dims. When she finds it again, the flames burst from her, so much that

I can feel the warmth on my skin, the audience can't hold their applause.

Tears well up in my eyes as she takes her final bow.

"What an incredible performance!"

"I knew you would enjoy it." He wraps his arm around my shoulder, and there is an audible gasp in the crowd. Whispers fill the air, but he doesn't pull away. He doubles down, pressing a kiss to my temple. "Keep your head up."

CHAPTER 40

Just as I start to let myself relax and enjoy everything around me, the woman comes back onto the stage.

"It is my pleasure to call the Sarrik." She is absolutely beaming.

Riven turns to me with a smile that takes my breath away. "This Sarrik is a traditional dance. It is to–"

Taking his hand in my slightly shaky one, I pull him up to stand. As I turn, I make brief eye contact with Sidra. She looks like she's about to bounce right out of her skin. Even Verrin gives me a tight nod. For him, that's a lot.

"What are you doing, Demi? This dance–"

"Shh." I don't trust my voice not to wobble, so I just roll my shoulders back and take the place that Sidra told me would be for Riven, the center of the dancefloor.

There is a shift in the room as I stand in the pose to begin the song.

"Demi." He sounds awestruck but gets into position as well.

Everyone is watching. I knew they would be, but it's still jarring to feel the weight of every gaze fixed on us. Their anticipation is almost tangible, crackling in the air like a current. I have no idea if they are hoping I succeed or fail.

The music begins—a haunting melody—ancient and other-worldly. I take a breath, steadying myself. There's no turning back now.

Dancing with him is very different than dancing with Verrin. With Verrin, it was all structure, like following the ticking of a clock. Riven doesn't just guide me; he anchors me. He holds me. His hands are firm but gentle, everything feels more intimate. His presence wraps around me like a protective shield, dissolving the edges of my anxiety. I feel stronger in his arms. The nervousness isn't as present. He's not going to let me fail.

The first steps are tentative, a test of how well I really know the dance. His movements are fluid, as though the dance is part of him, second nature. Each step he takes flows seamlessly into the next, effortless grace that both intimidates and inspires me. I focus on matching his rhythm; the steps I practiced endlessly finally slipping into place. He was the missing piece that I needed to feel like I really had it.

Whenever I look up at him, I catch him already watching me. His golden eyes hold a quiet pride, a smile tugging at his lips. Any lingering doubts melt away. There's something in his gaze —a warmth, a recognition—that makes my heart stutter.

As we move, the world around us begins to blur, the crowd fading away. It's just us now, gliding through the steps of a dance older than I can imagine.

His hand tightens slightly at my waist as we approach the final sequence or steps, and I follow his lead without hesitation. The last steps are intricate, but I trust him and my own feet. I can do this.

The final note of the music lingers in the air as we come to a stop, his hand still on mine, our breathing slightly uneven. For a moment, there is only silence. Then, the crowd erupts into applause.

As we leave the dance floor, the other dancers move to the sides, creating a walkway for us. As we pass, I notice several of them bowing their heads.

"You've won them over," he nudges my shoulder.

I bite my lip to hold back the smile that aches in my cheeks. I didn't learn the dance for them, I learned it for Riven. But if they hate me a little less because of it, I'll take that as an added bonus.

"Well done, your majesty." An older Ophidian with steel gray eyes and dark scales bows his head.

"Themus." Riven tips his chin. "This is Demi."

"Lovely." His eyes rake up my body in a way that makes me shiver—not in a good way. "Your reputation precedes you."

Giving him a tight-lipped smile, I don't say anything.

"I have a message for you, your majesty." He steps closer. "General Dyus sent me."

Riven stands up straighter, tugging me protectively into his side.

"Someone is helping Hydriss. They were together on Liemon. He was disguised, so his identity is unknown, but he had crown-issued weapons."

"So, a friend then." His jaw ticks. "Thank you, Themus."

"Anything you need, we are at the ready, sir." He bows his head. While he made me uncomfortable, I can see his loyalty to Riven.

"I may need to call on you." He quickly pulls me away.

As we bypass our seats, it dawns on me that the festivities are over for us.

"What happened?"

"General Dyus is in charge of the desert planet Liemon. It is vast and unpredictable. Hydriss was there with someone that I trust—someone that is close enough to me to have weapons that I only issue to my inner circle." He explains.

"Oh."

"I will protect you." He stops, turning to me and taking my chin in his hand. "He might have one friend, but I have more. Now that I know he's working with someone I considered a friend, I know that I cannot trust any of them, and I will treat them as such."

"Where are we going?" I rush into the pod, feeling his sense of urgency.

"Home."

The tension in the pod is thick and heavy as we weave through the maze toward the bridge. His brows are furrowed, and his finger taps against his knee. One of his arms is wrapped tightly around my waist.

"Come here." He tugs me up into his lap as we cross over the bridge. "I am in awe of you."

"Of me?" I jerk my face up to look at him.

"You don't know what it means that you learned that dance. I—" He sucks in a breath. "You are so strong in spirit. I cannot understate the respect I have for you, Demi. Your constant consideration for me and my people. I know you learned that dance for me, but my people saw it, and they now know the lengths you will go to to show honor to our traditions."

Snuggling into his chest, I rest my head over his heart.

CHAPTER 41

This isn't the first time we've been in this position, but it always feels like it. My body trembles, excitement and anticipation coursing through me, twitching and shaking deep in my muscles.

I'm seated on his lap behind his desk. He is lazily working, looking at screens that are much more advanced than anything I've ever seen at home. Watching him work, so calm and relaxed, makes me want to jump him.

Everything he does is attractive, powerful, and deliberate—even working.

When he moves both of his arms behind me, I feel the change in his demeanor. His body isn't loose beneath me anymore.

His fingers gently sweep over my skin as he slides my dress down. The low hum of appreciation in his throat makes the room suddenly warmer. He stands us, letting my feet down to the ground gently so that he can drop my dress into a puddle of fabric at our feet.

"Are you going to bite me?"

I never expected to like it so much. To crave it. It's like a drug; it spreads euphoria through my veins.

He groans and drops his forehead down, pressing it into my

shoulder. "Demi." There is a thick, needy desperation in his voice now. "I had plans. I wanted to take my time with you tonight. To show you slowly, over and over again, how much I appreciate you. You can't say things like that."

The over and over again part sounds good, but I could do without the 'slowly.' I want him right now.

"Why not?" I press back slightly, my naked body pushing into the front of his pants.

"Because," his breath falters. "It makes me lose control."

"Good." I press back again.

With fast, desperate hands, he tugs his pants down. "I don't want to pull out tonight." He presses himself against me. "I want to hook in."

After last time, I thought I would have reservations about letting him do that again. But now, I want it so desperately that if he doesn't do it, I think I might cry.

"Oh god, please!" I drop my head back, resting it against his chest. "Please, do it."

That's all the convincing he needs. He pushes in, the gnawing emptiness fading away in an instant.

He wraps his arm around me, holding me up against his chest. "You feel so…" he chokes, his voice breaking as he groans.

The idea of taking his time is forgotten completely as he starts to speed up.

Biting into my lip, I try to keep myself quiet as he builds the pressure; tighter and tighter, I feel like I'm pulling inward. Every muscle strains, growing painful but in the best way.

He releases me, and I fall forward, pressed flat against his desk. Holding onto it, I let him ram into me, and he gives me as much force as I can take. The sound of our skin slapping together fills the room, only slightly muffled by moans and panted breaths.

When his hand wraps around to rub my clit, his face flush against my back, I know I don't have long to brace myself. The weight of the wave about to crash down on me is going to crush me.

In a sudden, unexpected motion, he presses one of his hands to the back of my neck, holding me down against his desk. The pressure is just what I need. The possessive, dominant position is everything I didn't know I was waiting for.

I open my mouth, but no sound comes out. My eyes roll back into my head as my mind goes completely blank. Peace. I'm in the void again, far away from the ground, floating.

I'm completely unaware of anything until I feel a pinch in my wrist. It's so slight I wouldn't have even noticed, but for the warmth that starts to spread from the spot. He has my arm up, pulled back behind me, with his teeth buried in my skin.

I can feel him pulsating inside of me with each beat of my heart. The venom spreads, hot, rushing through me.

Immediately, even in this hazy state, I know it's more than he's ever given me before. He drops my arm and falls forward, pressing himself inside of me as deep as he can. He swells and releases; there is heat there too. He's locked in. This time, I know what that feels like, and I know exactly what's happening.

He breathes against my skin. "I didn't want to come yet."

I giggle, the venom making me feel loopy and loose. Immediately I regret it. "Oh! Shit!" Laughing around him between my legs like that makes the feeling even stronger. "You're really rooted in there." I clear my throat as the sobering effects of the pressure inside of me hit me hard. My skin still tingles, but my brain is clear.

"Come here." He wraps his arms around me and lifts, sitting in his chair with my body comfortable on his lap. He leans back in the chair, putting his feet up on the desk with mine resting above them. "Comfortable?"

"Very." I lean into his chest.

"How is the venom? That was ten full drops, nearly a complete release." He kisses my hair.

"It was really strong but good." I feel my cheeks heat, and I'm glad he can't see them.

He leans us back further, grabbing a book from somewhere behind him. Wrapping his arms around me, he opens the book, and I let my eyes drift closed.

"Before time, before the sky or the sun, there was a single planet inhabitable in this system." He starts to read. "The Ophidian race lived together, all species together under one sun."

I try to stay awake and listen to his history, but the sound of his voice lulls me to sleep. I'm safe in his arms, and the tingle in my skin is too hard to fight.

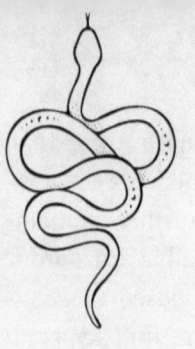

CHAPTER 42

"'ll be back as soon as possible." He kisses me again.

"Riven, go!" I swat at him. He has been attempting to leave for a meeting for at least twenty minutes. His procrastination is endearing. "Are you already late?"

"I'm the king. It's not as if they can start without me." He straightens his spine, and a slightly mischievous smile tugs at his lips. "But, I'll go."

"I'll be waiting here." I assure him again.

He hesitates for a moment longer before finally turning to leave. The echo of his footsteps fades down the hallway, and with it, the tension I didn't even realize I'd been holding in my shoulders. I take a deep breath and head for the bathroom. Some things about me need to stay a mystery, even to him. He doesn't need to see everything.

The shower is paradise, the warm water cascading over me in endless waves. At home, my bathroom was small, and the hot water would cut out after five minutes. Here, I can take all the time I need. It's like being pampered at a spa.

After taking much longer than necessary, I force myself out. I rummage through his wardrobe, looking for something to wear. That's when I hear it.

A thud.

It was one quick sound, like something hitting the ground. Normally I wouldn't give something like that a second thought, but now...

Frozen in the middle of the room, I listen.

Silence.

"Hello?" My voice is barely a whisper.

I know it was real, but it was probably nothing. I'm not the only person here. It was just a sound. No big deal. I'm just nervous.

Just as I let out the shaky breath I've been holding, there is another one.

This time it's louder.

"Riven?" I whisper, but I know in my gut it's not him.

Panic courses through me, and my flight or fight response gets all jumbled up. I don't know where to run or what to do.

Taking three steps back, then freezing again, my heart is pounding so loudly that I can't hear past it. All I can think is that someone is here to kill me. I'm not prepared to see Hydriss right now. Ever, really, but right now specifically.

"What do I do?" I panic, grabbing a shirt. I definitely don't want to have to fight for

My life while naked.

The balcony doors are open.

I hear the sound again, and this time I'm sure it's coming from right outside the door.

"Oh my god, oh my god!" My legs wobble.

Running toward the balcony I have a split second to make a decision. Do I lock it or try to climb down? I don't know if someone is trying to break in.

My breath catches in my throat as I reach the doors. Crouching down, I inch outside, craning my neck to look down without being seen.

"Sidra?" I don't mean to say it so loudly, but it slips out. She's standing in the garden below the balcony with several pieces of fruit cradled in her arms.

"Oh," she drops the fruit onto the ground, and they roll through the grass. She quickly smoothes out her dress. "Hello."

"What are you doing?"

She looks nervously toward the house.

Standing upright, I lean over the railing to see what she's looking at.

Verrin is standing at an open window, stiff and serious as he always is.

"Are you throwing fruit at him?"

"Not at him!" She exclaims quickly. "To him."

"Why are you throwing fruit to him from the garden?"

"Well-"

She starts, but he cuts in. "No reason."

"No reason?" I don't believe that for one second.

"He's hungry." Sidra scowls at him, placing her hands on her hips.

"What's going on?" I'm so confused. "Are you hungry? Why can't you eat? Why are you throwing the food at him?"

Verrin opens his mouth, but Sidra cuts him off.

"We just sat down to lunch when he was called to guard the door. No one is allowed up the stairs when Riven is away. So, I'm throwing him the fruits." She shrugs before bending down to grab one.

I clap my hands over my mouth as a snort bursts through my attempt at hiding my laughter.

"Verrin, I'll be right out. Let's go downstairs." I barely get the words out.

My big, strong, serious snake alien bodyguard is having food thrown to him, and I can't handle it. Now that the fear is gone completely, I can't stop laughing.

Taking a moment to gather myself, I feel composed enough to leave the room.

Opening the door, the sight of him sheepish and embarrassed makes me laugh again.

"Let's go. I can't have my bodyguard starving!" I walk down the hallway, and he follows, a few steps behind, as always.

Sidra is waiting at the bottom of the stairs. "Will you join us?"

"No, no. I'm going to wait for Riven. Please, enjoy your meal!" As much as I enjoy their company, I want to wait for him. Our meals together have become one of my favorite parts of the day.

Sitting with them at the table, I watch as they eat together. Her hand brushing his, the way he serves her. It's all so tender and wholesome. Verrin is the serious type, but when he looks at her, it's so clear.

As they finish eating, I know they're rushing; I recognize the same lingering hesitation in them that I see in Riven. They know it's time to go, but they don't want to separate.

"If this ever happens again, please knock on the door. I am more than happy to come down. You have to eat too." I look at him seriously. Even as I say the words, I know that he won't. "Or, Sidra, you can throw some fruit at my window to notify me."

"I will do no such thing!" She tuts, but a smile tugs at her lips.

CHAPTER 43

"You're not sleeping." His voice is soft in the dark. It wraps around me, comforting me.

"No." I sigh and cover my face with my hands. I knew he was awake, but I was trying to stay still and quiet. I don't want to worry him.

I can't sleep. I don't know how to tell him that every time I close my eyes, I have the most horrific nightmares. They came out of nowhere, but they're haunting me even after I wake up, they replay in my mind.

Hydriss finds me. Phaedra exacting her revenge. The people of Earth are being rounded up and brought here against their will for what purpose I don't even want to guess. I can't escape them.

They are awful, and I find myself unable to fall asleep.

"What's wrong?" His arms wrap around me, holding me tightly to his chest—the only place on this world or any other that I feel safe right now.

"Nothing." I crane my neck to kiss his cheek. I have to distract him.

"Did something happen?" My kisses are clearly not working.

I don't want to tell him that hearing an innocent and frankly adorable interaction between Verrin and Sidra almost gave me a heart attack.

I'm trying to ignore it, to be in the moments as they happen and focus on the things happening around me, but I think the dreams are a sign. I can't pretend forever.

"Nothing happened, not really, I just—" As I work out the best way to explain it, I'm zapped with an idea. It hits me like lightning.

Jumping out of bed, I stumble around in the dark.

"Demi?" I hear him, I know he's coming, but I can't keep still. Pacing around in the dark, I feel energized.

"We should set up a trap!"

"What?" The lights come on, starting low and growing brighter slowly.

"A trap! We'll plan a trip or something! We can set it up so that it's a big deal, everyone will know about it! Then, we send groups out ahead of us so that we're more guarded than it looks. Is there a cabin in the woods or something? Do you have those here? A remote place that might make him think he can get to me easily? If he really wants to get me, let's set it up!" I'm hardly breathing by the time I spill everything messily from my brain in disjointed, rushed, incoherent thoughts.

"Wait." His brow furrows as he takes my hands in his, forcing me to stop pacing around frantically. "Demi, I don't think—"

"Riven, it's perfect! We'll make him think that he can get to me easily! We can plan it out and set a trap!" My mind is racing in fifty different directions.

"Demi, that is too dangerous. We can plan and prepare, but there is no guarantee that he will do exactly as we want him to do. He is too unpredictable a variable to make a perfect plan." His voice is soft.

"Have you already thought of this?" I feel like my idea is actually not new.

"Yes, it's been discussed at great length. I can't risk it." He sweeps his hand up over my cheek into my hair. "If anything goes wrong, it will be—"

"Even if something goes wrong, his bite won't be able to hurt me. Is there a way you can put a tracker on me? That way, in the worst-case scenario, you'll be able to follow me? I just can't keep doing this. The threat of him constantly looming over my head is starting to make me feel…" Itchy. I don't know how else to describe it to him. I'm itchy. It's nagging in the back of my head all the time, creeping down my spine.

He sits down on the end of the bed and holds his head in his hands. "I knew it was bothering you more than you were letting on. I could feel it."

"I feel safe with you." I sit beside him, feeling defeated and small. "I mean that. But knowing that he's out there, waiting and watching, it's too much."

"The idea of using you as bait to draw him out is…"

I can only nod. I'm not particularly excited about the idea myself, but it's the only thing I can think of that might actually work.

"We have discussed a decoy, but there isn't anyone that looks similar enough to you, even from a distance, to make him believe you're there." He sounds more tired suddenly. The heaviness of all of this showing its weight.

"What if we sneak out there, to wherever 'there' is, and put my scent around, maybe leave a few items there?"

His head tilts to one side while he considers it.

"There is a woodland community that is remote, on the far end of this system, near the outer rim. We could take a small blood sample and spread it there. Then make a public announcement that I will be taking a short leave." He stands suddenly. "We won't release any other details; that will make it believable. Then, when we leave, we won't go there at all. We will send Verrin and a group of covert operatives. It could work. There is no guarantee, but even the possibility might be worth it to try."

"Ok." My shoulders feel lighter as I sit up, a sense of purpose filling my chest. "What do I need to do?"

He smiles, one of the soft ones that makes me feel warm again. "First, we should sleep. I will call a meeting with my most trusted inner circle in the morning. We will present our plan and listen to their input. Verrin is skilled in covert operations; he will have ideas and concerns to add."

"Sleep first, right. That makes sense." I crawl up to lie down, eager to fall asleep. Now that we have something, even an idea, to hold onto, I can't wait to start figuring it out. This has gone on long enough; it's time to end it.

CHAPTER 44

My knee bounces, all of my nervous energy seeking an outlet. I don't know why I'm so nervous.

Everything will be fine, probably.

If Verrin sees anything we missed, he will address it. This is going to work. It has to. Now that we have a plan, I can hardly keep still, it's like my skin is vibrating. I want to dive in right away.

As they enter the room, everyone looks momentarily surprised to see me but quickly masks it.

"We're going to set a trap." Riven gets right to it with no greetings or small talk given. Maybe he's as anxious as I am, or maybe this is always how he handles business. "Speak freely, if you see something that has slipped my attention, point it out. We don't have time for mistakes. This is a one-time opportunity. If we mess it up, he will see it coming; the element of surprise is on our side, but only this once."

While he explains the plan, I watch their faces. Each of them is a pillar of emotionless stoicism. I can't read any of them.

"Who will bring her blood?" Verrin immediately has questions.

"We will. I want him to smell us there. It's important that he only smells us." Riven sits back in his chair.

"Will you leak information?" Another guard asks.

"No. I do not want him to suspect. We will announce the leave days as is customary, but nothing else. If he takes the bait, he will have to seek out the details."

I wish one of them would say something to let me know what they're thinking. I can see them processing, but no one is giving anything away.

"As long as you are safely off-planet and we are able to hide our scents from him, it could work." Verrin speaks slowly after a long pause.

"What makes you hesitate?" Riven folds his arms over his chest. He looks so calm, not at all how I'm feeling.

"I'm not sure if we have the numbers to support this." He stops, and the tension in the room seems to triple.

What just happened?

He has armies at his disposal. Why wouldn't he have the numbers for a fairly small secret operation?

"Continue." Riven's voice has a sharp edge that it didn't have just one second ago.

"Your majesty, we will need a team of at least four on-site. Then at least four physically with her. Do you completely trust eight people? There are four of us here today. Do you have four others that you are comfortable sharing this plan with? We still don't know who the betrayer is." His words are measured.

My heart sinks.

"I believe I know who the traitor is."

My neck almost breaks with how quickly I snap it to the side to look at him. The tension in the room shifts again. Clearly, this is news to everyone.

"I haven't shared my suspicions because I don't want him to know that I'm watching him." He quickly adds as one hand slides up my thigh. He gives me a light, reassuring squeeze. "I want to move forward with this plan for now, if something comes up, we will adjust."

"Yes, your majesty." They bow their heads.

"You will be the team that accompanies us to leave behind the traces." He nods sternly before standing abruptly. He holds my hand gently and leads me out of the room.

We move quickly through the hallways, and I know the conversation isn't over. He's moving too purposefully.

We're not even fully in the bedroom when he turns, grabbing my face in both hands. "Murrious will be here tonight."

"Oh," I wasn't expecting that. The thought of seeing him again fills me with instant dread. Last time he wasn't exactly quiet about the way he wanted to make me his.

"Do you trust me?"

"Yes." I don't even have to think about it.

"He's not going to harm you. I will not let him out of my sight. I'm luring him in."

"So, he's the one?"

"There are more than one." He purses his lips.

A heavy weight presses down on my chest. He's being betrayed because of me. People are turning their backs on him.

"This is not your fault." The sternness in his voice catches me off guard. "If they are willing to betray me, then they were never loyal to begin with."

Wrapping my arms around his waist, I hug him tight. He's right. Their betrayals are their own, but I still hate that it's happening.

"Do you remember what I told you on Elapidia? After the confrontation with Kimora?" He looks at me with a softness that feels like it doesn't belong in this moment.

"Never rattle before you strike." I've thought about it daily since he said it.

"Never rattle before you strike." He nods. "I trust you implicitly. I am not withholding information from you because I don't trust you. I will tell you everything, but it's imperative that you are believably shaken and afraid when the time comes."

"Don't tell me." I almost laugh. He might know me better than I know myself. "But who can I trust?"

"Verrin and General Dyus. They will be by your side every step of the way. They are my most loyal and trusted guards."

Taking a deep breath, I nod. A few hours ago, I thought I had clarity. Now I'm not sure of anything but the fact that I trust him.

CHAPTER 45

There is something strange about sitting beside him while he pilots the pod. It feels almost normal—like we're just a couple in a car together.

We've never been this truly alone before.

Usually, he has an entourage of people around him. But now, it's just the two of us, apart from the world we know, adrift in the vast expanse of space. The silence between us isn't uncomfortable—it's charged, alive, carrying a weight I'm not sure I'm ready to unpack. I know he's stressed. I can feel it.

This plan can go wrong at any point.

It's frightening and nerve-wracking.

But there is something exciting about it.

We're doing something. Whatever happens now happens because we didn't just sit back and wait. The choice has been taken away from Hydriss and anyone else that is working with him.

Even with all of the unknowns, this feels like progress. We're moving toward something—possibly my demise, but at least it's moving forward.

"Why do you keep looking at me like that?"

"Oh," I feel myself blushing. Caught in the act. "I haven't seen you drive or fly before."

"And you like it?" His brow furrows.

"I mean, yeah." I bite back a nervous giggle. "It's attractive."

"This?" He looks bewildered as he gestures to the console in front of him.

"Yeah. Don't you ever see something that's completely nonsexual but, for some reason, it just does it for you?" I hope he has, because otherwise this is weird.

"Oh, yes. I do have a few of those." He nods thoughtfully. "I suppose I never thought of it in those terms before." He shakes his head slightly. "They do it for me." He whispers quietly to himself.

My interest is piqued. "What things?"

A small smile tugs at his lips, but he doesn't say anything.

"Oh, come on! You know one of mine!"

"When you are nervous or very interested in something, you tuck your hair behind your right ear, only the right. I like it. You are difficult to read sometimes; human cues are different from Ophidians. That is an insight into your feelings." He presses a few buttons on the console.

"I don't do that." Do I?

"You do it often."

The air in this small cabin feels warmer suddenly. There is a heat in his gaze that wasn't there before.

"What else does it for you?" His voice dips down into that raspy place that definitely 'does it for me.'

Really, everything about him is attractive. His eyes, his voice, the quiet, calm authority that wafts from him. He demands respect and attention, but not in a pretentious way; he just does.

We're going to this place to have sex and spread some of my blood around. That's the entire point.

After this conversation, I'll be ready the moment we land.

"How much longer?" I shift slightly in my seat.

A low laugh rumbles from him. "Soon."

He moves in my peripheral vision, and it catches my attention. He's shifting in his seat too, adjusting himself.

This is probably a very bad idea; that's why I don't let myself overthink it.

Reaching over, I press my palm down on the front of his pants.

"Demi!" His spine stiffens as he sits upright.

"Do you want me to stop?" I run the tip of one finger over the hard bulge.

"No." He groans and leans back. "We're almost there."

"I'll just make sure you're ready then." I slip out of my seat completely. On my knees beside his seat, I have better access to him.

He mumbles something under his breath, and his breath catches. I unbutton the front of his uniform and slide my hand inside.

Warm and hard.

Wrapping my hand around him, I watch his face. He shifts his hips forward, rubbing against me.

"This is dangerous."

I hum and move my hand again.

"I'm guessing road head isn't a thing here?"

"Road—what?" His hips flex again.

Giggling to myself, I lean forward and lick him, just the tips.

I'm really enjoying the upper hand here.

"Demi." He moans my name in that gruff, needy way that makes my insides melt.

"Yes?" I lick him again, swirling my tongue this time.

"This is highly—"

Whatever he was about to say turns into a grunt when I suck one of the heads into my mouth.

My heart pounds in my chest. This is new for him. I'm giving him something he's never had before.

The anxiousness I felt earlier is gone. This is the fun part of the plan. We get to go somewhere secluded—completely alone together and have sex. That sounds like the perfect night.

Working him in and out of my mouth, using my hands, I get him as close to the edge as possible, then back away.

Once, twice, three times.

By the fourth time, I feel the pressure of added speed. He's flying faster now.

I love it.

Each time I pull back, he makes a sound, a needy, desperate whimper that jolts like lightning in my belly.

"Please," he pants, squirming in his seat.

"How much longer?"

"It's there." He clears his throat.

Peeking up, I look over the console out the window.

Oh. So it is.

A massive wall of dark green and yellow spreads out in front of us. He told me this planet was used for food production and has more trees and plants on it than all the others combined. I can see it. It's so densely packed it looks like a solid mass.

"Land this thing." I clench my thighs together as I lean in to lick another long strip over his swollen cocks.

"Come here." He pulls my arm. "Sit here so I can hold you while we land."

Facing him, I settle onto his lap, resting my face in the crook of his neck. "I can sit down in my seat."

He grunts and wraps his arm around my waist tight, holding me in place.

He rubs against me, the friction against my aching clit drawing a moan before I can stop it.

"When we land, I'm going to make you pay for that teasing. You won't be able to walk by the time we leave." He thrusts his hips up again.

Sucking his skin softly, I move my hips in rhythm with his.

"I want you to bite me too."

CHAPTER 46

My body is tired, but my mind is racing.

We're hooked together, his body buried inside of mine. We've marked this place with so many scents I hope Hydriss chokes.

I've been given enough venom to kill me twice over, and the only effects I feel are some tingling in my limbs.

"What are you thinking about?" He hums.

"Can I say something crazy?" With some effort, I sit up enough to look at him.

His eyes narrow, but he nods, waiting.

"I know it's insane, and I truly don't want it to happen, but part of me wants to see the look on his face if he is ever actually able to bite me. All of this hiding, running, plotting, and scheming, and it's for nothing."

His lips twitch. "The thought of him biting you makes me want to remove his head. But I know what you mean, there would be a certain satisfaction in it."

Resting my head on his chest again, I let my eyes close. I know we have more to do, but for now, I just want to listen to his heart beating. This moment suddenly feels very fleeting.

I feel him releasing me, and I cling to him, holding tight to his chest.

"Is it time for blood?" I whisper, the words barely escaping, as if saying them aloud might shatter the fragile peace between us.

His chest rises and falls beneath me in a rhythm that feels steady, anchoring. "We can wait a few minutes," he says softly, his voice carrying a weariness. Still, there's a quiet contentment in his tone that I recognize because I feel it too. "Let's just sit."

I feel safe—wrapped in his arms, shielded from the chaos and threats. But my mind refuses to settle. It churns, cycling through every possible scenario, every risk, every tiny misstep that could unravel everything.

This has to work.

His hand moves slowly up and down my back. "Just a few more minutes."

"Demi." His heart rate picks up, beating hard against my ear. "I have—I need—" He stutters, hesitating.

Nerves creep in. He's usually so calm and collected. Knowing that he's rattled, for whatever reason, scares me.

Sitting up again, I search his face. He doesn't look like himself.

"Riven, what's wrong?"

"When the threat is over, when Hydriss and anyone that is conspiring with him have been dealt with, do you want me to find Earth?"

"Oh," a pit forms in my stomach.

"I will ensure your return is handled with the utmost secrecy," he tucks a strand of wild hair behind my ear. "Only my most trusted wardens will know anything about your location. You would be safe, I promise." His face softens, and there's a sadness in his eyes so profound that it twists like a knife deep in my chest.

The thought of going home has been a distant, unreachable dream, buried beneath the fear of Hydriss discovering Earth.

The idea of giving him a map to find and exploit my world—to steal more innocent lives—feels too selfish, too risky.

But if he's gone...

If the threat dies with him...

There would be no reason that I couldn't go back.

"I..." My voice falters. The weight of the decision feels too heavy.

"You don't have to answer now." He quickly takes my face in his hands. His voice is gentle, cutting through the panic rising inside me. "I just needed you to know. Keeping you here without giving you a choice would be wrong." His voice wavers, but the conviction in his words never falters. "Make no mistake: I don't want you to leave. If you stay—if you choose to stay— then my planet, my home, my bed, my arms—they'll be open to you, always. But it has to be your decision. Whatever you want, I will make sure you are safe enough to have it."

I can't think about this right now.

Tears sting my eyes as his words sink in, the honesty of his offer tearing me apart. How can I make this choice? How can I think about leaving when the battle isn't even over?

"I can't..." My voice cracks as I whisper, "I can't think about this right now. We have to get through this first."

His thumbs brush over my cheeks. "Then don't. Not yet. Focus on what's in front of us. We'll figure out the rest when the time comes. There is no rush."

He shifts slightly, his body moving beneath mine, and I know it's time.

"Blood?"

"Blood." He nods.

Untangling myself from him, more than ever, I want to stay exactly as we are.

"We need to be wise with the placement. I believe the most authentic scenario would be that you were injured by the water. We can walk down to the shore, swim, then make the smallest cut and leave droplets behind leading back to the cabin. If we overdo it, he will sense the trap. It has to be just enough to hold your scent, to lure him in, but not to make him think it was left intentionally."

"Ok, that sounds good." I gulp. I just assumed we would leave blood all over the place. This is better.

Walking hand in hand, we trek through the forest. It might be my imagination, but it feels like we're going slow on purpose.

"The day I first saw you, tumbling from the wreckage of that ship, I was intrigued. Your fear was palpable, but you never stopped running. I followed you through the forest in awe of your determination." He hums.

"I wish I knew then that you wouldn't hurt me. It could have saved me from a lot of running."

The trees break, stopping at the shore of a strange lake. It moves, large waves lapping at the shore like the ocean, but I can see the other side from here. It's a small, contained body, but it rolls and tumbles.

"Let's wade into the water, I'll hold you. He'll be able to smell it, it will sell the idea that the blood left behind was accidental." He turns, wrapping his arms around me.

"Don't let go of me." I shiver, stepping toward the rough water.

"Never."

CHAPTER 47

Clinging to him, I hold my breath as he wades into the rough water, each step cutting through the waves with an effortless strength that both reassures and unnerves me. The lake is warmer than I expected, its warmth a stark contrast to the chill creeping up my spine.

"Give me your hand." His voice is low and gentle, but there's a weight to it that makes my stomach twist.

"What now?"

"I'll pierce your finger," he explains, his fingers brushing mine, sending a jolt through me. "We'll let a few drops fall into the water."

"How can he possibly smell a few drops of blood in so much water?" I glance out at the water surrounding us.

"Trust me," his lips pull down into a faint, somber frown. "He'll smell it."

"Is it bad?" In a stupid way, I feel self-conscious. Who cares what my blood smells like? Apparently, I do.

His gaze meets mine, piercing and unflinching. "It's so good." The words are low, almost reverent. His fingers tighten on mine as his tone softens further, raw with honesty. "Everything about your scent is intoxicating—it's soft but completely unique. There's nothing on my planet like it. It's like a flower, but sweeter. I could pick a single droplet out of the air in a room filled with thousands of others."

"Oh." The word comes out small, almost breathless. My cheeks burn, a strange blend of embarrassment and endearment. Leaning forward, I press a small kiss to his lips. "Go ahead, bite me."

He presses the pad of my pointer finger against one of his fangs, nicking the skin.

Gently, he puts pressure and forces five drops out into the water.

Then, he licks my finger, erasing the blood from my skin. This feels so incredibly intimate. I'm not sure why, but even more than sex, even more than having him hooked inside of me, this feels like the most connected we've ever been.

It's almost frightening. The weight feels like pressure in my chest, pushing on my lungs.

"Riven," I whisper.

"I know." He presses a kiss to my finger before tightening his grip on me and carrying me back to shore. "We just have to make it through this. He will come. He can't help himself. This will work."

I don't know if he's trying to convince me or himself.

Wrapping my arms around his neck, I take comfort in his skin.

After we reach the beach, he bites again, leaving droplets of blood on the ground as we walk back to the little wooden cabin in the middle of nowhere.

"So that's it." I sigh. It feels anticlimactic. All of this build-up and just like that, it's over. The blood is out there.

"That's it." He cups my chin. "Are you ready?"

"I'm ready." I square my shoulders, trying to be brave.

He stares at me for a moment before pressing a button on a communication device. As soon as he presses it his facial expression changes. He's stern and serious, cold.

"Your majesty." Verrin's voice comes through the speaker.

"We're ready to start phase one. Make the announcement." His voice is absolute.

"Yes, sir. We are hovering near the planet, and we will arrive very soon."

Without another word, he ends the call.

There is a heaviness in the air as I sit down, knowing that right now, they are telling everyone, everywhere, that Riven is taking a day of rest off-planet. Hydriss will hear it come running. It's all part of the plan but knowing that he will be on his way to our exact location makes my stomach fold over on itself.

He looks at me, his softness returning to his face and voice. "Do you want to go over everything again?"

Even through my nervousness, I can't hold back my smile. "I remember it."

"If something starts to go wrong, if—"

"I'll do exactly as Verrin tells me to." I'm impressed with the way I'm able to keep my voice from wobbling. I sound confident. I hope he believes it.

He grabs my face, kissing me with so much emotion it takes my breath away. I want to pull away, to scold him for kissing me as if he's saying goodbye, but I can't. Instead, I kiss him back, giving him everything he's giving me. If this is goodbye, it had better be good.

A sound from outside makes my heart sink. They're already here? He said he was nearby, but we've only had a few minutes.

"I need more time." I cling to him, digging my fingers into his uniform.

"There will never be enough," Riven murmurs, his voice low and heavy with an emotion he rarely lets surface. His lips twitch into a fleeting smile, but his eyes betray him. He's worried. "This is better. Go, so we can be reunited."

"The sooner we separate, the sooner we'll be reunited." I nod, hoping to convince myself.

Rolling my shoulders back, I think brave thoughts as we walk out to meet them.

"General Dyus." I bow my head as we reach him, my voice steady despite the crack I feel threatening to open in my chest.

"It is my honor to be a part of this." He looks at me, then Riven.

"Your majesty," Verrin holds eye contact, and an eternal moment passes between them. Neither says a single word, but I can see the conversation happening. "We will meet you when this is done."

"When it's done." Riven's voice is so cold it sends a chill down my spine.

"Be careful." I whisper so that only he can hear me as I hug him tightly.

His embrace is swift and fierce, his arms lock around me like armor, and for the briefest second, I feel safe. "This is almost over," he whispers, but the way he's holding me feels like a goodbye, and I cling to him tighter, refusing to let the moment slip away.

As he pulls back, his gaze lingers on mine, and for a fleeting second, I think of begging him to let me stay here. But I can't. Not now.

"It's time." He lets go of me, and I force my feet to move, to carry me into the pod.

CHAPTER 48

General Dyus is the complete opposite of Verrin. He isn't chatty by any definition of the word, but even a few questions seem like a lot compared to Verrin.

"Fascinating." He listens intently as I explain the vast spectrum of human height, weight, and physical appearance.

He was particularly interested in our lack of venom or self-defense mechanisms.

"We can camouflage, people do it. But it's external. We use paint or clothes, it doesn't come from us."

"Fascinating." He says again.

"And you have no weaponry?"

"Again, we do. But it's not built into us. We have guns, knives, and bombs; we made them."

"So you are an ingenuitive people, then?" He looks impressed.

"I would say we are." I look at Verrin. His face is stoic, but he gives me a slight nod. He's listening even if he's not adding anything to the conversation.

Talking is helping. It's ridiculous, I just left him less than an hour ago, but I miss him. There is an empty feeling without him.

I try to imagine what my life would look like if I took the opportunity to go back home when this is over.

Both sides feel like a loss.

If I stay here, I'm here forever. My home, Earth, will be a distant memory. My life and everyone in it will be left in my past.

If I leave, I know, as sure as I'm breathing, that I'll never meet anyone like Riven. No man will ever be able to compare. I'll miss him as long as I live.

I can't decide which fate is worse.

An ache settles in behind my heart.

"There," Verrin speaks for the first time since we started this journey, to point out our destination in the distance.

I pull in a shaky breath, my lungs fighting against the tight knot coiled in my chest. The plan is simple on the surface—wait here until General Hydriss steps into the trap we've set. But nothing about this feels simple. My hands tremble, not just from exhaustion but from the knowledge that so much hinges on this one moment.

If everything goes according to plan, I should be with Riven by morning. The thought steadies me enough to keep a calm exterior. I can picture him there, waiting. He'll come for me. He always does.

Verrin shifts beside me, his gaze sharp and unreadable, scanning the terrain as if he expects danger to spring from the shadows at any moment. I envy his composure, his silent confidence. He doesn't falter. He doesn't let fear leak into his movements.

We touch down in a field of long, golden grass.

The door opens, and Verrin jumps out first, tension in his shoulders and neck. He stalks out, taking three big steps before spinning around. I can tell by his eyes—something isn't right.

"No!" He shouts, stopping me in my tracks. Pulling my leg back inside, I wait in the doorway.

"Phaedra." General Dyus hisses and grabs my arm, pulling me inside.

"She's here?" I turn to look at him, but a glowing light outside catches my attention. Looking over his shoulder, I watch it grow larger by the second.

"Out!" Verrin screams from outside, the urgency in his voice spurring us both into action without hesitation.

Dyus grabs my arm and pulls me out the door just as the pod is fried by an electrical pulse.

"Oh my god," panic courses through me.

"I'll stay behind her." Dyus calls up to Verrin, who is standing in front of me, a shield protecting me from whatever is out there.

Verrin presses buttons on his communicator with calm precision. It's as if he's been in this situation one hundred times before. He knows exactly what to do.

"Stay behind me, hold onto my shoulder." He looks into my eyes, and I know I'm going to be alright. "They're already here. But we know what to do, don't we?"

"Yes." I nod breathlessly. "We do."

This was always a possibility. I knew it. We all did.

Of course I had hoped that things would have gone the other way, but we planned for this.

"Let's move."

Dyus' hand comes down on my shoulder, gentle but steady.

We walk several steps in this formation before Verrin stops. "movement," he whispers.

"Come out, show yourself!" Dyus calls.

"I have to say, I'm disappointed." Phaedra stands. She looks absolutely gorgeous. Her stunning features accentuated by the gold all around her. Her stark white hair is pulled into a long, straight ponytail that sways when she walks. "I was to be your queen. How easily you cast me aside! Was there no loyalty between us?" The rage shakes in her voice.

Behind her, two people that I don't recognize stand, the

disgusted looks on their faces make it clear how they feel about me.

"My loyalty is to Riven alone. He is the king; you are a would-be queen." The bite in Verrin's voice surprises me.

A low, angry laugh passes her lips. "You have no ship, and you're outnumbered." She smiles. "Come, the others are waiting."

I cower behind Verrin, I know we're going to go, but I don't want to.

"Weapons, communicators, and trackers down. Throw it all here." The man with her tells, stepping toward us with a weapon drawn. It's much bigger than Verrins' weapon.

As they throw their things onto the ground, Dyus looks at me. It's the briefest glance, just a moment. But I know we're still alright.

Walking in a line, they stay in front and behind me, guarding me as we make our way to their pod.

"Just her." Phaedra steps in front of the door. "You two stay here."

"Phaedra, armed or not, you will not separate us. The only reason I'm complying is to keep her away from unnecessary violence and danger. Do not force my hand. I will kill you all easily. I am allowing this because I believe we can come to a resolution that does not involve her being out in harm's way." Verrin doesn't falter.

CHAPTER 49

I have to clap my hand over my mouth to stifle the screams threatening to escape. I can't control them.

It all happened so fast.

One moment, there were three of them—then, there was only Phaedra.

I'm still trying to process it all when Verrin gently takes my arm and tugs me into the pod.

There was a sound, like a swish. Then, a splash of blood. A head rolled across the ground. Simultaneously, there was a hiss, then a flash of copper. A loud crunch followed as General Dyus impaled one of the men through the chest. Both bodies hit the ground at the same time.

I can't make sense of it. Even as I witnessed it, the events seemed hazy, disjointed in my mind.

Now, sitting in the pod, Phaedra is directly across from me. She looks cold and deadly, but I saw it—just for a split second. When the situation started slipping from her control, she panicked. It was just a flicker, but it was there.

Verrin confiscated her communication device with cold smugness.

Riven is unreachable, and it's making me nervous. I try to

convince myself there's a good reason for it—a reason that doesn't involve him being injured or dead. But I can't think of any.

The flight is tense.

Phaedra stares at me, unblinking, for the entire duration. She never looks away. Her hatred is palpable, radiating off her like a tangible force, wrapping around my throat like an invisible hand.

"Who is waiting with Hydriss?" General Dyus growls. "Murrious? Kimora? Who else?"

"Riven has more enemies than you think." Phaedra's gaze never wavers from me, even as she speaks. A wicked smile tugs at her lips, revealing her long fangs. "You might have won this round, Dyus, but by the end of this, I'll have your head."

Her confidence is unsettling.

Fear coils in my chest like a thorny vine, squeezing my heart. Verrin tries to contact Riven again, as if he can hear the silent pleading in my mind. Why isn't he answering?

"What's the matter, Verrin? Can't reach him?" Phaedra's smile widens, and the thorns twist tighter.

I feel sick. My head spins, and a dull thumping pounds behind my eyes. I won't give her the satisfaction of throwing up —unless I can aim for her lap.

For the next hour, it feels like we're standing still. Can't this thing move faster? Every few minutes, she sighs contentedly or chuckles softly, as though amused by a private joke.

What the hell is so funny?

I want to slap the smug grin off her face. But I know she's watching me, so I keep my expression neutral, though I'm sure the lines of worry crease my brow anyway. She can probably hear my heart hammering in my chest, each beat screaming my anxiety.

Everything feels tight—my head, my chest. Even my skin itches like it's about to split. Just sitting still takes all my strength.

"There," Dyus says gruffly, breaking the silence.

I jerk my head up and fix my gaze on the rapidly approaching planet. I don't look away until we've landed.

There's no one waiting. No pods. No people.

The landscape looks different now. When I was here with Riven, it was beautiful, peaceful. Now it's ominous and desolate.

"Where are they?" Verrin hisses.

"Let's go find them!" Phaedra grins. "It'll be like Seeker! Oh, I haven't played that since I was a child!" She claps her hands in mock glee.

I imagine her as a child playing hide-and-seek, but I shake the thought from my mind. Don't humanize her.

General Dyus's lip curls in disdain, but he doesn't speak. Instead, he grabs her arm roughly, yanking her upright and out of the pod.

Taking a deep breath, I follow them.

"Wow! Do you smell that?" Phaedra sniffs the air theatrically. "Sex and blood. Delicious."

Normally, I'd blush and shrink back in embarrassment. But now, it only fuels my anger.

"Phaedra, shut the fuck up!" I snap, at my wit's end. I can't listen to her voice for another second.

Her mouth falls open, stunned into silence. For a solitary moment, there is peace. I don't think she's used to being spoken to like that.

"I can't wait to watch you die," she hisses, turning her nose up as she stalks away.

"That won't be happening today," Verrin mutters quietly, leaning toward me.

When I glance at him, he gives me a small, almost imperceptible smile. To anyone else, it wouldn't qualify as a smile, but for him, it is—a subtle tug at the corners of his lips.

I think we're still alright. This is within the bounds of the plan.

The weight in my chest doesn't lift, but I manage to take a deeper breath.

Silently, we trek through the forest as the light fades. It's clear by the way none of them stumble that they can see much better in the dark than I can.

"Welcome!" A voice cuts through the shadows. "We've been waiting for you!"

Murrious steps into the path, a wide grin plastered across his face.

"Our king is waiting inside." His eyes rake over me, appraising. "Let's not keep him waiting."

With Verrin in front of me and Dyus behind, we head toward the strange rock structure I was in with Riven just hours ago.

"You know," Murrious says, holding the door open like some kind of gentleman, "your strategy was sound. Too bad you have a leak inside your ranks."

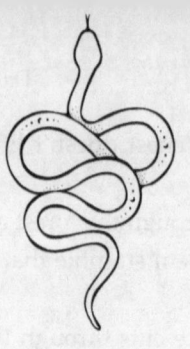

CHAPTER 50

Verrin stiffens, his body tensing.

I can't see around him, whatever he's looking at, it's bad. The muscles in his back and shoulders are coiled into knots.

I step inside and my body freezes, my feet rooting into the ground so that I can't take another step.

"Sidra?" It slips out. I don't mean to say it but the ache in my chest blurs out all reason and thought. My eyes well up with acidic tears that leave a painful trail down my cheeks as they fall. Of everyone I've met, I could not have seen this coming. Not from her.

"Demi." Riven's voice snaps me back to reality. I search the room and find him sitting at the small table. His face grounds me.

The second our eyes meet, I know everything is going to be alright. With or without Sidra. Wiping my face and rolling my shoulders back, I lift my head. He's here, he's safe. I'm here, I'm safe. He's not going to let anything happen to me.

I won't cower or cry.

Murrious gestures for me to sit in a seat across the room from Riven.

We're outnumbered again. They have five to our three. Phaedra and Kimora sit together on either side of Riven with Murrious watching over Dyus. The other man is new. Another enemy I didn't know I had.

Where is the rest of our team?

"I'm going to kill you with my bare hands." Verrin hisses at Sidra.

"You'll be dead long before you have the chance." She smiles.

My heart hurts for him. She's betraying all of us but him more than anyone.

The door opens and Hydriss walks in, his face split by a wide smile.

"My darling," he sniffs the air. "I've been waiting for you!"

"You're going to have to kill me." Riven speaks calmly, the weight of his authority heavy in his voice.

"Oh, don't worry your majesty, I plan to. I just have a few things to do first!" He starts to walk toward me and something flashes in my peripheral vision.

A blade flies through the air.

It happens so fast I almost miss it.

Verrin catches it out of the air and before anyone even realizes, it's planted in Murrious' neck. Blood sprays across the room, drenching everything in front of him, me included.

"Be careful with her!" Riven shouts as Sidra kicks her foot up, knocking Kimora out of her chair.

Hydriss grabs my arm and yanks me up over his shoulder. The world rolls my body in a freefall as I am knocked out of his arms.

The shock of hitting the ground dazes me for a moment, as I sit up, watching as Dyus and Riven attack him from both sides.

I was only in his arms for a moment, a single second, but even that was too much.

"Come on, you can't sit there, they'll hurt you!" Sidra grabs my arm, pulling me up.

I know this is not the time, but I can't stop myself from

throwing my arms around her. She returns the gesture, hugging me tightly.

"I doubted you! I'm sorry I doubted you!"

"Verrin really sold the betrayal." She smiles, clearly not holding any grudges.

Phaedra lets out a scream that curdles my blood. She flies at Sidra and the two of them crash into my body, sending me flying halfway across the room. Shielded by the table, I huddle on the ground. The impact rattles my bones. Pain radiates from every part of me. I can't even pinpoint it, it's everywhere.

Crawling toward the door, I watch as Verrin holds Hydriss by the neck. Riven moves with deadly precision, the tip of his laser-like weapon gleaming in the dim light. The strike is quick, surgical, and the sizzling sound that follows is sickening. Hydriss's lifeless body crumples to the floor, smoke curling from the wound into the air.

"He was supposed to be mine!" Phaedra grabs me again, her nails digging into my skin as she drags me upright. Her body coils around mine, suffocating and unrelenting. "You filthy little beast! I was supposed to be queen! You don't deserve a swift death but it will have to do!" Her teeth plunge into my neck and I feel the venom instantly.

She releases me and laughs loudly. She releases me with a triumphant laugh, her breath on the back of my neck.

"Come say your goodbyes, Riven!" she taunts, her voice laced with a cruel snarl. The malice in her tone is so profound, so devastatingly cruel. I can't help the smile that tugs at my lips.

She thinks she won.

Falling limply from her arms onto the floor, I wait until Dyus grabs her to pull myself up onto my feet.

Her laughter dies abruptly as I cross the room, my gaze locked on Riven. Her eyes widen in disbelief as I step over Hydriss's smoldering corpse, ignoring the metallic tang of blood in the air.

Without hesitation, I launch myself into Riven's waiting arms, the world around us fading into insignificance.

"How?" She screams, thrashing against Verrin's chest.

Turning to face her, my eyes land on all the bodies scattered around the room.

"Your majesty, we caught him trying to flee." One of the wardens forces the man I've never seen before back into the room. I didn't even realize he left.

"Bind them and bring them to the pod." Riven's voice is stone cold and it shakes slightly. He's so angry I'm worried he's going to crack his teeth the way he's clenching his jaw.

"How are you still alive?" Phaedra screams, throwing her head back into Dyus' mouth. His lips split open on contact but he doesn't flinch. Her tantrum isn't affecting him at all. "Explain it!" She's like a toddler who didn't get her way.

"Precautions were taken. Phaedra." Riven tightens his grip on my waist.

She thrashes and screams then goes perfectly still and quiet. Her mouth drops open and her eyes go wide. "You broke the law for her."

CHAPTER 51

There is a pause. An audible shift that makes my stomach drop. Nausea and unease churn in my stomach.

Even Verrin and Sidra are staring wide-eyed.

Everyone knows what he did. They know that he broke the law. It's out in the open now.

"You trained her with venom." The rage is gone from her voice now. There is no anger or fury–just bewilderment. With the realization of what we did hitting everyone, the room is unbearably uncomfortable.

"Your Majesty?" Verrin is the first to speak. His tone holds no accusation–he's giving him the benefit of the doubt even with the truth sitting in the room with us.

"I couldn't allow her to be bitten. It was the only way." He doesn't waver. There is no shame or regret anywhere that I see. He's standing behind his choices.

"Riven, why didn't you tell me?" Sidra's expression is different from the rest. She doesn't look shocked but sad.

Riven doesn't seem to hear any of them. His eyes move over my body, checking me for injuries. His thumb runs over the bite mark in my neck. It stops there, brushing over the wound and sending a shiver up my spine.

"I'm alright." I reassured him even though my voice trembles. Later, when my mind has a chance to catch up, I'm sure I'll feel more but right now I'm numb.

Riven's jaw tightens, and for a moment, it's as if the rest of the room ceases to exist. His fingers linger, a silent apology in his touch. But there's something else there, something darker—a possessive kind of protectiveness that I've grown to love.

"You'll never get away with this! I will make sure everyone knows! You will lose everything! You broke our laws for her? You preach of the sanctity of our history and traditions yet you would so easily—" Phaedra's screams come to a jarring and abrupt end.

My eyes jerk up at the gasp followed by a gurgling sound.

Blood pours from a wound in her neck that wasn't there just a second ago. General Dyus is still holding her up, his face completely unreadable. If he's shocked he doesn't let it show.

Sidra is clutching a blade tightly in her fist. As Phaedra falls to the ground, she turns, stepping over her body. "Does anyone else have anything to say about this?"

"No." Everyone in the room shakes their head and looks uncomfortably at the ground.

"This secret dies here. Anyone that has anything to say, speak it now or let it lay." Her eyes dart around the room.

The man being held by the warden backs up, pressing his body into him. "I won't say anything!"

Sidra hums, stepping forward but Verrin grabs her, whispering in her ear. Her eyes narrow but she stops.

Riven wraps his arm around my shoulder, partially shielding my body.

"Take him back to the Fenlands." He gestures to the warden.

I almost feel sorry for him.

When they're gone and it's just us left here, a strange feeling washes over me.

Hyrdiss is dead. Murrious is dead. Phaedra is dead.

We're surrounded by bodies. Violence and chaos still hang in the air, even in the silence, the memory of it is here--the smell. But I feel a sudden and unexpected calm. It washes over me like warm water, easing any lingering fear or worry.

"Riven, I want to stay here with you."

I decide to stay, and the choice feels unexpectedly natural, as though it had always been written in the stars, just waiting for me to see it.

The life I'm leaving behind pales in comparison to what he's offering me. This doesn't come without sacrifice but I'm willing to make it. He's worth it.

The words slip from my lips effortlessly, like they've been waiting on the edge of my tongue all along, waiting for my heart to catch up. There's no hesitation, no fear—only a strange, grounding certainty that feels terrifying and freeing.

It's my choice.

And I chose him.

A moment passes in silence. It's like the whole room is holding their breath.

His lips twitch and he tightens his arm around me.

"I knew she would." Sidra whispers to Verrin who nods knowingly.

"Let's go home." He lifts me and I don't protest. If he wants to carry me, I'll allow it. I want to be close to him too. After everything, I think we both just need to feel one another.

Sitting in the pod, I feel clear. The future is stretched out in front of me and I can see it. The clouds that blocked my view before have vanished leaving behind blue skies.

I can do this. Whatever it is, I can handle it. We'll handle it together.

"We have one more pressing matter to attend to before we can be alone." He tucks a loose hair behind my ear. "Everyone must be informed of the attack. It has to be swift and public. I have already drawn up the preliminary information. We just have to fill in the blanks. I know that it is a lot to ask of you..."

His face is so serious. "But I need one more thing. One more brave moment from you."

I nod, bracing myself for whatever he's about to ask.

"Stand beside me while I address the people. They need to know that it was not just me that was attacked but both of us. The plot that was formed against you failed and you are still standing tall. I want them to see it."

"I can do it." I mean it. I'm not just saying it to make him feel at ease. I can do it.

He smiles, nodding in approval. "Let's show them who you are."

CHAPTER 52

t could be the attempt on my life. Or Riven standing by my side. Or the fact that my mind is made up and I'm staying.

Whatever the reason, an eerie calm washes over me, so steady it surprises even me. My heartbeat slows, my breath is even, as though my body has accepted its role in what's to come.

In mere moments, we'll step out into the grand hall, where a sea of dignitaries and political figures are waiting. They are going to take what we share with them and spread it across the galaxy.

"Ready?" He looks at me, steady and resolute, like always.

"I am." I nod, really meaning it.

We step out together, and the room, lightly buzzing with quiet conversation, likely speculation, goes silent. There are about fifteen people here in person and twenty people here via a telecommunication system. Their stoic faces plastered across one wall.

"Thank you for gathering so quickly." He addresses them right away. "What I am about to share with you is both difficult to share and difficult to hear. The course once set for our galaxy and for my reign as king has been significantly altered by the actions of a small group of disloyal subjects."

I watch their faces. They are serious and elegant—as all of them are.

As he recounts the mostly true events of today, leaving out the fact that a trap was set and a plan was made, their expressions change to ones of shock and horror.

"Phaedra attempted to bite Demi, her intention to use her venom was clear. She was swiftly dealt with. As you process the truly vile nature of this attack, I want all of you to be assured that I say this with a clear mind—any such actions will result in a swift death sentence. Spread that loud and clear through the galaxy. The use of venom is outlawed for a reason. There will be no leniency on those that disregard that." He stares them down, making and holding eye contact with each of them as he speaks.

"As for the future," his voice resonates, steady and unyielding, "we have made the decision, together, that Demi will remain here even in the absence of a threat to her planet and people. She stays by choice."

The room reacts in ripples. A few eyes widen, the shock barely hidden behind a veil of civility. Others remain stoic, their practiced composure giving nothing away, though I can feel the weight of their scrutiny bearing down on me. The silence that follows is sharp, teetering on the edge of judgment and acceptance.

"Thank you for your time," he continues, the command in his tone is final. If anyone has anything to say, they're going to have to wait. "I will not be answering questions today. At a later date, there will be another meeting set where I will allow time for questions for the sake of transparency. Until then, I wish you well. Be safe, be strong."

My breath catches as he steps down from the podium, the quiet authority of his movements drawing every gaze as he approaches me.

I don't even realize it's over until he takes my hand. His grip is firm, grounding me as the murmurs swell behind us. Without a word, he leads me away.

I keep my head high; every step is a reminder that I've chosen this. Him. This place. But the questioning glances from the crowd linger in my mind, their unspoken doubts a weight I can't shake.

As we pass through the arched doorway, I finally exhale, the tension of the moment beginning to unravel. His hand tightens around mine, a silent reassurance, and when I glance up at him, his expression is unreadable.

It isn't until we are up the stairs, safely behind the closed door, that he lets out a breath.

"Come here." He grabs me, his lips coming down on the wound on my neck. He kisses it softly.

I know he's going to coddle me, to fuss over the bite, and I'm going to let him. He needs it, and so do I.

"In that moment I felt fear unlike anything else I've ever experienced." The tip of his nose runs over my neck, up to my cheek. "I saw it all in slow motion. I knew we had built up your tolerance, but I just saw it all go wrong."

"It didn't go wrong, though." I hold his shoulders. "I'm here, I'm fine."

He hums, continuing his soft exploration. "I'll be the judge of that. I'll have to inspect every inch of you, just to be sure."

"You probably should." The familiar heat creeps up my spine. His touch ignites a fiery feeling in my blood. "Riven?" I'm already panting.

He hums, a low vibration that resonates through my bones, his lips tracing a path from mine, lingering softly before beginning to move downward. The warmth of his breath fans across my collarbone as he kisses a line of devotion, each touch unraveling a knot in my chest.

"Do you think this feeling can last forever?" My voice is barely a whisper.

His lips pause just above my heart, and he looks up, his gaze steady and unyielding, filled with something that makes me feel both exposed and cherished.

"Yes." His answer is immediate with no hesitation. "I know it can."

The conviction in his words pierces through my defenses, and something inside me shifts, a fragile bubble of emotion breaking open, flooding me with hope. His hand finds mine, fingers intertwining as if promising he'll never let go.

That's all the reassurance I need—the truth in his eyes, the certainty in his touch.

Part II

The Queen Trials

CHAPTER 53

"**R**iven?" I creep my fingers up the bed toward his sleeping body. I only feel a tiny bit of guilt for waking him.

He hums, rolling onto his back beside me.

"I can't sleep." I sit up, sliding my leg over his stomach.

His eyes open quickly, finding mine.

"I need help."

A groan rumbles in his throat as I slip into position, straddling his hips.

"How can I be of service?" His fingers bite into my thighs, holding them tight.

"Can we try something?"

"Anything." He doesn't hesitate. Deep down, I knew he wouldn't but I'm still nervous to ask. To actually say it out loud.

I'm grateful for the dark, it's hiding the blush on my cheeks. I don't know where this forward, confident feeling is coming from but I want to try something new.

"I've always wanted to try a specific position." But none of my previous partners would have been strong enough to do it. I know he is .

He sits, his body shifting beneath mine so that we're sitting face to face. He wraps his arms around my waist and holds me close. "What position?"

"Can we stand?" I clear the nerves from my throat. "And you hold me."

His lips twitch before they crash into mine. Without breaking the kiss he lifts me, standing up in the middle of the room.

Sleeping naked with this man is the best decision I have ever made.

He handles me like I'm featherlight. When he slips his hands down behind my knees, a rush of excitement courses through me.

He's going to be able to do this with ease.

Hooking his arms behind my knees, he holds me in front of him. "Like this?"

"Yes!" I gasp as he rubs himself against me.

He pushes forward, leaving nothing between us.

I can see his face so clearly from this angle. God it's too perfect.

Fully planted inside of me, he stills, letting me feel all of it.

"The way you pull me in and squeeze..." his head drops forward.

I can't look away. There's something hypnotic about him, something that pulls at me, luring me closer. It's always there, I always feel it but right now, alone in the dark, vulnerable and open, I can't escape it.

His eyes gleam with a golden light, a flicker. His beauty is alien and human—snake and man.

His skin, so smooth, seems to shimmer under the dim light, his muscles taut with the ease of power. There's a quiet strength in him that speaks louder than words ever could.

I can feel it in the air between us, the tension, the energy. It's like the pulse of something alive, something wild and untamed. His breath is steady, but there's a flicker of something darker in his gaze.

When he moves—slow, deliberate—there's a grace to it, like a predator on the hunt, a quiet, almost imperceptible slither. The way his body shifts with such fluidity, the scales underneath, the snake part of him that is so much a part of his being, yet so foreign to me.

I can see it, feel it, even in the way his posture bends, the curve of his spine, like something coiling, waiting.

Reaching up, I trace the line of his jaw before moving down to the scales on his neck.

A part of me craves it, but another part of me feels small in the face of such raw, untamed beauty. There is power in every inch of him, in every calculated move, and I feel that power reach out, touching something deep inside me, coaxing me to give in.

It's not just his strength, though. It's the way he carries that strength, the way it's woven into every part of him, from the sharpness of his gaze to the sound of his voice. His venom has been in my veins. My pulse quickens just thinking about it. We don't need to continue to incorporate the venom but I will be sad to see it go.

"What's wrong?" He notices the slight shift in my mood immediately. Of course he does.

"Nothing." I shrug it off. We're already doing the position I asked for. No need to be greedy.

"Demi."

Leaning in, I kiss him, hard while squeezing my muscles around him. The hiss beneath his breath, makes my heart rate spike.

He groans, pulling away. "You're not going to distract me. What happened? Your face changed."

"I'm going to miss the venom. I liked it." I cringe.

"We don't have to stop." He uses his hands on my hips to slide my body up, then back down onto him.

"We don't?"

"No." He moves me faster, thrusting his hips to meet me each time he brings me back down.

"I don't want you to get in trouble." I pant completely breathless.

"We'll be careful." He groans. "I don't want to stop either. Biting into you is..."

"Oh, god! So good. It's so good!" I finish his half-moaned sentence.

"Maybe I can try the soft skin between your thighs. I would love to take a bite after making you come on my tongue." He is bouncing me so quickly now, I'm struggling to breath.

"Yes!"

I want to watch him but my senses are overloaded. Pinching my eyes closed, I let myself feel everything.

"I'm—"

He makes a sound, pleasure and pain—a wild animal.

He stills, holding me against him, "I have to stop or—"

"Don't stop!" I'll beg him if I have to. I want him to come and anchor himself inside of me. The way I want it—need it— feels biological. I crave him in my cells, in my blood, in my bones.

He lets out a whimpering sound, a soft, desperate plea as he lifts and lowers me over him three times. On the third, I feel him twitch inside me, the strange pressure of his body locking into mine.

His mouth drops open, his fangs on display.

I feel every pulse.

Feeling exhausted now, I lean forward against his chest as he walks us back to the bed. Sprawled across his chest I let my heavy eyes close.

With our bodies still connected, I drift away.

CHAPTER 54

There is a loud, swift knock at the door that would ordinarily not frighten me, but Riven's reaction has me instantly worried.

"Stay here." His voice is clipped, his usual calm replaced with an edge that prickles my nerves. He steps out of the shower in a rush, water still streaming down his toned frame as he disappears from the room.

The door closes quickly behind him, leaving me alone with nothing but the sound of the shower filling the silence. I poke my head out cautiously, straining to hear beyond the rush of water. I hear the muffled sound of voices but I can't make out what's being said.

They aren't screaming, so that's probably good.

A few agonizing minutes pass before the door swings open again, and he steps back into the bathroom, his posture tight. His face is etched with frustration, his jaw clenched tight. He doesn't even meet my eyes at first, running a hand through his damp hair.

"What is it?" I press, unable to wait another second.

He stops staring at me for a second before sighing. "The

heads of state are demanding a meeting with me." His tone is sharp and laced with annoyance.

"Demanding it?" I echo, my heart skipping a beat. "That's bad, isn't it? They don't just... demand things from you."

Riven exhales a sharp breath and rolls his neck. "No, they don't."

His words send a chill down my spine, but there's no time to dwell on it. He's already moving, grabbing clothes in quick, efficient movements, and I follow suit. There is urgency in the air. I'm not waiting around for instructions.

The tension is thick as we dress in silence, the gravity of the situation weighing heavily on both of us. My hands tremble slightly as I pull my shirt over my head, but I force myself to focus. This has to be about me. There is no way it's not.

I have a thousand questions. But I don't ask them.

Now doesn't feel like the right time.

When we step out of the room and head down the grand staircase, my breath catches in my throat. Standing in the lobby below is a face I recognize in an instant. We've only had contact ones, but it was memorable.

His mother.

Her striking features are carved from the same sharp lines as Riven's, but where his expression is often unreadable, hers is a storm of fury barely contained beneath a composed facade.

Her piercing gaze snaps to me, then to Riven, and the fury in her eyes is unmistakable. The air feels like it's heating up, like we're standing in an oven.

"Riven," she says, her voice smooth but ice-cold. "We need to talk. Now."

Her presence is commanding and fierce. Long, dark hair pulled back into intricate braids, her sharp features a mirror of Riven's.

"Mother," Riven mutters under his breath, his tone barely masking his frustration. "Do you have a meeting scheduled? We are just leaving."

"A meeting? With my own son?" She scoffs, her hair swaying over her perfectly poised shoulder. "I demand a moment."

"Demand?" He growls. "I am hearing that word a lot lately. Maybe it's time I have a meeting to remind everyone who they are speaking to."

She ignores him, stepping toward us, her eyes raking over my body. "What are you doing?"

There isn't even an attempt to hide the disgust in her voice.

"I have made my inventions clear." He is a wall of impenetrable steel. The only thing he's giving away is anger.

Her expression intensifies as she crosses her arms. "I thought you were a king, Riven. Not a fool."

"You are my mother but do not forget your place." His eyes flicker.

She waves her hand, completely unaffected. "I heard about the incident with Phaedra." She looks at her nails, almost disinterested. "I suppose you were right about her all along."

"I suppose I was." He bites back.

"I would like to speak to her, Riven." She looks up at him with uncovering confidence.

"She's dead." He growls. "You're too late to-"

"Not Phaedra." She cuts him off. "Demi."

A sharp, cold feeling runs the length of my spine. I don't move or flinch but every part of me is screaming to turn around and run back upstairs–to hide from her.

The hissing sound and rigidness of his posture make me panic. He looks like he's about to fight her.

"I won't hurt her." She's still unphased by his rage.

"I'll speak to her." My voice takes me by surprise.

Call it morbid curiosity or stupidity, but who knows? I want to know what she has to say.

He turns, scrutinizing me, searching my face.

"I'll speak to her." I whisper again, watching the anger on his face fade.

"You don't have to."

"I know." I nod. "But I'll do it anyway."

"As I said, you came unannounced and we are busy. You have five minutes." He turns back to her, his voice ice cold.

"I'll take what I can get." She turns to me. "Are you comfortable in the dining hall?"

"Sure." I swallow the lump of nerves in my throat.

Walking slightly behind her, I watch the way her hips and hair seem to sway in unison. Her long, thin body looks straight off of a runway. She's stunning. But I suppose that is to be expected. So is he.

We don't sit, just stand slightly uncomfortably in the middle of the room.

"My son seems to have chosen you." She looks down at me over her nose. "I will never understand him but I know my son. If he wants you, there must be some redeeming qualities that I am not privy to."

There is a slight pause before she continues.

"He must be a king first. Always. His duty to the Ophidians must come first. His infatuation with you cannot distract him from the long legacy of rulers that have led us out of the fields and into what we are today. Can you stand beside him? Or will you drag him away from his duties?"

"I want him to be great." I mean this so fiercely that my voice doesn't tremble despite my nervousness. "You're underestimating him. I don't want to interfere with his ability to rule. And he wouldn't let me."

Her head tilts slightly to one side as I speak, her lips tugging upward into the smallest most imperceptible smile. "Good."

"Good." I stand taller.

"I won't keep you any longer." She steps aside to let me leave.

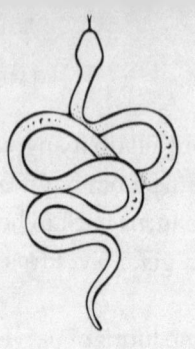

CHAPTER 55

With one fire put out, we're into the next.

The hum of the pod fills the small cabin as I stare out at the endless expanse of space. It surrounds us in every direction.

I don't know if that makes me feel better or worse.

My stomach twists, a mix of nervous energy and dread gnawing at me.

We're heading to the Fenlands—the same Fenlands that Hydriss dragged me to. Memories of that place creep into my mind, sticky and dark, but I push them aside. This time, it's different. Riven is beside me. I know he won't let things turn out like last time.

He's silent for now, his gaze fixed ahead as he pilots the pod with steady hands. The air between us feels taut, heavy with unspoken tension. I know he senses my unease, though I try to mask it. My fingers drum against my thighs, and I've chewed the inside of my lip raw.

"Come here," he finally says, his deep voice breaking through the hum of the engine.

I glance at him. "What?" I'm so wrapped up in my own head I barely heard him.

"Come sit with me," he repeats, softer this time, but no less commanding. Releasing the controls with one hand, he makes space for me on his lap.

Without hesitating, I get up. I know I'll feel better—safer—with him. The pod tilts slightly as I move, but he steadies it with ease, his eyes locked on mine the whole time. When I reach him, he takes my hand and guides me down onto his lap.

The tension in my chest loosens immediately, like a string snapping. His arms wrap around me, strong and protective, and I lean back against him.

The tension in my chest releases, and I draw in an easy breath.

"You're safe with me, Demi," his lips brush against my ear. "I'd lay down my life before I let anything happen to you. Do you understand that?"

I nod, swallowing the lump in my throat. "I know," I whisper.

The view outside the pod shifts as we descend into the atmosphere. The stars fade, replaced by swirling clouds and the faint glow of the swampy planet below.

The sight is breathtaking—misty marshlands bathed in pale, eerie light, sprawling as far as the eye can see. For a moment, I forget my fear, captivated by the beauty of it all.

His hand strokes my arm gently, grounding me, reminding me. "It's not so bad, is it?" he asks, his tone lighter now.

"No," I admit, surprising even myself. "Not with you here. It's actually beautiful."

"Do you remember what I told you? About keeping your head high. Don't bow to them. Don't let them see fear. You have nothing to be afraid of."

"I'll keep my head up." I promise.

"Good." He squeezes me.

My breath catches as the row of huts comes into view far below us. "There they are."

"I won't leave your side. Not for a second."

"I know."

The pod slowly lowers toward the ground, bringing me back to a place I never thought I would go.

We stop on the dock, the same dock I escaped from. It feels like years ago and yesterday all at once.

Hydriss is dead. He can't hurt me now. As long as I remember this, everything will be alright.

Rows of Fen Wardens are lined up on the dock, in full uniform. They look cleaner and more professional this time.

General Dyus is standing at the end of the first row. That explains it. He's come here to whip them into shape, and by the looks of it, he's done it.

They don't move as we step out into the docks. A stoic wall of silence and precision.

"General." Riven greets Dyus first.

He bows his head, but when he looks at me, he gives a little, reassuring nod.

"The Heads of State have gathered at the Hollow." General Dyus ushers us forward.

We walk side by side behind him, down the dock and onto a strange pathway elevated above the marshes. It's like a bridge, or a dock, with reeds and long grass growing on either side.

The Fenlands stretch out around us, an endless expanse of mist and shadowed water. The marshes feel alive, humming with energy.

The air is thick and warm, after only a few seconds, sweat gathers on my forehead and neck.

I glance at Riven, his tall frame cutting through the haze like a shield. The wardens behind us are silent, their movements precise and fluid, like they've walked this path a thousand times before. I'm less sure-footed.

The water shimmers, the water rippling in the breeze.

I never thought I would feel anything but fear here, but I am completely calm.

We walk for what feels like forever but realistically is about ten minutes. The humidity here is suffocating.

At the end of the walking path, there is a cluster of boats. They look normal until we get closer. They're like snake-skin canoes with a high stern and bow that coil like a snake about to strike.

"Sit on my lap." Riven growls under his breath.

It only takes a second to understand why. These are no slow, ambling canoes. They are fast-paced speedboats that cut through the water with enough force to throw anyone not holding on tight into the water.

Looking around, I can't tell who is steering, but they do it with expert precision, cutting around the reeds, rocks, and trees growing up from the water.

Last time I was here, I didn't get to see all of this. In the depths of the Fenlands, there is so much more. I'd thought it was a desolate, miserable place. But now? I know that it is full of wide-open waterways and blue skies. It's wild and dangerous, yes, but also breathtakingly beautiful.

Ahead, the path widens, and through the reeds and grass, I catch a glimpse of the great hall.

A building built on stilts, just like the huts, but this is massive.

"Ready?" He squeezes my hand.

CHAPTER 56

I t's like a switch being flipped. As soon as we step out of the boat, Riven is the king.

His posture changes, his face is still his, but there is an unrecognizable look to him now. I feel his anger; it's palpable, and it makes me cower back slightly.

I know he's not mad at me and I have nothing to fear, but... damn.

The Fen Wards that escorted us here seem to notice it too, and they step aside, giving him a wide berth.

The hall is massive, its wooden walls polished to a sheen that gleams even in the muted light streaming through the tall windows. Wide windows on every wall give views to the marshes on all sides. I try to focus my attention on that as we enter.

The weight of so many gazes lands on me as soon as we step through the double doors. It's a mixed crowd—some faces are blank, others carved with lines of disapproval or outright anger. My pulse races, but Riven's hand on my lower back steadies me.

He guides me to a chair near the center of the room, one that feels too exposed for my liking, but I bite my tongue and let him settle me into it. His touch is gentle, but his tension radiates from his skin.

He doesn't sit in the seat beside me.

Instead, he stalks to the center of the room, his presence commanding, dangerous. His movements are sharp and purposeful, his jaw tight and his eyes cold.

"You've demanded my presence here. I'm here now. Let's begin." His voice booms through the hall, bouncing off the rafters. "To demand my presence without warning, as if I am one of your peers." His gaze sweeps the room. "I am your king," he continues, his tone sharpening with each word. "Not a colleague. Not a subordinate to be ordered around. Air your grievances; I look forward to hearing them."

His fury hangs in the air, heavy and electric. And as I sit there, I can't decide what terrifies me more: his rage or whatever they have to say.

A tall, thin man with bright yellow scales and black hair stands, walking toward Riven. He doesn't look afraid, which only worries me more.

"We have met, your majesty. And the heads of state have concerns." He holds eye contact as he speaks.

Riven's jaw clenches, but he doesn't speak.

"We," he gestures to everyone in the room. "Would like to know your intention."

"You question me?" Riven's lips tug upward, almost into a smile, but I know that he is anything but amused.

"Respectfully, yes."

"Continue."

"We received word of the attack perpetrated against you. We are disgusted. However, Phaedra was to be your queen. Our queen." He takes a breath. "Now that she is no longer a viable candidate, we have questions that you have not answered. It is our prerogative as the heads of state in this system. Our people —your people—want to know what lies ahead."

Phaedra. I can't escape her apparently, even in death.

"Is she your nomination for queen?"

The question hits me like a punch to the stomach. Me?

"It has been two days since the attack." Riven sounds as bewildered as I feel. "You gather, discuss matters, or state among yourselves, then dare to call and demand my time for an answer that I cannot give you because I do not know it!" His voice gets louder with each word. "If weeks had passed, I might understand your frustration and impatience, but the dust has hardly settled on the ground where we fought!"

"Your majesty, while it is true that the attack was mere days ago, this situation is not new. Phaedra was removed from your home and your court. The people have felt this state of limbo for some time now." He looks from Riven to me.

"There are matters that need to be discussed between us before I can answer that." His rage has dialed back to a simmer instead of a full, rolling boil.

"We trust you." He starts. I hold my breath, waiting for the inevitable 'but.' "But this inconsistency is unsettling."

"The only inconsistency has been in my personal life. I have been ever present as King of this system. Nothing has gone unnoticed, no duty undone. There has been no reason given for this mistrust and impatience. I will not rush and declare myself before we have had the chance to fully discuss all of the implications. I will speak freely, in the confidence of this room, that yes, it is my intention to ask Demi to stand beside me. But that decision is not one that can be made lightly, she has to know all of the facts before making that commitment."

The room spins slightly. He just told all of the heads of state for this galaxy that he wants me to be his queen. Their queen.

I feel like I'm about to be sick, but then he turns to look at me.

The peace on his face instantly soothes my fears.

"I can appreciate your position, your majesty." He bows his head.

"And I can appreciate yours." His tone is much calmer now.

"I will not rush her. I will not rush this. But know that there are steps forward being taken."

The atmosphere in the room changed so suddenly it's like night and day.

"I am glad to hear it," he bows his head. "We are standing by to begin preparation as soon as you are ready."

"Preparation?" Riven's head tilts slightly.

One of the men stands, his pale eyes meeting mine. "Your new queen, whoever she may be, must complete the Queen Trials."

The what?

CHAPTER 57

The next several minutes are a blur. I hardly notice that I'm being led out of the hall and back into the boat. My breaths come short and shallow, too fast, like my lungs forgot how to work. My hands shake as I press them against my chest. My heart is beating so quickly it's going to give out. My vision is blurry, my stomach is in a knot. Everything in my body is on high alert and panicking.

I have to fight against the urge to run—to just sprint away.

"Trials?" I choke out the word, staring at him. "What does that mean? Am I going to prison?"

He holds me against him, his expression grim but calm. I'm unraveling.

"Demi, it is not a trial for punishment." He leans down like he's about to kiss me.

"Don't," I snap when he tries. "Don't try to make me feel better with cuddles or whatever. What is happening?" My voice breaks, and I hate how desperate I sound.

He sighs, running a hand through his hair. "Demi, the place of the queen isn't given here. It's earned. A queen here has to win the people's favor."

"Earn it?" I repeat, like the words are in a language I don't know. "How? What does that even mean? What do I have to do? I don't—I can't—" My chest tightens, and a strangled gasp escapes.

He grabs my shoulders, but I flinch away, shaking my head. "Don't touch me unless you're going to fix this," I snap, tears pricking my eyes. "I need—" My hands fly up to cover my face as the panic builds, a wave threatening to pull me under.

"Calm down," he says softly.

"Calm down?" My voice pitches higher. "I can't calm down! Hypnotize me. You can do that, right? Just... please! Please, I'm begging you."

He hesitates, his jaw tight. "Demi, you told me never to do that to you again. Transfiction is–"

"But now I want you to! Please!"

My throat feels like it's closing. I can't get any air. I try, but I can only hyperventilate.

"I can't breathe!" I think I'm screaming. "Riven, help me! Please!" I beg him.

For a long, agonizing moment, he stares at me. I keep expecting to feel something, for that soothing sensation to creep through me, but it doesn't.

"Please. I know what I'm asking for. You have permission."

He cups my face gently. "Breathe with me," he whispers, his voice low and steady. His thumbs brush my temples in slow circles, and I feel the faint hum of his power slipping under my skin like a warm tide.

"Focus on my voice," The words thread into my thoughts–weaving into my brain. The humid air feels like a straitjacket, and everything starts to fade. The panic retreats. My shoulders sag, and my breathing evens out. I feel myself starting to lose consciousness. It's slow and fast at the same time. I'm drifting in the clouds.

I blink up at him, my vision softening as the trance takes hold. "You're okay," he whispers. "We'll figure this out."

"We will." I hum, dropping my face into the crook of his neck.

I can feel things happening around me, but I'm like a blob. Skin and bones that have no purpose. I can't move or speak. I'm just here, existing.

I don't know where I am, but I know Riven is still with me. He's holding me. The soft thump of his pulse and his smell are mixed into the haze in my mind.

People move and speak, things are happening, but I'm unaware beyond that basic knowledge. It's nice.

"Demi?" Riven's voice cuts through the fog, a hand reaching out to pull me back into the world.

Read or not, I'm waking up. I have to face this.

"Oh," I sit up, still disoriented but surprised. "We're here?" I look around his bedroom.

"Yes, I didn't want to wake you until we were in a place where I know you feel safe." He looks tired. Like there is a weight on his shoulders.

"Can you just explain it to me?"

He nods. "The Queen Trials are a series of five hearings that any future queen must stand for. It is a mostly closed event, only the judges and heads of state are present. You will be given a series of questions about how you will rule. These questions can range from cultural, historical, social, and into the executive processes you will or won't utilize. It is a way for the people to know that their queen has their best interests at heart."

"Why didn't you tell me about this before?"

"Please don't misunderstand this." He takes a breath, almost like he's nervous. "I want you beside me. But we have not discussed what your role would be here. It was for selfish reasons that I hadn't mentioned it yet. I didn't want to scare you away. To say that I am shocked by their swiftness in this matter is an understatement. A Queen Trial is a huge undertaking, and they just held one. I incorrectly assumed they would be slow to act."

"So Phaedra did it and passed?"

"Yes."

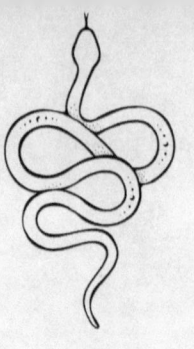

CHAPTER 58

T he room is quiet. It's like the weight of everything is sitting on both of us.

Riven stands before me, the golden flecks in his eyes holding my gaze. He's steady but unreadable. I don't know what he's feeling. It's as if he's willing me to understand something unsaid.

"If I don't want to be the Queen, what happens?" The words scrape my throat. I don't want to ask this because the answer is potentially devastating.

"In our history–" He stops, running his hand through his hair. "We have never had a king whose partner did not pass the Queen Trial. We have had Kings without a partner but those that have one have never had her be just a citizen with no role."

That makes sense. Obviously, the king would want a partner that is fit to be the queen.

"We never really talked about this part. I heard what you said to the Heads of State but…"

"I just want you." He looks certain.

"What are you trying to say, Riven?" My voice cracks, betraying the whirlwind in my chest. It's a miracle that I'm sitting upright. I feel like I've been flattened by all of this.

"I want you beside me." His words are deliberate, soft, but they hit me like a bolt of lightening.

"Beside you?" My laugh is brittle, disbelieving. "Damn it, speak clearly. What does that mean?"

He tilts his head, his lips pressing into a thin line. "I want you to be my queen."

"Your queen?" I repeat, my voice barely above a whisper.

"Yes."

I slide out of bed and take several steps away from him, as if distance will help me process the enormity of what he's asking. It doesn't.

"Riven, I—" My chest tightens, panic clawing up my throat. "I'm just a girl from a small town in Wyoming. I don't know how to be a queen. And now I'm being asked to fight for the position?"

"It's not a fight." His tone is calm, almost coaxing, like he's trying to soothe a wild animal. "It's just a series of trials that will test your mental and emotional ability to lead."

Just. Just a series of trials.

I stare at him, incredulous. "What if I can't do it?"

"You can," he says firmly. "You're more capable than you think."

"If I don't pass, will I have to leave?"

"No. I will never send you away." He flinches, like his muscles want to move, but he stays, giving me physical space.

"Is this all a front? Are they bringing it up so quickly because they want me to fail and move on to a more suitable candidate? A human as queen? Won't they revolt or declare war or something?" Each time I start to calm down a little bit, another thought pops into my head that freaks me out all over again.

His lips curve into a small smile. "It's never been done, no. But there's no law against it. And I don't care if it's tradition or not—I'll make it happen. I just need you to consider it."

I shake my head, the room tilting as my thoughts spiral out

of control. "I can't just consider this. It's my life! It's your king-dom! What if I'm terrible at it? What if—"

"Demi."

The way he says my name stops me mid-spiral. There's something raw in his voice, something vulnerable that I've never heard from him before.

"Take your time," he stands, closing the space between us. "I won't push you. I won't force you. But I need you to know how much I want this. I want you. Not just as the woman I..." He falters, just for a second, a crack in his usual collectedness. "As the woman I need beside me, but as the kind of queen my people deserve."

I want to argue, to deny him, but the words catch in my throat. How can anyone stand in front of this man, hear him say those things, and not melt into a puddle in his arms?

"I need to think," I whisper, my voice shaking.

He nods, his expression unreadable again. "Then think. But know that no matter what you decide, I'll wait. And I'll stand by you, whatever comes next."

"Get in bed." I point.

"What?" He seems surprised by my sudden shift.

"I just want to get under the blankets and pretend there isn't anything outside of this room. And I want you to hold me while I do it."

Lying in bed with the blankets covering us completely, I rest my head on his chest.

"I wish you would have mentioned this."

"I should have."

"Can you give me an example of one of the trials in the past?" I still can't really wrap my head around it.

"The king is not permitted to be present, but the queen has a team of her choosing standing beside her. I will be able to review all of the transcripts after. One of Phaedra's trials was about the preservation of our traditions. If she was to be queen, how would she aim to move our people forward while still holding onto the traditions of our past?"

"Will I know the questions beforehand?"

"No."

"Shit." I clear my throat.

"You will be well prepared. Whoever you choose as your team will make sure you're prepared. I will spend every minute of every day teaching you and answering your questions. You're not alone here." He kisses my hair. "I can't be with you in the trials, but I'm with you–right behind you."

I feel calmer. "Would Sidra and Verrin be on my team?"

"I'm sure they would be honored."

I'm not ready to say the words out loud, not yet. But I know the way my heart is leaning –the answer is on the tip of my tongue.

CHAPTER 59

I feel terrible. This strange mash-up of panic and guilt. Riven's so sweet, so loving, so perfect, and all I want to do is be near him, to let him hold me and make everything feel better.

But right now, it's like there's this weight on my head, pushing down on my brain. I can't think with him so close. He's distracting me. It doesn't matter what my heart says. I need to use my head this time. I need to think about this.

My heart needs to shut up and step aside.

"Riven," I whisper, my voice trembling. He looks at me, waiting for me to continue.

Why am I nervous about telling him what I need? He has never given any indication that he would be anything other than fully supportive.

Just spit it out.

"I need some space," I finally whisper, barely hearing the words myself. "I need time to think. Without feeling like you're waiting on me--watching me. I can't do this with you right here."

His eyes search mine, his brow furrowing.

I hurt him! I shouldn't have said anything!

"I know it's not fair," I panic, trying to make him understand. "But I need to go into this with a clear head. Being a queen is not a small task. Especially not..." I don't want to say 'snake alien queen.' But that's what it is. I would be the queen of the snake aliens. How has my life come to this?

"Demi." He smiles, instantly easing my mind. "I have asked something impossible of you. If you didn't have to think about it, then you wouldn't be taking it seriously. I want you to take all the time you need. This is no small matter."

"I'll be back soon." I lean in, kissing his cheek but he grabs me as I try to slip away.

"One more."

"Take two." I kiss him, soft but still needy.

I have to force myself away. He could easily distract me into staying for the rest of the night.

I need to talk to Sidra. She'll have advice. She will be objective and straightforward.

Creeping down the hallway in the dark, I realize that this might be a bad idea. Verrin is probably asleep. She's probably asleep. I doubt she will want to come over here now.

Then I hear it. Her loud, boisterous laugh.

She's already here.

I knock lightly on the door, waiting for someone to answer.

Verrin opens the door with a jerk, his eyes darting around suspiciously before he realizes it's me.

"Demi?"

"Hi, sorry to bother you." I feel like an idiot.

"It's not a bother!" Sidra calls from inside the room.

"I was wondering if I could talk to you." I peek past him. "I just need some advice."

"You've come to the right place! I'm absolutely wonderful at giving advice!" She jumps up. "We will have a snack and talk."

I follow her down into the kitchen.

"You look troubled." She opens several doors, pulling things out. "Come, sit."

This looks like enough food to feed five people for a four-course meal, but I'm ready to eat my feelings.

I don't need to be told twice. I sink into the seat and hold my head in my hands. I don't know where to start, or how to really explain everything in my head. My fears, hesitations, concerns, there are too many.

"I don't know what to do, Sidra," I finally just blurt something out. "I need help. I feel like I'm..." I pause, swallowing down the emotion in my throat. "I don't think I'm good enough to be Queen. It's such a huge responsibility. And I guess part of me thinks it's not fair. I'm not from here. I shouldn't get to swoop in out of nowhere and take such a significant role."

Her eyes soften. "Those thoughts are valid."

I wait, I know she'll be honest. She won't sugarcoat it. I need the truth, hard and fast.

"If I'm completely honest with you," she starts to make a plate, putting fruits and desserts onto a tray. "I don't know if you can do it. Our customs, our culture—they're so different from yours. And I'm not just talking about politics. The way we live, the way we think–it's different from you. If you can't adapt to that, if you can't accept the weight of it all, the choices you'll have to make, I don't know how this will work." She looks at me before turning her attention back to the tray of small desserts and choosing a few.

Her words hit me hard. She's so casual about it. It's not mean spirited, it's just honest. I can't cower back just because the truth hurts.

"But," she says, leaning forward slightly, her voice a little softer now, "I don't think that means you shouldn't try. Not if you want him. Not if you want a future with him. I believe that the questions you're having are not questions that Phaedra ever had. She never questioned whether or not she was fit to rule. That in itself makes her a poor choice, if you ask me."

I swallow the lump in my throat. "I want him. I really do. But is that enough? Am I enough?"

Sidra studies me for a long moment, her eyes moving over me in that almost predatory way that only an Ophidian can. "That's something you'll have to answer for yourself. It's not just about being enough. It's about making a choice, and living with that choice. If you want him, if you want a life with him, make the choice and stand firm in it. For what it's worth, I believe in you." She smiles.

"Thank you, Sidra."

"Take your time and think about it." She reaches over, taking my hand. "I'm going to bring that burly man a midnight snack." She takes the tray of food and leaves me alone in the dim light of the kitchen.

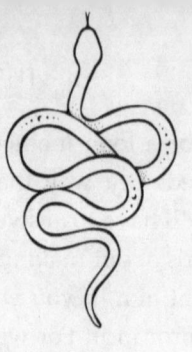

CHAPTER 60

Sitting in the kitchen, mostly in the dark. I pile my plate full of food.

I don't know what I'm doing anymore. My mind feels like it's spiraling in a hundred different directions.

For some reason, a memory keeps popping into my head. When I was in fourth grade, Mr. Blanchard, the elementary science teacher, would split the room up to play a science trivia game. He would always divide us into boys versus girls. I never wanted to be on the girls team because he gave us harder questions and then chastised us for not answering them correctly.

We would be asked, "What is sphenopalatine ganglioneuralgia the scientific term for?"

And the boys would get questions like "how much of the earth is made up of water?"

I asked to be on the boy's team once, and he scoffed. He told me that boys are just better at science and math, too, for that matter.

From that point on, my grades started to slip, and my care and attention to detail in science were less and less. He didn't believe in me, so I stopped believing in myself.

Riven believes in me. Sidra believes in me. I just need to believe in myself.

I don't know why I keep remembering that. It was so long ago. It just changed the way I saw myself. I was suddenly less capable in my own eyes.

Taking a bite of a thick, creamy pudding, I let my eyes flutter closed. This is almost as good as when I eat it with Riven. Almost, but not quite.

Lost in my thoughts, I don't realize how much I've eaten until my spoon scrapes the bottom of the bowl.

I'm not sure why. I don't think it's because of the pudding being gone, but before I can stop myself, I break. Tears spill down my cheeks, one after another. This feels like such a heavy weight to carry.

I chose him. I picked him. I chose to stay.

If I asked him to, he would help me carry it. I know he would. He isn't setting me up to fail. He wouldn't do that to me.

I hiccup, wiping my cheeks with the back of my hand, but it's no use. The tears keep coming. He's so kind. So patient. But I'm so afraid. Afraid of failing. Scared of not being enough for him. But I chose him.

What if I'm not enough and he's disappointed in me? What if he regrets choosing me?

Now I'm just being mean to myself.

I can do this. He will help me.

"I'm not going to run away," I whisper to myself, the words shaky at first. "I chose this. I chose him. I won't back out now. I won't leave him."

There has to be something about me that makes him think I can do it. He wouldn't pick me if he thought I would be an unfit leader for his people.

I take a deep breath and stand a little straighter, as if I'm trying to will some strength into my bones. This is my life. This is my choice. I can't keep doubting myself.

"You're stronger than this, Demi," I force the words out, loud and clear, clenching my fists. "You're not a coward. You're not going to let fear control you. You want him. You want this. So chase after it. No more second-guessing."

I will be fair and honest. I know my character. I can be a worthy Queen. And if I falter, I'll have him by my side.

I wipe my face one last time, take a deep breath, and make my way upstairs. Stopping at the door, I listen. The soft rustle of movement comes from the other side. Just knowing that he's there waiting makes me feel a sense of calm.

Pushing the door open, I find him immediately, and my heart feels mushy.

Pacing the length of the room, his broad shoulders tense. The sight of him like this makes the weight in my chest return, but this time, it's different. It's not fear. It's longing.

He stops, turning to look over his shoulder. His eyes meet mine, soft but strained.

He exhales, almost like he's been holding his breath, and runs a hand through his hair. "I wanted to come to you, but I didn't want to rush you into making a choice you aren't ready for."

I shake my head quickly, stepping closer to him. "No. I am ready. I've made my choice, Riven. I'm not backing down from it."

His eyes search mine, and for a moment, the room feels too small, like the weight of everything between us is too much–too heavy. We step toward each other at the same time.

"Come here."

I crumble into his arms, letting myself be engulfed by him— all of my thoughts clouded by his closeness.

"We can wait to make the announcement." He starts to kiss a slow, deliberate trail down my neck and onto my collarbone. "Give ourselves a few days."

"Yes." I'm already panting. "Let's take a few days."

CHAPTER 61

His lips press against mine, hot and demanding, as his strong arms carry me up the stairs toward the room we now share. My fingers grip into his shirt, pulling him closer, feeling the steady thrum of his heartbeat beneath my hand. We barely make it to the room, bumping into the doorframe as his mouth trails a line of fire along my jawline.

"Hold still," he hums, his voice low and teasing, but his grip on me tightens.

The door clicks shut behind us, and the world outside disappears. It's just us, his careful movements as he sets me down on the edge of the bed, his hands never leaving my waist. My breath catches as his eyes meet mine—intense, deep, powerful–full of something that makes my chest ache.

His forehead rests against mine, our breaths mingling in the silence. My hands slip to his neck, tracing the line of his jaw. For a moment, neither of us moves. The heat between us is fading into something soft, something tender.

He pulls back slightly, brushing a few strands of hair from my face. "Are you ok?" He's studying me. I couldn't lie if I wanted to.

I nod. He cups my face in his hands, his gaze searching mine as if he's looking for something deeper. Maybe he's looking for fear or hesitation.

"Come here," he says softly, guiding me to stand. His hands slip down to mine, intertwining our fingers as he leads me toward the bathroom.

There is something so calming about this place. I feel myself immediately relaxing before we've even touched the water.

Everything he does is slow–measured and controlled. He's purposeful in each action. Filling the small pool, slowly stripping my clothes, running the tips of his fingers over my arm–he's not rushing anything.

"I like to look at you." He hums, undoing his own buttons to remove his clothes.

Heat creeps up my neck. It's more than insecurity. There is something so vulnerable about this. He's not just looking, he's memorizing. He's noticing every detail. I can't hide anything, not with the way he's searching for it–actively seeking it out.

"You scare me," I whisper, barely audible, but I know he hears me.

He tilts his head, pressing a soft kiss to my temple. "You scare me too," he admits, the rawness in his voice making my heart flutter. I know he understands me. It's not fear, it's love.

Taking my hand again, he leads me into the water.

When he sits, I know his intention is for me to lean against him, but I have other plans. His brows move upward in surprise as I sink down onto his lap, bringing our faces together.

He groans and lets his head fall back.

"I want you like this." I whisper against his skin as I leave a trail of kisses against his exposed neck.

He swallows and nods. I can't help but smile. I know what he's feeling. It's the same thing he makes me feel all the time. This all-consuming, needy, desperation that makes my throat feel too tight to speak.

Rising up enough to sink down onto him, I watch his face as I slowly take all of his inches.

He brings his hands up out of the water, putting them behind his head like he's struggling to keep control. I love it.

"You feel so good." I lean in, pressing our chests together. We're as close as possible. He's inside of me, our bodies are pressed together, we're breathing each other's air. But I still want more.

"Before you come, I want you to bite me."

I'm barely able to get the words out. A sound, a moan wrapped in a sharp gasp, heaves from his chest and his eyes fly open to meet mine.

"Demi." He pants, bringing his hands down to my hips.

"Please." I'll beg if I have to, but something tells me that won't be necessary.

He moves up to meet me, each time I come down, his hips press upward.

"Anything you want." He groans. "I'll do anything you want."

Time drifts away. I don't know how long we stay here like this—wrapped around each other. We kiss. His fingers trace patterns on my skin, our hearts beat together. We talk and laugh, then get lost in the moment again.

The whole time he holds me like I'm something precious to him. I know I'm safe.

Eventually, I know he can't hold on much longer. There is only so much he can take.

"Riven," my voice wobbles. "Bite me."

The desperate, whimpering sound he makes vibrates down between my legs.

He leans forward and scrapes his fangs against my neck. With a tight grip on my hips, he holds me down as he lets his teeth break through the skin.

He doesn't give me much venom but he doesn't need to. A few drops is all it takes. I'm flying and falling, floating and sinking, I'm caught in between every sensation at once. It's too good.

My eyes pinch closed and let myself feel everything. He

hooks in and I feel the full, contentedness of being connected to him completely.

He drops his forehead to mine and we sit together, coming down from the high.

"Can you tell me something about your people? Something you think is important to know." I keep my eyes closed.

He is quiet for a moment before taking a long breath. "There is a coldness to Ophidians but do not mistake that for disinterest or detachment. We are a fiercely protective race–proud of our heritage and history. If anyone has objections to you it will be due to fears that you will uphold our traditions or understand us." His voice is thoughtful.

"Thank you." I needed to hear that.

For the next hour we sit together, talking about everything— his people, mine, the good, the bad, the ugly. With each passing second I fall deeper. He doesn't hold back from me. We share it all.

I've never felt so close to anyone. My decision feels more and more like the right one—like the only one.

CHAPTER 62

The pages in front of me blur together, the endless names of planets swimming like the letters are taunting me.

Each page I study feels like it goes on forever and somehow, the more I research, the less I know.

The pile is growing instead of shrinking.

A water world, a jungle moon, the Fenlands…

How am I supposed to keep them all straight? The names alone feel like an alien tongue—half of them sound like someone sneezed and the other half are a jumble of consonants that I can't say without tripping over my own tongue.

"Demi." Sidra's voice snaps me back to the present. Her sharp, no-nonsense tone grates on my nerves. "Focus. The queen trials aren't going to slow down because you're overwhelmed."

Overwhelmed? I'm drowning.

There is a reason we learn over the course of several years, starting with the basics and building on that foundation.

They've got a good cop-bad cop thing going and Sidra's bad cop is starting to grate on my nerves. I'm trying. I'm taking it seriously. I'm giving everything I've got. This is so much harder than the Sarrik. I wish all I had to do was learn a dance.

This is everything, all at once, all jumbled together. I want to say something sarcastic but instead, I clench my jaw and stare harder at the holographic map projected in front of me.

Planets spin in slow orbits, their details scrawled in shimmering letters beside them. Each one is a potential death trap—or worse, a test of just how spectacularly I can embarrass myself. And not just myself. Riven.

The thought makes my stomach lurch. I can't mess this up. Not with his name and reputation on the line.

But no matter how hard I try, the words just won't stick. The Fenlands. Elapidia, the water planet. The largest planet in this system...something with an "N"? No, wait, was that the jungle world? It's all running together.

"Stop overthinking." Verrin's calm, measured voice cuts through the haze of panic, but it doesn't help. He steps closer, his piercing gaze locking onto mine. "Don't panic. The names matter less than understanding the terrain. Water means currents. Fenlands mean marshes and mud traps. Jungles mean high heat and humidity. You'll survive if you can adapt."

"I can't do this," I mutter, slamming the map shut. "There's too much. How am I supposed to remember all of it? I'm not—I'm not like you." My voice cracks, and heat rises to my face. Great. Now I'm losing it in front of them. It's been four days and I don't feel any more confident than I did on the day we started.

Sidra arches a brow, unimpressed. "Then get better. Fast. Or you'll fail."

My chest tightens, the weight of her words pressing down on me like a boulder. Fail. I'll fail.

The word echoes in my head. If I screw this up, I won't just be failing myself. I'll be failing Riven. And I don't know if I can live with that.

She sits down beside me, taking my hand. "You're making this more difficult than it has to be. If your brain can't handle the details, we'll trick it into doing what we need."

"Trick it how?"

She smiles, moving to the console, to pull up the map again.

This time, instead of spinning planets and walls of text, each world is represented by a distinct image—visual snapshots of their environments. Rolling waves, tangled jungle canopies, sprawling deserts. My breath catches at how vibrant and real it all looks–like it's sitting right here in front of me.

"We'll associate each planet with something you already know," she points to the images. "Did your planet have anything like this?"

"We had oceans."

"Good. Oceans." She nods, saying the word slowly. "Is there anything about oceans that would make you able to remember it?"

"The ocean smells like salt."

"Close your eyes and think about the smell. Elapidia smells like salt water. It is not a freshwater planet. Think of the smell. Elapidia." She repeats.

"Elapidia." I whisper, thinking about the smell of ocean water.

"What else?" Verrin's voice cuts in. "Tie the planets to places, smells, sounds—whatever makes it stick."

Sidra hums. "The Fenlands? Find the emotion. They will help you remember."

"In the Fenlands I felt fear." I shudder just thinking about the time I spent there alone.

"Fear," Verrin agrees, his voice low. "That one will be one that you won't forget."

The weight in my chest eases, just a little. It's still over-whelming, but now it feels like there's a thread I can grasp, something to pull me through the chaos. "Ok," I nod. "I'll try again."

Sidra smirks, her sharp eyes gleaming with something almost like approval. "You'll do more than try. You'll get it right." She nods. "Or else."

I roll my eyes, but for the first time, there's a flicker of hope. Maybe I can do this.

CHAPTER 63

"We should take a break." Verrin's voice is full of both hesitation and exhaustion. I can see the pity on his face.

"No. She is going to answer one of these to an acceptable degree. Then she can have a break." Sidra presses her palms flat onto the table. I know she's frustrated.

"Ok, ask the question."

"What is the current policy regarding venom?" Her words are measured. We all know this is a sensitive subject.

Clearing my throat, I mentally sift through all of the information. "It is illegal to use venom unless it can be proven that the threat of death was legitimate. Venom is generally considered to be barbaric and uncivilized." I let out a shaky breath.

"And would you, if you were queen, choose to uphold these policies?"

"If I were queen I would never try to foster policy change that goes against what Ophidians want." I hope that was diplomatic enough.

"And what if Ophidians wanted to use venom against other races? What is the policy on that?"

"The policy is the same," I think. "The use of venom against any enemy, Ophidian or otherwise is prohibited."

She sighs. "We can break for the night but that answer won't stand up in the trials. You can't just say you wouldn't change policy because it's what we believe. You have to believe it too."

Shit. "You're right." She's showing me mercy. I only got it half wrong.

"Of course I'm right." She smiles for the first time in hours. "We'll begin again tomorrow morning."

I'm already dreading the morning.

I slowly organize all of the materials, waiting until they're gone to let myself fall apart. Dropping my forehead onto the table, I close my eyes and let my tired brain sit. I can't even remember two plus two.

Everything I've ever learned is being pushed out by all the new information being stuffed into my head. There isn't room for all of it.

I'm never going to remember everything.

"Demi?" His voice is soft. Jumping up, I turn to find him standing in the doorway watching me with concern on his face. He was so quiet I didn't hear him come in.

"Hey!" I try to smile. "I was just regrouping. I'm alright."

He doesn't believe me. "Come upstairs. I'm exhausted and you clearly are too. I can't sleep without you."

"Sleep sounds amazing." I'm grateful he doesn't push or ask questions about how the studying is going.

As we walk up the stairs, some of the weight on my shoulders lessens. Just being close to him makes it better.

We shower quickly and silently. The same tiredness that I feel is reflected back at me in his face. The quiet is nice.

I follow him into the bed, wet and naked, we curl around each other, seeking refuge and comfort. I find it immediately. My eyes are heavy and closing them feels so good.

Physically, I feel him close. His heart beats against my ear, a soft rhythm that lulls me to fast sleep.

But the peace is short lived.

His breath is steady, his chest moving slowly up and down beneath me— soft and safe. But dreams come for me, clawing at me and pulling me down.

I can feel the soft thump of his heart, and I know that's real but it's not enough. The moment my eyes close, I slip.

It's dark. There is a quiet murmur, the hum of a whispering crowd behind me. I'm alone, standing in a spotlight.

There is a flicker, then the lights come on.

I'm standing before the judges. A panel of them is seated before me.

The stone walls of the trial hall loom around me, cold and suffocating.

Hydriss is directly in front of me—tall, venomous, eyes narrowed with that calculating gleam I've come to fear. Phaedra sits next to him, her features cold and hard as marble. She's smiling, but it's the kind of smile that makes my skin crawl. Kimora is on the other side, arms crossed, her gaze piercing through me.

It's them but somehow not.

They don't look like themselves. They look like snakes, all of them, their faces elongated, their expressions twisted in ways that make me feel small, insignificant. The air around me thickens, suffocating. My throat tightens. I can barely breathe.

I want to scream, to run, but my body won't move. I can't do anything except stand here.

"You'll never be queen," Hydriss hisses, his voice echoing through the room.

"Your blood is weak," Kimora adds, her eyes flicking over me with disgust.

Phaedra stands as she speaks, her body slithering upward. "You are a threat to us all. Your sentence is death."

My heart stops. I try to wake up but I can't.

I know it's not real. I know it's a dream, but the weight of it feels so suffocating. I need to wake up, I need to get out of here. I try to focus on Riven's heartbeat, to let his steady thrum pull me back to safety, but it's slipping away from me, fading as the dream tightens its grip.

And then, just as the darkness begins to close in, I hear his voice. Barely a whisper, but it's there, real, calling me back.

I gasp, jolting awake. My eyes snap open, my heart pounding in my chest, the dream fading as I blink away the pieces that are trying to cling to me.

Riven's warmth is still beside me, his breath against my skin. I'm safe. But the fear lingers in the pit of my stomach, rolling around and making me nauseous.

I hold onto him, feeling the reassuring beat of his heart against my ear. It's enough to remind me that, no matter how real the dream felt, I'm still here, still breathing. It was just a dream.

CHAPTER 64

Untangling my limbs from his, I slip out of bed quietly, and sneak out of the room. He needs sleep.

I need to study.

I can sleep when the trials are over. I'm wasting valuable time.

The trials are not a death sentence. If I fail, they aren't going to kill me. I know that. But I can't shake the dream away as I creep down the dark hallway.

They are dead. They won't be the judges.

But maybe their influence is still alive and well. The judges might be friends of theirs. I need to be perfect in every way. I can't give them a reason to vote against me. My answer from earlier keeps coming into my mind. I should have been more clear and precise in my answer. I can't try to pander to either side. I have to make my feelings and intentions known without a doubt.

Places, leaders, history, policies, laws. There is so much of it and most of the names are confusing and hard to pronounce.

Dropping down into my seat, I open the holographic map. I'll warm up with one of the places that I'm having an easier time with. I've been there after all.

Elapidia, the water planet.

Closing my eyes, I try to remember their most pressing issues.

"They need more money and resources than other planets due to the cost of maintaining their underwater cities." I whisper to myself.

"That's right." Riven's voice whispers back, reassuring me. "What are you doing in here?"

Opening my eyes, I sigh and look at him. He's watching me with a soft smile. "I couldn't sleep. I need to study more. The truth is, it's not going very well, Riven." I confess to him. "There's so much to learn and I'm struggling. I'm afraid I'm not going to pass."

He walks with a calm, easy gait and comes to look at the map.

From behind me, he leans down, pressing a kiss to my shoulder.

"Stand up." He whispers and the air feels suddenly warmer.

With my hands flat on the table I stand, leaning slightly over the hologram.

The chair scraps against the ground as he pulls it away. My skin pricks, excitement creeping down my spine.

He stands behind me, his chest pressed against my back.

"What is this?" He points to an area on the map.

"That's the outer rim." I appreciate that he starts by throwing me an easy pitch.

"And what is the outer rim?"

His fingers graze my thighs as he inches down my body to lift the hem of my nightgown.

My breath catches. "Um, the outer rim is—"

One of his hands presses flat against the middle of my back with enough pressure to push me forward. I'm face to face with the map.

"The outer rim is an uninhibited expanse between Ophidian territory and—"

The tip nudges against me and I lose track of my thoughts.

"What is the outer rim, Demi?" He slides into me, a rough, steady stroke that has him all the way seated inside.

"Ungoverned territory not owned by any empire." I pant.

"Good," he groans. "And this, what is this?"

"The Fenlands."

"And what was their position during the Great War?"

"They—"

He starts to move, a hard, fast pace that forces me even farther forward.

"Answer me."

"They were divided!"

"Why?" His voice is tight, trembling slightly with the effort of talking and pounding into me at the same time.

"Some of them believed that the Fenwardens should have more power and authority."

"Why do the Fen wardens and the citizens of Elapidia have a tumultuous history?"

My mouth falls open but the only thing that comes out is a moan.

"They— Oh god, Riven!"

He grips my hips and uses the leverage to pull me back as he rocks forward.

"The Fen Wardens-" He grunts, helping me to make sense of the mess in my mind.

"They are angry that Elapidia gets more money because salt-water is more damaging to infrastructure than freshwater!" I drop my forehead onto the table.

"So good." He growls and I can't help but think he's not talking about my answer.

Everything fades away, the room, the map, the questions—all of my stress.

Forgetting about the trial, even for a few minutes, is exactly what I need.

He moves faster, forcing me to grip the table. I have to bite into my lip to keep from screaming and waking everyone else who's here.

The thought suddenly occurs to me that anyone could walk in. We're not in the privacy of our room. There is a full staff here at all hours. We're exposed–out in the open.

"Riven! Harder!" For whatever reason, this excites me beyond what I ever thought was imaginable.

"You feel so good." His forehead presses between my shoulder blades. The rough, desperate sound of his voice unravels me. "Demi!" My voice rips from deep in his chest and I know he's close - he's holding on, waiting for me.

"Come with me, Riven, please!" I'm out of my mind. The pressure in my stomach is so acute, so consuming that I can't even take in a breath.

Colors burst behind my eyes, lights and warmth that swallow me whole. I'm floating and falling and soaring–all at once.

He twitches and plants himself inside of me.

With my face flat against the table, I suck in a heaving breath. "At least I'll never forget those things again."

"I'm available whenever you need me." I can hear the smile in his tone.

"You might come to regret that offer."

CHAPTER 65

I know they're trying to help. If I'm comfortable with the layout of the room, I'll be more at ease when the real trial begins. Nothing will be a surprise. No sudden shifts to throw me off balance.

But standing here, under their scrutiny, it doesn't feel like practice. It feels real.

The weight of it presses down on me, tightening in my chest. The circular chamber, with its sweeping arches and open-air design, should feel freeing, but instead, it makes me feel exposed. Too many eyes will be on me. Too many people waiting for me to fail.

I don't belong here. Not yet. Maybe not ever.

"You will sit here." Riven's voice is calm but firm, his fingers briefly grazing my wrist as he gestures to the table in the center of the room.

I lower myself onto the wooden bench, my palms flattening against the smooth surface. My heartbeat is too loud in my ears, drowning out the rustling of the treetop canopy above. If I weren't here for a mock trial, I might be able to appreciate the beauty of the space—the way the sunlight filters through the leaves and paints the stone floor with golden dots. But right now, it feels like a stage, and I'm the unwilling performer.

Riven, Verrin, and Sidra settle into the judge's box, their expressions unreadable. I know this is practice, a chance to prepare, but as their gazes lock onto me, my chest tightens.

I'm not ready.

"On the first day of the trial, there will be a ceremonial entrance of the judges, introductions and opening remarks from the elected speaker of the panel. After the fifth day, they will call rest. They have one day to deliberate over your responses. Then on the seventh day there will be a ceremonial entrance and the speaker will announce whether you pass or fail."

"Let's begin!" Sidra stands. "Your first trial question–" She pauses, her flair for dramatic effect shining through. "Traditionally, Ophidians have held strict restrictions on warden training and qualifications that begin at the age of three. There have been groups that protest against the rigidity of that policy. Do you believe there should be reform there or would you agree with the law as it currently stands?"

Taking a breath, I try to calm my trembling hands. I don't want my voice to shake when I speak.

"The tradition of starting warden training at three ensures discipline and mastery, but it also assumes that every child is suited for such a path from birth. I believe reform is necessary— not to weaken the institution, but to refine it. There should be allowances for aptitude and for choice. A rigid system risks losing potential just as much as it seeks to find and cultivate it. For example, the Ashiana desert planet is known for producing some of the physically strongest Ophidians, but they are generally slow to reach their adult height. A three-year-old Ashian would be smaller than a three-year-old Elipidian. Eventually, the Ashian would grow head and shoulders above their counterparts, but they have aged out of being allowed to train as a warden. We are losing out on capable wardens by judging individuals to the same scale."

I hold my breath, waiting for her reaction. Instinctually, I pick my cuticles beneath the table.

Riven's lips twitch, but he straightens his spine and looks down at the table.

"To follow up, what would you say to the people that strongly advocate continuing with this tradition?" Her voice is serious and cold.

I know she's playing a role, but it's jarring.

"I would say that I understand their desire to uphold the traditions of their people but would counter that sometimes, what was once good and right, can become wrong with time. This tradition served the Ophidians well, but holding on to something that is no longer working is cutting off progress."

Breaking her character, her mouth spreads into a wide smile. "I would say you passed that. Thoughts?" She turns to Riven and Verrin.

"She would get my vote." Verrin nods.

"Mine too." Riven never takes his eye off of me.

I let out a breath, and my chest deflates. It was just one question, and they aren't exactly unbiased judges, but it feels good to know I didn't completely fail.

"My turn." Riven tilts his chin up slightly. "Under my rule, we have seen an era of unmatched strength, but also one of swift and often ruthless justice. Some believe that my iron-fisted approach is necessary to maintain order, while others argue that it fosters fear rather than loyalty. Do you believe absolute control is the key to a strong kingdom, or should mercy have a greater place in my reign?"

I know the weight of my answer. Riven won't be upset with me no matter how I answer. But I can't help but wonder about his intentions with this question. Is he just trying to prepare me or does he really want to know what I think? I press my hands together to steady myself and take a breath.

"Fear is a powerful tool—it ensures obedience and deters rebellion. But loyalty? True loyalty cannot be built on fear alone.

Strength is not just in the might of a ruler's hand but in the willingness of his people to stand beside him, not just beneath him. Your justice is swift because hesitation is seen as weakness. There is a delicate balance between justice and mercy. I think there is more mercy in your reign than you give yourself credit for. I would say that you have found the balance and shouldn't change it."

Sidra giggles, clapping her hands together. "I will only admit this to you now, but I started to have doubts. You have proved yourself today. You're going to be fine."

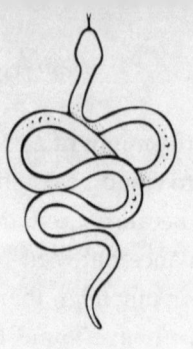

CHAPTER 66

"You look beautiful." He leans down, pressing a kiss to my temple.

I've never questioned Sidra's judgment before. She's never steered me wrong. But this dress feels too flashy for the occasion.

It's too bright and much too sheer for the swearing in of a new general. Call it my human prudishness and sensibilities, but this feels too risque for a government ceremony.

"It's perfect." Riven whispers again. This time, he runs his hand over the bare skin of my back.

"Wow." All thoughts of my outfit fade away as we step into the grand hall.

Everything is dark, but there is a faint shimmer in the air.

The vaulted ceiling stretches high above, adorned with luminescent, vein-like threads of silk that pulse with a faint, eerie glow. Dark stone walls, smooth and polished, reflect the flickering light of small fiery orbs that hover in strategic clusters, casting long, shifting shadows over the assembled guests.

Around the edges of the room, towering figures draped in ceremonial battle silks stand motionless, their plated armor whispering as they shift, the sigils of their houses glinting like dark constellations. The guests, a mix of Fen warriors and high-ranking officials, murmur in hushed voices. Everyone looks stunning, even the ones in uniform are spectacular.

At the front of the hall, a raised platform is waiting. A throne of gnarled wood, like the roots of a tree, is waiting in the center. It's empty, held for Riven.

A man in full uniform and armour is kneeling before it. The new General.

The man we're all here to watch as he swears fealty to something greater than himself.

Riven kisses my cheek and leaves me standing with Sidra. Her eyes are glassy as she watches him take his seat.

It's obvious that this is not just a ceremony. The air hums with quiet reverence, the weight of tradition pressing down on us like the thick scent of burning sage and polished steel. The Fen Wardens stand in perfect formation, their dark uniforms crisp, their silver insignias gleaming under the torchlight. There's a stillness to them—a discipline that speaks of unwavering loyalty, of a respect so deeply ingrained it's practically woven into their bones.

Riven pulls a silver blade from a sheath and makes a small cut to the palm of his hand. He lets the droplets of blood fall into a small basin at his feet.

The new general lifts his head, holding his hand up, palm open to Riven. He slices his skin with the same blade, and the blood runs into the basin.

"Extrenus, do you swear your allegiance not to me, but to the health, safety, and prosperity of every Ophidian?"

"I do."

"Do you vow to use your life for the service of every Ophidian, forsaking selfish pursuits?"

"I do."

Every eye is on them, and every breath is held in silent anticipation. The High Warden begins the oath, his voice ringing through the courtyard, clear and steady.

My chest tightens. This isn't just a ceremony. It's a vow, a binding promise that every single one of them believes in, down to their souls.

"Give your oath." Riven holds his head high.

"I, Extrenus Naes, pledge my unwavering loyalty and obedience to serve with honor, strength, and unyielding resolve. I will uphold my duty, forsaking fear and doubt, standing steadfast in the face of all who would oppose. My word is my bond, my actions my legacy, and I shall not falter."

"Bring the blood that everyone that stands beside you may give their blessing." Riven sits on the throne as the general takes the basin in his hands and rises to stand.

As he walks past the rows of Fen Wardens, they cut their hands, adding drops of their blood to the basin. Every one of them gives their stamp of approval by way of blood donation.

"You have been unanimously accepted, General Naes." Riven gestures to a much larger basin where an orange flame is flickering.

General Naes steps toward it, pouring the blood from the basin over the fire. It flickers blue and grows taller.

"From now, until the end of our days, you will be known as General Naes. Take your positions among your ranks." Riven's voice booms, loud and strong, through the hall.

His words echo, bouncing off of the walls. The Fen Wardens drop to one knee in unison, fists pressed to the ground. A pulse of something raw and unspoken moves through the crowd, something sacred. My throat tightens as I realize this isn't fear-based loyalty. It's not obedience forced by power.

I've never seen anything like this.

It's honor personified.

"You are dismissed." Riven stands ,and everyone bows their heads. "Enjoy today. This is a momentous occasion."

He steps down from the raised platform and walks directly toward me.

"That was amazing." I whisper.

"There will be a ceremony for you as well."

"What?" My mouth goes dry.

"After the Queen Trial. You will have a ceremony too ,but it's different from this."

The thought is terrifying, but at the same time, I can't help but wonder what it would feel like to belong to something like this.

CHAPTER 67

can't sleep.

It's been hours, and no matter how many times I close my eyes, I just end up staring at him.

He's always handsome and commanding in a way that borders on terrifying. But there's something about watching him sleep that shifts the balance. It softens him. The sharp angles of his face seem less severe, and the weight of authority that hangs from him during the day is less noticeable. The tension in his brow, the one I've learned to track so closely, is gone. His breath is slow and steady, the rise and fall of his chest a strange comfort I hadn't expected.

He's still Riven. He's still the king. But right now, he's just a man—one who seems almost vulnerable in the quietest part of the night.

Guilt tugs at my stomach–guilt and the now ever-present fear of failure. I did well during the mock trial–at least, that's what they said. Sidra didn't say it outright, but I saw the approval in her eyes—a flash so brief it was gone before I could catch it.

But what happens if I fail when it really matters? The trials ahead aren't just theater. They feel like life and death, and not just for me. I can't stop thinking about what would happen to him if I fail. Would they respect him less? The weight of it is suffocating.

In just a few hours, I'll be expected to wake up and spend hours on end studying. I'm exhausted. So exhausted that I can't sleep. My brain feels heavy–physically and mentally.

I've never been involved in something where so much of the outcome depends on me.

I care so much about this it actually aches in my chest.

I draw my knees to my chest, wrapping my arms around myself. There's no comfort anywhere. I just want to sleep. To let this momentary peace last. But sleep feels like a distant, impossible thing when every thought spirals back to him—and the shadow of failure hanging over me.

Slipping silently from the bed, I pull on a robe and open the door as quietly as I can.

I need fresh air–I need to touch grass. I've been inside, studying, for so long.

Creeping down the hallway, I move with silent, purposeful steps down the stairs. The house is quiet. In a strange way it's both peaceful and scary.

As soon as I pull the door open to the back garden, a rush of fresh, cold air chills my skin.

It's invigorating.

My bare feet sink into the cool, slightly dewy grass, and the scent of something sweet fills the air. Flowers the size of my head open wide, petals in shades of blue and iridescent white, glow under the moon.

I almost recognize the smell but not quite.

With each step, I feel a bit better. The cold is what I needed–the grass and plants. I feel connected to something for the first time in days. I've been so lost in the books I forgot why I like it here to begin with.

Trees with golden leaves sway gently in the breeze, their branches forming delicate arches that shimmer under the night sky. I walk beneath them, the house disappearing behind me.

Everything is asleep. The entire world beyond this garden feels far away, a fading memory of noise and chaos. Here, it's just me, cradled by nature's lullaby. I'm in the garden of Eden. A secret place where I can hide from the world.

I wander further in, following the gentle sound of rushing water.

I amble slowly, stopping to look at different leaves and flowers. It's nice to have nothing to do, no set pace. Maybe I should have come out here sooner.

The path is longer than I expected. When I finally reach the end, there is a streak of light in the sky. I think the sunrise is only a few minutes away.

Hidden beneath low hanging trees with thick, gnarled roots coming up out of the mud, the water spreads out in front of me. A small waterfall drops into an emerald-colored pool on the other side. It flows gently here, moving slowly.

Finding a spot among the roots, I sit on the bank of the river. Little clusters of white flowers grow in bunches around the water. Their petals are soft, and they smell like honeysuckle.

I love it here immediately.

I know it isn't true, but I feel like the first person to ever see this place. It looks untouched.

Closing my eyes, I just listen. The water and the occasional rustling of leaves are the only sounds. No talking. No rush. No history, politics, or culture. I'm alone.

The tension that has taken root in my shoulders feels relaxed. Stretching my legs out, I let my feet dip into the water. It's arctic.

Leaning closer to look for fish, something catches my eye.

A man is standing below the low-hanging branches, watching me.

CHAPTER 68

A s he approaches, I don't scream or run. A strange sense of calm takes over. I'm afraid, but my body is relaxed. I know I can't outrun him, so I'm not going to try.

"Good morning." He sits down beside me. Not close enough to touch me but still much too close. I can't get a good read on him. He doesn't obviously and immediately seem to hate me. It's not there like it was with Phaedra. He doesn't seem violent or unhinged like Hydriss.

"Good morning." My mind races, I don't recognize him. He looks like he might be from Elphdia. A desert planet with harsh conditions. The people from there are generally long and lean, as he is, with fair skin and blonde hair. He might kill me but I feel silently proud of myself for remembering those details.

"You look distressed."

I bark out an unexpected laugh. Distressed? The understatement of the century. I'm way beyond distress at this point. Where to even start? Present situation aside, my whole life is in distress right now.

"Yeah, you could say that."

"Why?"

"Well," I adjust the sleeves of my robe. "Are you going to hurt me?"

"I don't know."

I hum. At least he's honest. "I'm Demi."

"Salus." He gestures to himself. He seems surprised. He probably expected me to scream and panic. "You looked distressed before you saw me. What else is bothering you?"

"I'm afraid that I'm going to fail the Queen Trials." I just let the words tumble out. He was honest with me, I'll be honest with him. "It's not even that I really want to be Queen. I want Riven. Power and control are frightening—they change people. I'm putting so much effort into this and in the end, I still might not be good enough. I'm cramming all day, every day, to understand your history and culture, the politics of this place. It's a lot. Then, I have to sit before a panel and be judged of my worthiness. In a strange way, I think it's kind of a good system. If I was a third party watching from the outside without having to participate—I would find the whole thing fascinating. Right now, it's just terrifying. I'm afraid that people will look at Riven differently if I don't do well. He picked me and I can't stand up to the challenge—what does that say about him?" I suck in a deep breath.

"You are very forthcoming." He looks confused.

"I'm not trying to hide anything." I shrug.

"You don't want to be queen?" His silvery eyes meet mine.

"Don't mistake that for a lack of respect for the position. I am just a normal person where I'm from. I wasn't going to do anything particularly notable with my life. This is all very unexpected. When I decided to stay with Riven, I guess I was naive to what I was choosing but I didn't realize that choosing him meant choosing the crown."

He nods but doesn't speak.

We sit for several minutes in silence. I feel like I just took a ten pound weight off of my chest. I don't know him. It might have been a very bad idea to tell him all of that but it felt good. I needed to say it to someone, and this stranger who may or may not kill me seems like the perfect person.

"Have you shared these concerns with Kind Adder?"

"To some degree." I lie. I don't want to add more stress to his plate. He already has so much to deal with. I know the trials are on his mind as much as they are mine but if I'm not confident, he'll be more anxious too. I don't want to do that to him.

He hums, staring out at the waterfall with a thoughtful look on his face.

"I am a stranger to you. I'm sure my opinion matters very little but I believe you might be better suited to the role than you think."

He stands, dusting off his pants. "I will see you again, Demi. It was nice to meet you."

I consider my response. "It was nice to meet you too, Salus."

"You should tell King Adder how you're feeling." His lips tug into a smile.

"Maybe I will. Thank you for letting me dump my fears and frustrations on you."

"It was my pleasure." He smiles, his fangs are long and thin—much more prominent than Riven's.

And then, just like that, he's gone.

When he disappeared behind the trees, I let out a long, slow breath. That could have been bad. Maybe this wasn't the best idea after all.

I'll stay for a few more minutes, then I have to go back before anyone starts to worry. After pushing it as long as I possibly can, I stand and start to make my way back to Riven. Walking slowly, I let myself enjoy the planets again, stopping to smell them and study them.

I'm stalling.

CHAPTER 69

The grass is dewy beneath my feet as I rush back toward the house. It didn't feel like long but I know I overstayed my window for causing concern.

I should have been more careful.

There is no way Riven isn't awake. I just hope he isn't panicking.

Pulling open the door that leads into the dining room, I hear the sounds of rushing.

People are not only awake but they're running around. Voices and footsteps are coming from all around the house.

Shit.

Walking quickly, I keep calm. If I'm freaking out he will be on even higher alert when he sees me. I have to de-escalate the situation.

As I step out into the foyer, I see Riven immediately. We make instant eye contact and his shoulders lower slightly—an almost invisible sign of his tension releasing.

"I'm so sorry! I went walking in the garden and lost track of time!" I rush toward him.

He grabs me, pulling me into a tight hug.

"I've looked everywhere for you, Demi." He breathes against my neck.

"I'm sorry! I shouldn't have stayed out so long. I couldn't sleep and needed fresh air. I'm sorry!"

"Stop apologizing. I understand if you want a moment but next time can you tell me you're leaving? Waking up to an empty bed is upsetting enough but not being able to find you..."

"I'll tell you from now on."

"Are you alright?"

"Yes." I take his face in my hands. "I'm fine."

The uncertainty in his eyes makes me feel guilty.

"Do you have a few minutes to come upstairs with me?"

He groans quietly and his eyes narrow. "I can always spare a moment for you."

Taking his hand, I turn and quickly run up the stairs with him right on my heels.

In our bedroom, I spin around in time to press him into the door.

"Today I'm learning about how you became king." I slip my robe off. "I want to hear it directly from you."

"I'll tell you anything you want to hear." He reaches out to slip my nightgown off one shoulder.

He's already in uniform. This damn uniform makes me feel like a feral animal. As quickly as my fingers allow, I undo the front of his pants.

"Sit down on the chair." I let my eyes trail downward, watching the front of his pants specifically.

He never disappoints.

With a suspicious look in his eyes, he sits in the chair waiting for me.

" start from the beginning." I walked toward him slowly.

" My father was the king before me. He was beloved by the people."

I nod. I know this.

"When he began taking the steps to pass the phone to me,

there was an uprising of Fenwardens who had been secretly plotting against him. By the time they moved to strike, I was in the middle of the transfer of power."

Lifting my nightgown up my thighs, I straddle his lap.

"Continue." I run the tips of my fingers down his chest.

He clears his throat, looking down at where our skin is touching.

"I had to come out strong. I knew that, how ever I responded to their uprising and would set the tone for the rest of my reign. I couldn't allow them to continue to grow."

"So what did you do?" I reach down, sweeping his tips against the wetness that had already accumulated between my legs.

He lets out a rough breath and lets his head lean into the chair. "I—"

I slide down, just enough for the tips to slip inside.

His hands come to my hips, gripping my skin hard.

"What did you do?" I wait, holding myself there.

He hesitates, he knows what's coming.

Leaning forward, I press a soft tail of kisses on his cheek, over his lips, and down his neck.

"Demi."

"What did you do, Riven?" I whisper against his ear.

"I gathered a small—"

I sink down completely, taking him all the way.

His grip tightens and he chokes on his words. "I gathered a small patrol and had them set up a station in the Fenlands. It was peaceful, they were there to gather intel and report back to me directly but—"

I roll my hips, holding onto his shoulders to steady myself as I ride him.

"But then?" My voice trembles.

"They took this as an act of aggression. They believed I was invading their territory." The roughness of his voice makes my stomach clench.

"But you're the king. Isn't every territory your territory?"

"Yes." He growls.

"What happened next?" I move up and down faster, sliding over him and pulling him deep.

"A line was drawn. I couldn't allow them to continue to spill their rhetoric into other territories. They are so firm in their beliefs that they truly thought that they would have support within the other territories."

"But they didn't." I bounce faster.

"No." he pants. "They didn't."

"Riven." I moan, starting to lose control.

"The Great Wars were less of a war and more of a massacre. They didn't stand a chance. They had very few supporters in the other territories and those that they did find quickly turned on them when it was clear that this was a battle they could not win. They wanted more freedom to govern themselves but they proved with their hasty and il-thought-l thought out plans that they need a ruler."

He's close. And I'm closer.

It's not just how good it feels, but it's the sound of his voice, the power radiating off of him, and the way he's struggling to maintain control.

All of it together is an unbearable torture—it's too much.

"They tried to attack you here." I whimper.

"They thought they could surprise me at home. They thought my defenses would be down."

" but they weren't."

He shakes his head and bites into his lower lip, his fangs pressing into his skin.

"Oh, fuck," I lean forward, pressing my forehead into his shoulder as he thrusts his hips up to meet mine.

And that's all it takes.

He groans my name and I cry his, our mouths pressing together in a sloppy kiss.

Panting and shaking, I force myself back to look at him. I know he's holding back.

He doesn't have time for the connection right now.

But I want him to come.

Lifting up, I drop to my knees in front of him and suck him into my mouth.

"Demi!" He slams his fists into the armrest and presses his heels into the floor.

It only takes a second, and my tongue is coated in the subtle taste of his release.

Careful not to waste a drop, I slide him out of my mouth. "I'm sorry I scared you this morning."

His eyes flutter open, a hazy, relaxed smile on his face. "I don't know if I will ever not worry about you."

"I know that. I shouldn't have gone out without telling you or leaving a note." I come up on his lap again.

"I don't want to go to these briefings."

"And I don't want to study. I think I've got a pretty good handle on the material anyway."

He hums, "I'm glad I was able to help."

CHAPTER 70

"Ok," I mumble to myself. "This is—" slowly moving the hologram around. I name each planet, the different territories, and the current leadership.

I'm slow and I know some of my pronunciation is off but I got each one correct.

"I told you you would get it." Sidra smiles from the doorway.

"I'm getting there." I try not to let myself blush at her compliment. She gives them out so rarely that when she does let one slip I know I've really earned it.

"Would you come have lunch with me? I would like to speak to you about something."

She doesn't look nervous exactly, but something about her expression has my heart rate spiking.

"Sure." I wipe my sweaty palms on my pants.

As we walked toward the kitchen, a thousand scenarios play in my mind. It's probably nothing. I try to calm myself down, but I'm starting to feel lightheaded.

The only possible thing she could have to say that would make her face look like that is that she doesn't think I'm ready for the trial.

Or exponentially worse she doesn't think I deserve the position anymore.

"Sit here." She points to a chair that already has a plate in front of it.

She's trying to soften the blow with desserts.

"I would like to ask you something." She starts immediately wasting no time.

"Ok." I brace for impact.

"Verrin has asked me to join him in a commitment ceremony." A shy, sweet smile spreads across her lips.

"A commitment ceremony? Like a marriage?" Excitement blooms in my chest.

"We will be joined together to live out our lives in union politically, socially, physically, and emotionally. He will be my partner."

"Oh my God, Sidra congratulations!"

"Thank you." The smile is still on her face. " I wanted to ask if you would be willing to sign as a witness at our ceremony tomorrow."

"Of course! I would be honored!"

"Oh, good!" She lets out a relieved breath.

That was what she was so nervous about talking to me about. I wipe my hand over my damp forehead and try to calm my racing heart.

We sit down together and enjoy the dessert in peaceful, comfortable silence. I don't want to disturb her or burst the sweet love bubble. She's currently floating in.

"If you don't mind, I have a few maps for you to read over and study but I'm going to take the rest of today off."

"I don't mind at all. I'm sure you have a lot of things to prepare!"

The thought of Sidra and Verrin essentially getting married makes me feel fluttery inside.

"I spoke to Riven and he wants you to come and finish your studies in his office."

Now I'm the one smiling like a fool. Just the thought of seeing him makes me want to squeal and kick my feet.

I feel the same rushed energy from her that I feel. I want to get to him. She wants to get to Verrin.

"I will bring you a dress in the morning." She stands, barely calling over her shoulder before she rushes out the door. I clean our dishes as quickly as possible and run out into the hallway.

The foyer is quiet as I creep through to the professional wing. Listening at the door, I lift my hand to knock and the door swings open just as my fist touches it.

"Come here." He grabs me, lifting me up against his hard, warm body.

"Hi."

"Hi." He sniffs my neck. "You still smell like me."

"Do you smell like me?" I feel mixed emotions about this. I like it but if other people smell it I wonder if they're grossed out.

"Yes." His voice drops. "I've been breathing it in all afternoon."

Leaning in, I press my face into his neck and breathe. I know I won't smell what he smells but his scent is good enough.

"I have to complete a briefing. As soon as it's done, I'm taking you back upstairs." He carries me across the room.

We settle in behind his desk. He has work to do and so do I.

Opening the holographic map, I start to read the different pieces Sidra has selected for me to study. It's a lot. I'm not surprised.

"What are you working on?" He stops writing his brief.

"Hey, eyes on your own paper."

He turns back to his work but he keeps looking at me. I can feel his gaze on me.

"Riven!"

"What?"

"Finish your work or we'll still be sitting here tomorrow!" I push his shoulder back toward his screen. The thought pops into my head, suddenly. "Oh! Hey! Sidra asked me to be one of the witnesses for their ceremony tomorrow!"

"Did she? Verrin asked me to as well." The soft smile on his face makes that fluttery thing in my chest.

"Really?"

"Yes. It is a great honor."

"Yeah," I sigh. "I feel honored too."

"Demi, it is one of the highest honors someone can bestow here. To be the witness to a lifelong commitment to another almost as sacred as the act itself. Did she explain it to you?"

"No." I sit up straight. "What do I have to do?"

"We will wear special ceremonial robes and stand beside them as they are committed to each other. Then, we will be asked to speak for them."

"What does that mean?"

"The judge will ask if we accept their union. And you answer yes or no."

" If one of us says no are they not allowed to continue?"

"No. That is why it's such a high honor to be asked to witness. We hold the power to hold them back from their chosen happiness."

"Oh my god. I can't believe they trust me with that. I was honored before but now…" my eyes start to well up.

He has a look on his face. Almost like he wants to say something, but isn't.

"What?"

He shakes his head, a smile tugging at his lips. "Nothing."

CHAPTER 71

T he room is colder today.

Not the kind of cold that settles on your skin, but the kind that seeps into your bones, making it hard to breathe.

It feels different standing here. Last time, Rive, Sidra and Verrin sat in the judge panel box. The room was lighter. The sun was beating down from the open ceiling.

We practiced here so that I wouldn't be afraid. It didn't work. I'm terrified.

Riven can't stand with me. He's somewhere off to the side, just out of sight, but that doesn't stop the weight of his presence from pressing against me.

A reminder that I'm not really alone at this moment. That whatever happens next is mine to bear but he's with me.

I have to actively remind myself not to lock my knees. Passing out would be bad.

In the shadows, I watch for movement, for any sign that they're coming.

There is a sound behind me. The loud rumble of an ancient door opening. Light comes in, a single beam spreading across the floor.

Five towering figures come around from behind me, moving to the podium.

The judges.

Draped in long, ceremonial robes, they move with slow precision, each step heavy with meaning. The air hums with an unspoken expectation as they take their places.

My legs wobble. There is a chance I'm being dramatic, but I feel like I'm standing in front of a group of executioners.

From somewhere in the room, a voice rings out, sharp and crystal clear.

"Today, the judges for the Queen Trial take their vows. We seek truth and honor with this trial. We seek our future queen. It is with the utmost respect and reverence that we stand here today, prepared to make judgments on Demetria Winston."

Hearing my full name makes my stomach flip-flop.

"General Naes, step forward."

One of the figures steps into the light. I recognize him immediately. The new general of the Fen Wardens.

"Do you swear to put Ophidians first in this trial, and to make just and swift judgments that would be for the greater good, putting personal feeling or bias aside?"

He holds his closed fist to his chest. "I swear to uphold truth and honor."

The next three step forward, two women and another man. I don't recognize them. Each of them makes their vow.

Last night, I looked over all the current and past territory leaders. I thought I might see some of them here. But none of the judges seem to be heads of state.

They never look at me. It's like they're looking past me, over my shoulder, to whatever is behind. They seem so harsh. There's a cold, clinical quality to them. Their voices, their posture, even the cadence they speak in.

"Salus. Step forward." The voice calls out.

Everything he says after is distorted and distant. Salus?

When he steps into the light, I try to keep my expression neutral.

With his fist to his chest, he swears his oath. "I swear to uphold truth and honor."

He's a judge?

My already queasy stomach ties itself in knots. I don't know how to feel about this. He just swore an oath of truth and honor, but will he keep it?

How can he be neutral and unbiased when we've spoken?

The things he said come flooding back to my mind.

Is he a friend among the judges or an enemy?

"Do you swear to do your due diligence?" The voice calls out.

They all speak at once, their voices layer over one another, a chorus of solemn oaths.

"I swear my due diligence."

"We will hold you to these oaths."

The final oath is spoken, and silence stretches across the chamber.

I force myself to stand tall, to keep my expression blank.

I tried to keep my mind on other things. Sidra and Verrin have their ceremony tomorrow. I think about that instead of waiting for the long pause to be over.

"Dismissed." The voice calls, and with slow, deliberate steps, just how they entered, the five judges exit the chamber.

I don't know if there are more eyes on me. I know Riven is here, but I don't know if there are others. So I stayed perfectly still.

"Demi," he calls to me after the heavy door rumbles closed.

My shoulders sag just hearing him speak pulls the weight off of them.

Turning towards the sound of his voice, I squint in the dark, searching for him.

He pulls me into his arms, hugging me tightly against his chest, comforting me.

"You did well."

"Did I?" my voice shakes. I tried.

"You did."

Leaning into him, I take a deep breath against his chest.

"Do we like these judges?"

"I am very pleased with this panel." His tone is reassuring. He isn't lying just to make me feel better.

"Ok, good." I'm starting to feel less jittery. "I'm glad that's over."

Now, onto the hard part.

CHAPTER 72

"Riven." My voice is barely a whisper. I can hardly formulate words. The dress that arrived this morning is unlike anything I've ever seen.

I can't believe I get to wear that.

Ophidian traditions are different from earth's; that is already clear but...

It's obvious that the bride doesn't have any worries about being overshadowed at her wedding.

This gown is the softest, butteriest silk I've ever touched. The thought of slipping it on my body is exciting. It's like little clusters of glass beads are sprinkled over in swirling patterns. It looks like stardust.

He comes in behind me, holding me against him as he studies the masterpiece in front of us.

"I can't believe I'm lucky enough to stand beside you while you're wearing that dress." He hums, running the tips of his fingers down my arm.

"Stop it." I blush.

"No." He pulls me even closer.

"Yes." I laugh. "Or we'll be late."

"Fine, but later. You're mine."

I won't argue there.

"Can you help me put it on?" I'm almost afraid to touch it.

"Of course." He takes it down, carefully holding open the skirt for me to step into. The train will flow behind me for what looks like miles. Two thin straps over my shoulders hold the dress up while showing maximum skin. That is a Sidra signature. She wants as much skin showing as possible at every occasion.

"Shoes?" I look around, but there aren't any. A strange panic twitches in my brain. I don't have shoes that will work with this dress!

"We don't wear shoes. The ceremony is on the sacred grounds." He is gentle, as always.

"The sacred grounds? Really?" I was already excited about this, but now I can hardly contain myself.

"Yes."

"Oh, my god." I feel flushed. "Are we standing in the center?" My heart is racing.

"Yes." His lips twitch.

"Oh, my god."

"Take a breath, Demi."

"I've wanted to go there since I learned about it!"

I'm practically bouncing out of my skin as we down to the waiting pods.

We are whisked away, zipping through the air so that everything we pass is blurry and gone in a second flat.

The city fades in the background, and the lush green forest is all around us.

Above us, dark skies stretch on forever. The world feels endless and beautiful.

Sometimes, at a random place or time, I'll be hit with how extraordinary my life is. I've been dropped into a dream.

The trials feel less frightening suddenly. I have to earn my place in this wonderland.

Snuggling into his side, I press a kiss to his chest. He wraps his arm around me, holding me close.

We don't have to say anything. I don't want to ruin it. The silence is perfect.

A beam of light in the distance cuts into the darkness, shooting straight up into the air. My breath catches in my throat.

"There it is." He whispers.

All I can manage is a silent "wow."

Before us, a formation of smooth rocks is stacked into a perfect platform. They aren't man-made—they just are. There is no history of their construction. The center of the rock is a flat stage with glowing water pooled at the center.

There are hundreds, maybe thousands, of people standing around the base of the platform. I shouldn't be surprised that an event thrown by Sidra would be highly popular.

We step out of the pod, and he leads me up. There are stones carved into the stone, wrapping around the circular base up to the top.

It's smooth under my feet and cold like marble.

When we reach the top, we step into the center. The water is warm, just lapping at my ankles. Where does it come from? There is no explanation. Even at midday in the sunshine, it's here—it never dries.

It feels ancient and powerful.

Another pod arrives, Sidra and Verrin step out.

She takes my breath away.

Her dress looks like fire. Hues of yellow, orange, and red. They wrap around her like flames.

There is someone else with them. Someone I don't know. He's wearing long black robes.

The three of them climb the platform and stand perfectly in the center.

Sidra smiles at us, but she can't take her eyes off of Verrin.

"Today," the man in the robes cuts through the silence. I know his voice instantly. He is the voice from the judgment chamber, the one that prompted the judges to give their oaths. "We are here to join Verrin Orlovs and Sidra Garter. Their commitment to each other will be recognized from this day until they are gone."

He turns to us. "Riven Adder, do you accept this commitment?"

"Yes, I do."

"Demetria Winston, do you accept this commitment?"

"Yes, I do." I try to stay stoic, but I can't hold back my smile.

There's a ripple through the crowd. They must've seen me here, walking up the platform with Riven, but for some reason, they're only reacting now.

"There is nothing here or anywhere that can separate you." The man continues.

I feel love all around me. It's physical, it's palpable.

This is the most incredible thing I've been a part of.

"Honored guests and witnesses, I present to you, forevermore, this pair, united."

The crowd, a group of at least a thousand stomps into the ground, a single time creating a loud rumble that vibrates the platform and echoes through the air.

The three of them proceed down the stairs first, and Riven and I follow.

"Now what?" I whisper as we slide into the pod.

"Now we celebrate."

CHAPTER 73

I thought the solstice celebration was magical. This party is probably the most beautiful, extravagant event ever held on any planet in any universe. This is so far beyond anything I've ever seen.

Everywhere I look, there is some other-worldly thing to see. It's almost overwhelming. The seamless blend of nature and man-made design is something the Ophidians really do well.

We're celebrating on a small sandbar in the middle of a large lake between two waterfalls. It doesn't even look like a real place.

Lights in different hues of purple float in the air, hanging from nothing—they're just suspended above us.

Smooth, round stones are set out in the water in swirling patterns. People are using them as a walkway, standing out in the middle of the iridescent lake—floating on the surface of the water.

Everyone seems so happy. There isn't a single scowl on any of the faces. Laughter rings through the air. Even Riven's mother looks pleased. I guess it's hard to be in a place like this, surrounded by love, and still be angry.

"Riven, oh my god!" Strange alien fish are swimming in the water. They're brightly colored, and they glide like eels. "Wow."

"Are you hungry?" He runs his hand over my shoulder.

"Oh," I feel flushed. "Sure." Not for food… I swallow down the sudden flutter of desire in my belly. He means for actual food. Get a grip.

The tables are set up buffet style, row after row of trays stacked high with beautiful miniature foods. Everything looks amazing.

"Are you enjoying yourselves?" Sidra pops up out of nowhere. I haven't seen her since they left the Sacred Grounds.

"Sidra! You've outdone yourself! Everything is perfect!" I can't help but gush about it. "It's the most incredible thing I've ever seen."

She smiles, obviously pleased. "Eat and enjoy yourselves! The second course will be set out soon!"

Second course?

Riven's arm wraps around my waist, holding me tightly to his chest. "I can't take my eyes off you tonight. I've hardly noticed the party."

Humming, I spin around to wrap my arms around his neck. "Is there somewhere we can sneak off to? Somewhere private?"

His breath catches, and his spine straightens as he quickly looks around. Biting back a laugh, I look too, searching for somewhere we can slip away unnoticed.

"Here." He leads me away quickly, whisking me across the sandbar.

On one side of the lake, there is a small cove with a bridge over the water. It's partially hidden by long hanging branches from the trees on the shoreline. It's not completely private, but it's far enough away to steal a minute alone.

The bridge is different from others that I've seen here. It's not modern looking. The roots of a tree have been twisted and pulled upward to create a path over the water.

Standing with my back to him, I let my head rest on his chest.

The water stretches out in front of us, and the trees hang above. This feels like a little hidden paradise.

"Riven?"

He hums, tightening his grip on me.

"Do you think we're far enough away that people wouldn't notice if we misbehaved?"

"Misbehave?" His voice drops down lower.

"Mmhm."

"Demi." He groans.

"Would they? I mean, if we stand like this, they wouldn't know, would they?"

He groans again. One of his hands slips down, gripping the skirt of my dress. "I could just pull this up."

"You could," I whisper. Please do it.

Slowly, he pulls the material up, gathering it over his arm. "You are…"

"A bad influence?" I finish for him when his voice fades.

"The most incredible thing I've ever seen." His fingers skim my thigh.

When I'm ready, exposed, he presses himself against me again. My head is spinning. There isn't ever enough time.

Forcing my eyes to stay open. I look out at the beauty of everything before us as he slowly pushes into me.

We both moan together. His hand comes around me, wrapping around my chest, and his face drops into my neck.

"Fuck." I whisper.

This might have been a bad idea. If someone does look and see us, they might not be able to see anything, but they'll definitely know.

At this point, I don't care.

He moves his hips slowly, but it's enough.

"God," I drop my head back. "Why does this feel so romantic?"

"It's the lights." He huffs a strained laugh.

He speeds up, the careful, slow strokes becoming much less careful.

"Oh, please." I bite into my lip. We're far enough away that no one will hear us, but we still need to be quiet.

"Demi." His fingers bite into my skin. "I—"

"I know." I do. It's not enough. It never is.

We don't have much time. His absence will be noticed quickly.

But I'll take every single second he will give me.

"Riven," I press back into him. "I love you." My voice shakes, but not because I'm afraid. I mean it.

He freezes, his arm tightening around my body. "I love you. More than anyone or anything else in my life."

CHAPTER 74

"This is for today." She hands me a silky pink outfit. "I have each day coordinated in a very specific order. I will be here each morning to help you dress. The clothes are symbolic." She looks at me sternly.

"I'll stick to the schedule." I look at the outfits. "What does today's outfit symbolize?" I need her to keep talking. It's the only thing keeping my breakfast down. If I think about this after-noon–even for one second–I'm nauseous.

"Pink is the color of the Hyaseth flowers that bloom on Sarcadia. Judge Naes is from there. He will see the homage paid to his territory. These flowers are special–powerful." She looks at me, a glimmer of hope in her eyes.

"I remember. They can be eaten, and the high water content cures dehydration. They also have enzymes in the stems and leaves that fight infection."

"Yes!" She closes her eyes. "I knew you would remember!"

I needed this moment. A reminder of everything I've learned. I just have to take a breath and focus.

I'm grateful for the clothes as I slide into them. They are a perfect distraction. I still can't get used to the fashion here. I trust

Sidra. I know that she would never put me in anything inappropriate. But this is hard to get used to.

This is not the sort of outfit that we would wear to an event like this.

It's floaty and sheer and looks more like a high fashion runway outfit than something to wear to a serious trial.

It's soft though and comfortable. The silky layers of fabric make me feel sort of like a flower. I'm sure that was intentional.

When we step out into the hallway, Riven is waiting.

He's a pillar of strength. If he has any nerves or anxiety, he doesn't show it.

Taking his hand, we walked down the hallway. When my fingers tremble, he squeezes them tighter, giving me a reassuring nod.

I can do this.

Every step feels heavy. My legs aren't cooperating with my brain. Every instinct in me is telling me to turn and run— to find somewhere to hide.

There isn't anywhere to hide. I have to face this head-on. Right now.

When we reach the circular room beneath the canopy of trees, I swallow and tighten my posture.

"I'll be right here waiting." Riven takes my chin in his fingers. "I'm with you."

"I know."

Walking into the room alone is terrifying. But I remember the other terrifying things that I've been through. This pales in comparison to being kidnapped or watching someone's skin melt after they've been injected with venom. A little perspective here.

I've already lived through worse. They're only going to ask me questions. Five judges, five days, one question each.

When I take my place under the single beam of soft light, the doors rumble closed behind me.

The long, dark shadows of my judges move around me, walking in a line.

"Today, we begin the Queen Trials."

The voice rings out in the silence. It's less frightening when there's a face to go with it. He's not just a disembodied voice echoing in the air.

"Step forward."

I feel outside of my body. Like I'm hovering above myself as I take a step toward them.

"Today we hear from Judge number one. General Naes."

The general steps forward, and I bow my head. He does the same.

"My question is this: If betrayed, how would you respond to maintain order while preserving strength?"

Taking a breath, I try to appear calm while my brain works in overdrive. I know his strategies—I've studied them.

Tough but fair. Rational. Slow to react but ruthless.

"There isn't a blanket answer for this. Betrayal needs to be dealt with on a case-by-case basis. Some are worse than others. To maintain order, in any event, justice must be dealt out as quickly as rational thought and study of evidence will allow. A punishment, once handed down, can't ever be taken back." I take a breath. "The appropriate sentence can only be given with a clear mind. That is a show of strength. Reacting rashly, out of anger, that doesn't require strength. Holding back, seeing the full picture, that takes self-control and commitment to truth and justice—not just revenge."

My knees wobble as he bows his head and steps back into his place in the line.

The judges turn in perfect unison and walk around the perimeter of the room. The door rumbles open behind me, a streak of light shining through.

"You are dismissed." The voice calls.

It takes everything in me not to turn and run. Walking steadily, I know I am going to Riven.

Outside, we collide. He has me in his arms with his face in my neck immediately.

"One down, four to go." I whisper.

"Four to go."

CHAPTER 75

"Day two." I stare at myself in the mirror. My bluish military-type uniform is stiff and uncomfortable. Since I've been here, I've never seen anything like this.

"Judge Lious is from Inner Mornia." She whispers.

Ok. This makes sense.

Stoic, rational, cold. I look it. I feel it.

"A small but fiercely proud territory of mineral miners."

"Yes!" She smiles. "Blue Azur is the number one export. They are incredibly proud of it."

Running my fingers over the fabric, I list the qualities in my head. I know he isn't going to ask me something about Blue Azur. That would be too easy. But it's helping me relax.

"Ready?" Riven peeks into the room.

"Does it matter?" I smile. "It's time to go."

He wraps his arm around me in a way that feels protective. I lean into it. I wish he could stand beside me. I know he feels that.

"It's faster than I thought it would be." I attempt to seem positive here.

"It is." He agrees, a small tug pulling at his lips. We walk down the hallway together, his arms around me.

"And it's so dark, I can really only see the judge who is speaking."

"It is very dark." He nods.

"Right, which is good. It's better not to see all of them." I roll my lips into my mouth.

"Definitely."

A giggle wiggles in my throat. "Riven, it's so awful!"

He lets out a laugh. "I know. You don't have to try to find positive things to say about it, Demi. You can vent your frustrations. Tell me the truth."

"This outfit is hot and itchy."

"And you look like you're preparing to mine Blue Azur." He runs his hands over my shoulders.

"Well, good. That's what it's supposed to look like." I look down at it.

"It will be over quickly."

"It will be over quickly." I nod.

"And I will be waiting here."

"I know." I come up onto my toes to kiss him. I just meant for it to be a quick peck, but he pulls me in.

The world melts away. The trial, the judges, everything waiting behind this heavy metal door is gone.

His hands come up, holding my face, fingers weaving through my hair. "I don't want to go." I pout. This is so much better than what I have to do.

He hums and continues to kiss me, leaving a trail down my neck, his warm breathing fanning my skin. "I'll be right here."

Pulling myself away, I smooth out my clothes and stand in front of the door.

"See you on the other side." I wink before turning around and straightening my spine. "Let's go."

The door opens, and the rumble vibrates in the floor beneath me.

It might be false confidence, but I feel less fear today. The unknown aspect is gone now, I know what to expect.

Maybe it's that I'm more prepared, or maybe the novelty has simply worn off. The weight of the first day, with its ceremony and unspoken expectations, has settled into something quieter. The air still hums with anticipation, but it feels different—less like standing before a divine reckoning and more like being tested by men who have already decided my fate.

The judges enter, their dark cloaks whispering against the marble floor. Their presence is no less imposing, their hoods casting deep shadows over their faces, but the spectacle feels restrained, the edges softened. No grand pronouncements, no slow, deliberate theatrics. Just purpose.

"Today, we hear from Judge number two. Judge Lious." The speaker's voice rings out.

His figure steps forward, his movement measured, and controlled. He bows, but his eyes never leave mine—crystal clear beneath the heavy hood, sharp as glass. There's something hypnotic about them.

"My question is this: How will you deal with those who challenge your authority?"

Well, shit.

Taking a breath, I force my shoulders back.

"I'm not Ophidian. I expect that this may arise at some point. A strong leader understands that challenges to authority are natural. And, if handled correctly, it can be beneficial. My approach would be to listen first. A challenge doesn't have to come from a place of disrespect or anger. I will ensure that I understand the concerns or perspectives being raised. I am not a perfect person, I can make a mistake. If the challenge is constructive, I would engage in open dialogue to find common ground and address any valid points made. If the challenge is disruptive or harmful, I would assert my position calmly and decisively, reinforcing the principles and expectations that guide the current ruler. Ultimately, my goal would be to turn opposition into an opportunity for growth for all parties involved."

His sharp eyes watch me, pinning me to this spot. We're

waiting in the heaviest, most intense limbo. I don't know what to do.

Is he going to ask a follow-up question? Is he even allowed?

My nails press into my palms. Sweat gathers on my neck, the itchy collar of this uniform chafing my skin.

Finally, he bows his head and steps back into his place in line.

"Dismissed." The voice calls quickly, and they leave.

That felt strange. I can't be sure, but it seems they felt it too. There was a shift, a shuffle, that happened.

When the door rumbles open, there is a rush of noise from outside.

Spinning around, I find Riven, his silhouette in the doorframe.

Something is happening.

CHAPTER 76

R iven wraps his arms around me, a wall of coiled strength shielding me from whatever chaos is forming beyond us. His touch is firm, and grounding, but beneath it, there's a tension in his muscles—something restrained.

"Riven?" I tilt my head up, searching his face. His expression is unreadable, but his grip on me tightens for the briefest moment before he speaks. He's trying not to scare me, which only scares me more.

"Come."

He leads me through a small, rounded hallway, the dim lighting casting long shadows along the curved walls. The air hums with distant voices, a low murmur of something growing just beyond our reach. My heart pounds against my ribs.

"There is a crowd gathering," he finally says. His voice is calm, but there's an edge to it, something measured. "They are peaceful. But they are here for you."

My stomach knots. "In support?"

His brow furrows. "Most. Yes. But not all."

A breath catches in my throat. I expected this. Knew it was inevitable. And yet, standing here now, I can feel the weight of it pressing down on me. Fear twists low in my stomach, a small voice, a whisper of doubt urging me to turn away, to retreat into the safety Riven provides.

But I won't. I can't.

I inhale slowly, steadying myself. "Then I need to meet them."

His gaze sharpens, something flickering in his golden eyes. "You don't have to do this."

"Riven. I know you're trying to protect me, but I need to meet them." I square my shoulders, pressing past the weight of my fear. "Hiding won't change anything. If they're here for me, then I need to face them."

Riven exhales, his jaw tightening as he studies me. Then, after a beat, he nods. "Fine."

But his arm doesn't drop from around me. If anything, his hold becomes more crushing. He's on edge.

When we step outside, it sounds louder. The crowd gathered in the small courtyard is filling it to capacity. The building on one side has open terraces that overlook it. There are people lining the railings there too.

"Your Majesty. She has completely the second day of the Queen trials. Will she speak?" Someone calls out. Her voice is clear but kind.

He steps back, still holding onto my shoulder.

"I will." I look out at the faces in the crowd.

"How are you doing? The trials are a lot of pressure." Someone calls out and the knot in my stomach loosens. They might not all be here in support, but I'm not alone. Some of them care.

"I'm alright. It is a lot of pressure, but I'm well prepared. I don't want to let him down." I look over my shoulder at him.

The energy softens, I feel it. It's like the entire group exhaled simultaneously.

There are still a few faces in the crowd that seem unhappy,

their faces are etched with concern and mistrust. Not concern for me but about me.

Questions are thrown out left and right, most are simple and personal. They want to know more about me. What I like. My favorite Ophidian customs, dishes, and events. It feels very surreal to have a group this large care about my likes and dislikes.

"Do you think you're strong enough to be our queen?" A voice calls out.

Riven's fingers tighten around my shoulder.

Looking through the crowd, my eyes land on a familiar face. Sidra. She's smiling. She gives me a slight nod.

"I do." I don't mean to, but I smile. This question is meant to rattle me, to shake my confidence. But I've already doubted myself enough for every person here. "I asked myself the same question. I doubted my ability to do this. I wasn't trained for this. On my planet, I was not someone with any authority. I had no experience with it. But strength, physical and mental, can be learned. I am fair and reasonable. I will give this my all. For you, for Riven, and for myself. I might not be as physically strong as you, but I can promise you that I won't be cruel, or self-serving. I won't lie or betray you. I will earn the position and then spend the rest of Riven's reign earning it every day."

His hand relaxes on my shoulder, and Sidra places her hand on her chest.

"She has faced her trial today." He says behind me, stern but not angry. I recognize this tone. I've heard him use it before. It's not warm, not like I'm used to, but this is how he addresses his people. "Thank you for your show of support."

Tucking into his side, I let him lead me away.

As we round the corner, shielded from the crowd by the building, he picks me up. His mouth is on mine so fast it takes me by surprise.

"You are wonderful."

Wrapping my arms around his neck, I lean into this warmth.

"They see it now, as clearly as I do." He continues, each word punctuated with a kiss.

"I wish that counted as a trial day."

"It might not officially count, but trust me, that was a trial day. You stood before the people and earned their respect." He starts to walk, carrying me toward his office. "Now, let me help you relax. You earned that too."

CHAPTER 77

feel like the marshes.

Mossy green and muddy brown.

I know what this means. Today, my judge must be from the Fenlands. I know that Hydriss was not the representative for all Fen Wardens or people from the Fenlands, but knowing that I'm about to be judged by one has my stomach in knots.

After today, I'm on the downslope of this. More than halfway through. Two days left.

Running my fingers over the gauzy material on my skirt, I look at every little detail. The fabric is dotted with piles, weaving a texture into the skirt that is barely noticeable. It reminds me of marsh water, though. With its silty bottom and floating debris.

Sidra really never misses. The message is always there, loud and clear.

"I can do this." I whisper, straightening my spine.

"Yes, you can." Riven startles me from the doorway.

Spinning around, I wrap my arms around his waist and press my face into his chest. "I look like the marshes."

"You look lovely." He runs his fingers through my hair. "After today's trail, I would like to take you somewhere."

"Where?" I feel my body perk up.

"Patience." He smiles, squeezing me one more time before we have to walk out the door.

Each day, this walk feels shorter. Before I know it, we're standing in front of the door, hugging.

It feels like a blur today. I walk in–taking my place. They enter, floating to their place at the front of the room.

"Today, we hear from Judge number three. Judge Columme." The speaker's voice rings out in the dark.

The judge steps forward, his golden eyes glowing beneath his hood. Unlike the others, when he steps forward, tall and proud, he takes his hood down so that I can see his face clearly.

I'm not sure what is motives were in that but I feel more at ease. Somehow, seeing his face makes this less frightening.

"My question is this: Will you involve the Fenlands in decisions requiring delicacy, or will you relegate us to the outskirts of your vision?"

Son of a bitch.

Heat flares in my chest and creeps up to my cheeks. I wish I could step forward and slap his visible face.

Sucking my teeth, I straighten my shoulders. If he wants to ask this question. I'll answer it.

"To be clear, I do not believe that, in any way, shape or form, the Fenlands have been relegated to the outskirts of anything." I hold eye contact with him. With each word, my irritation becomes more apparent. How dare he.

Calm down, Demi. This is a trial. The whole point is to test me.

Taking a breath, I relax my clenched fists. "The Fenlands are an integral part of every decision that is made. They are neither blind or silent. And as Queen, I would advise that they be treated with the respect they are owed. Your counsel will be sought where your wisdom is required—and make no mistake, I recognize the value you bring. As does Riven. Do not mistake caution for neglect. Everyone here is well aware of the Fenlands and their tumultuous history with the rest of the territories."

His jaw clenches. I almost smile. Good.

"Decisions that affect the population as a whole require delicacy and clarity. The Fenlands is one territory–they will be treated with the respect and consideration that they deserve –not more or less. The goal will never be to pander to their egos but to ensure the safety and prosperity of every territory."

Lifting my chin, I hold eye contact with him, waiting for him to step back into the line with the other judges.

This is the most confident I've ever felt giving an answer.

He was trying to rattle me.

It didn't work.

"Dismissed." The speaker's voice breaks the tense silence in the room.

I feel his eyes on me as he leaves with the rest of the judges.

My body feels light as I practically bounce out the door into Riven's waiting arms.

"You look confident." His smile makes me feel mushy inside.

"I feel confident. I don't know if this question was just to rattle me–to really test my diplomatic abilities–or if he actually wanted to know. But I think I did well."

"I can't wait to read the transcript." He pulls me into his side. "Let's go."

"Can I change first?"

While I appreciate Sidra's efforts. I really don't want to go out dressed like swamp water.

"Actually," He runs his thumb over my lower lip. "What you're wearing is perfect."

"Riven, are we going to the Fenlands again?"

"Yes." He bites back a laugh. "Don't make that face. You'll like it, I promise."

"Fine." I lean into his side, still pouting.

It's just the two of us in the pod today. He is laid back and comfortable, maneuvering us out of the city and into the air.

Letting my eyes close, I lean toward the windows, letting the sun warm my face.

"Look." He reaches over and touches my leg.

When I open my eyes, I see hundreds of other pods stopped in the marshes below.

"What's going on?" I wasn't expecting other people. Especially this many.

"You'll see." He lowers us to the ground.

Everyone seems to be walking out into the fields, a large open clearing surrounding by trees. He helps me out of the pod and wraps his arms around me.

"We have to be quiet." He whispers against my ear.

"Ok." I follow his lead.

"Step carefully." He shows me a small hole in the ground. "Don't step on them."

The holes are everywhere. It's hard not to step on one, but we make it out into the field, eventually.

"We only have to wait a few minutes. We almost missed it."

"Missed what?" I crane my neck to look back at him.

"You'll see." His eyes glint with mischief.

There is an excitement in the air. Everyone here is silently humming.

Standing in the middle of the slightly muddy field, we wait.

Then, a single white bird flies upward from somewhere inside the crowd.

Then another.

They're tiny, little fluffy looking chicks—white streaked with gray.

Soon, there are so many of them it looks like it's snowing in reverse. They're flying out of the holes in the ground.

"Oh, my god." My mouth hangs open.

"It's Mynor hatching day." He holds me tightly.

"Wow." I stare up at the sky and thousands of them take to the air. "This is amazing!"

"I thought you would enjoy it. It happens every other year."

Every time I come here, I like the Fenlands a bit more. It's so much more than the bad memories.

CHAPTER 78

"Holy shit." I stare at myself.

I have never worn anything like this. I feel like a medieval Q-Tip. My dress is made of soft, malleable metal. It's long, and the silhouette is like a slender line. A hood comes up over my head, covering my hair. It's almost like chain mail, but not.

The color shifts when I move, rolling effortlessly between a deep gray silver and a shimmering lavender.

The Eukaryota Territory.

I'm particularly nervous about this judge. I did well yesterday, but today is a new day. Eukaryota is very small and there wasn't much information about them. They aren't involved in anything particularly significant. They have almost no exports. They are born mostly blind but have heightened hearing.

The way Sidra explained it, the judge will be able to hear me taking a breath or my heart rate spiking from across the room.

They are a calm, quiet people that mostly stick to themselves. They aren't outspoken about many issues that seem to incense other Ophidians.

My dress feels strange against my skin as I walk out into the hallway. Riven and Sidra are waiting.

He stops speaking when he sees me, his eyes flickering.

Sidra's scales are painted silver today. She is the only one here I've ever seen change her colors like make-up.

"You look wonderful!" She claps her hands together. "Do you know why I chose this dress?" She tilts her head.

I feel put on the spot. "Well, you've represented all the other judges so far. He might not be able to see my outfit, but that doesn't mean we shouldn't give them the same representation."

Her smile widens, the little gems on her fangs glimmering in the light. "You are ready!"

"You look..." he clears his throat and wraps his arm around me.

"Snake-ish?"

"Delicious." He growls.

"Later." I whisper, my cheeks warming up.

His hands are all over me as we walk down the hallway. It's a good thing this dress is slightly cool to the touch because he's making me burn up.

When we reach the doors, he holds me back, pinning me to the wall. Sidra doesn't even try to act like she's not watching.

"I can feel your nervousness. The Eukaryotans are very loyal to me. His question will be difficult, but his judgment of you will be in my favor. They are quiet and secretive but remember, that is not a weakness. They are strong without the need for show."

"Thank you." I whisper. I needed to hear that.

Shaking out my hands, I hold my head high and enter the room alone. I feel Riven's eyes on me until I'm completely out of sight.

When everyone is present, the speaker calls out. "Today, we hear from Judge number four. Judge Rena."

He steps forward, his slim build and slight frame noticeably more lean than the others.

"My question is this," his voice is so pleasant. Soft and kind– it catches me off guard. "How will you reconcile the predatory instincts of our kind with the cooperative needs of the society?"

For a moment, I'm gripped by panic. But just as quickly, it disappears. I can answer this.

"While humans and Ophidians are different, in almost every way," I can't help but smile at the heaviness of that truth. We are so different. "We are similar in this way. Humans are predators. We seek to own and rule over everything. We want land, resources, and power. We've fought countless wars for it. There is no way to reconcile predatory instincts and the needs of a large group. There will always be those that step out of line, that allow their ambitions to overrule the needs of the majority. As long as there is greed and ambition, there will always be conflict. All we can do is prepare for it. As long as we know that it's inevitable, we can set up a society that can bounce back from those kinds of fights. And, I believe that is already firmly in place here. It has been tested, and in the end, the needs of the majority won."

His lips tug upward into a smile, and he nods his head.

I know he'll hear it, but I don't care. I let out a relieved sigh, all the pressure in my chest releasing at once.

He steps back into his place among the other judges, but his face stays trained on mine. I know he can't see me, but he's listening.

"Dismissed."

I want to run out, but I wait, holding myself tall and still.

When it's my turn, I walk as fast as I can out into the hallway.

"I passed that." I launch myself at him.

"I never doubted you."

"I felt confident yesterday, but today I know, for sure. I passed."

"Let's go peel you out of this stunning dress." He lifts me up, throwing me over his shoulder.

"Don't you have things to do? King duties?" I laugh.

"Yes. I can do them and you at the same time."

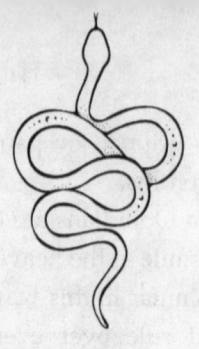

CHAPTER 79

My body is actually bouncing. I'm going to jump out of my skin. This is it. It's only been a four days, but it feels like years. All the preparation leading up to it, the nervousness and sleepless nights–it ends today.

Day five.

Salus is the last judge.

I wonder if he did that on purpose for dramatic effect. Or maybe it's just a coincidence.

Before I open the protective cover over the outfit Sidra brought me, I close my eyes. Elphdia. A desert planet. The outfits–costumes–have been more elaborate and beautiful each day.

Opening the tabs, I gasp. What is this?

"Pretty fantastic, right?" Sidra is standing in the doorway, watching. "I figured you might need help with this one."

"Sidra! How?" My brain can't quite fathom what's in front of me. Inside the garment bag, there is a pile of sand. "Is this a joke?"

"Of course not!" She steps up to the bag. "Take it by these straps." She reaches into the bag and pulls two clear straps up.

"This can't be real!" I reach out and touch it.

"Step into it." She holds it open.

Somehow, the sand bends to her will, opening like a dress for me to slide into it.

"What material is this?"

"It is Elphdian sand. I molded it with a polymer." She shrugs like it's simple.

"I've never seen anything like this!" It's not just a representation, it's actually made of Elphdian sand.

"Of course you haven't! No one else has ever made anything like this." She laughs.

She sweeps my hair over my shoulder and pins something into it, a clip holding it over to the side. "You're ready!"

"I'm ready!" I know she means physically, but I mean it in every way. I'm ready. Let's finish this.

"You look like a desert queen." She helps me spread the train out behind me as I walk.

"You do." Riven's voice makes me blush. "You never fail, Sidra." His eyes darken as he takes in my dress.

Tucking into his side, we make this journey one more time.

"Ready?" His hand pressed to the exposed skin of my back makes me feel warm.

"I am. Let's get this done."

He looks proud, which only makes me feel warmer.

There is a crowd gathered outside today. Hundreds of people, quietly watching us–watching me. I feel their support. As I make eye contact with a few of them, they lift their chins.

At the door, Riven holds me, just for a moment, but it feels longer than normal.

"See you on the other side." I pull myself away and hold my head up as I walk inside. Only when I'm sure the crowd can't see me, I allow myself to let out a shuddering breath. This is it. Day five.

The air feels thicker as the judges make their way, in a perfectly straight line, steps in unison, to the front of the room.

"Toady," the speaker's voice is different today. There is a hint of something there that normally isn't. Maybe he's excited that this is the end, too. "We hear from Judge Number five. Judge Salus."

He steps forward, his eyes meeting mine beneath the shadow of his hood. "My question is this." He jump in immediately. "We have laws and restrictions placed on the use of our venom. While it is deadly, it is a part of us, given by nature. There are some in opposition to those policies, specifically that our venom is prohibited from use in almost any case. How do you feel about that?"

Did all the air just get sucked out of the room?

What the fuck? Does he know?

I teeter on my feet, feeling wobbly.

"I–" my throat is too dry to speak. Closing my eyes, I take a deep breath. "I am aware of the opposition to the current policies regarding venom." I feel like the world's biggest hypocrite. "I stand behind the policy, as is currently written." I roll my shoulders back. Time to sell this. "When I was taken from Earth by Viris, it was an act of violence perpetrated against me. He scared me, tormented me and treated me like a possession that was his to trade. I had no choice in the outcome, no say in my future. He was cruel and frightening. When Hydriss killed him, he used his venom to do so. Viris was, in my limited experience, not a good or honorable man. But, watching him die was the single most horrifying experience of my life. I've dreamed of it since." I look into his light eyes, watching the way they flicker. "Having seen that firsthand, the horror of it, I cannot stand to change the laws. Watching someone meet their end in that way…" A chill rolls down my spine. "It was…"

He's holding eye contact, the golden scales on the sides of his face almost glimmering in the light. I can't read his facial expression–good or bad–I can't tell.

"Venom, while natural, should be closely regulated. The consequences of a more relaxed approach could be catastrophic."

He nods and steps back into his place in line.

I'm a hypocrite. If venom is used for my benefit, I'm all for it! I hope they can't see my panic.

"Dismissed." The speaker calls and they leave unceremoniously, like all the other days.

Taking a breath, I spin around.

As soon as we make eye contact, his body tenses. He reaches for me, shielding me from the crowd.

"Come with me."

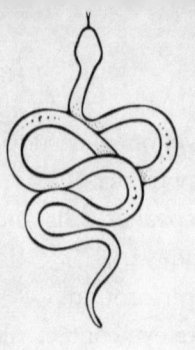

CHAPTER 80

H is hand is firm around my wrist as he pulls me into the hallway, his grip steady but not tight. My breath is coming too fast, too shallow, and I feel like I can't get enough air. My pulse pounds in my ears, and my thoughts race too quickly to catch any of them.

"What happened?" His voice is low and even, but there's a crease between his brows. He's concerned. He's so still. I'm frantic, moving in all directions at once, sheer panic.

"The final question was about venom! Salus asked about the policy and if I would want to uphold it." I grab his arm tightly, my nails biting into his skin. "Oh my god, Riven. I was honest. I told them what I really thought, but I'm such a hypocrite! We used venom to save me. We broke the law! I—"

"Demi, stop. Take a breath."

I barely register his movement before his hands settle on my shoulders, drawing me forward into his warm chest.

"I wasn't expecting that question."

"It's alright," he reassures me, his voice never rising, never breaking from that quiet steadiness. "I'm sure you did—"

"My heart was beating so loudly. Judge Rena had to have heard it. He knows I panicked."

"He probably did." There's the barest hint of amusement in his voice, but it isn't mocking. Just a quiet acknowledgment. "That doesn't mean anything, Demi. Relax."

"I'm sorry." I press my face into his chest. "I panicked."

His arms tighten around me, and I feel myself calming down slightly. "You're allowed to panic, Demi. These trails are stressful."

I sag against him, letting him hold my weight.

"How long do we have to wait for the verdict?"

"It will be quick." He kisses my hair. "They have been thinking about this for days. All that is left to do is to come together and discuss. Each judge will weigh in on each day, but the opinion that really matters is the judge that asked the question. He will hear the panels thoughts though."

"Ok." I shake off the nervous feeling in my stomach.

"Let's go shower and change. Sidra made another dress for the verdict."

"Of course she did." I don't move. "I just need another minute." I'm not ready to walk past the crowds yet.

"Take as long as you need." He's steady, calm and solid. If he's nervous, he doesn't show it at all.

We stand in silence, our bodies pressed together. With my eyes closed and his heartbeat against my ear, it feels like we're the only people here.

I don't want to leave this little bubble. But we have to.

"Let's go." I sigh.

Hand in hand, we walk out to face the waiting crowd.

Steady. Keep it together.

I hold my head up, making eye contact with them as we pass, smiling. He rubs my hand with his thumb, gluing me together as he leads me through the courtyard.

I feel slightly dazed as we make our way through the house. When the door closes behind us and I'm sure we're alone—completely alone, I let my shoulders slump.

"Holy shit."

"Demi."

Humming, I absentmindedly start to peel the dress off.

"Demi."

"Yeah?" I spin around and the look on his face stops me dead in my tracks. My heart starts to race immediately. "Riven, what is it?"

"I–" he smiles, a sweet, nervous smile that makes my legs feel wobbly. "I want to commit myself to you. To stand before everyone and vow to spend this life and any other together."

My mind glitches. "What?"

Is he proposing? Right now?

"Riven? What if I don't pass? I–"

"I believe in you, Demi. But I want you to know, regardless of the outcome of the trial, I want you forever."

Standing in front of him, half-dressed, trembling, full of nerves and fear, he's asking me to spend my life committed to him.

A giggle slips out before I can stop it.

His smile grows as I try to contain it, but can't.

"Yes. I'll commit myself to you."

He wraps his arms around me, kissing me breathless.

"You could have at least been partially naked, too." I come up on my toes and wrap my arms around his neck.

"I suppose that would have made things more even. I couldn't wait."

He carries me into the bathroom and helps me out of the dress. It drops to the floor, a perfect pile of sand.

"Sidra is a genius." I stare at it.

"She is." He pulls me into the shower. "We'll have to have her design something extra special for our commitment ceremony."

"Actually, I have a few thoughts to share with her about that."

The nervousness about the trials seems like background noise now. Holding him makes other things seem smaller somehow.

CHAPTER 81

My fingers trace over the little swirling patterns on the fabric of my dress. Over and over again, I twitch my fingers over the material.

Riven is a pillar beside me, strong, sturdy, and unmoving. He's not fidgeting with his fingers or shuffling his feet.

I'm so grateful that he's here beside me. When they announced that the judge's deliberations were over, my legs almost gave out. I don't know how I would stand here without him.

I barely doing it now.

The door rumbles open behind us, opening the same way it has every day. Now, it feels louder and heavier. The vibrations in my feet seem to last longer.

The robes they're wearing are deep red instead of black. They float past us, up to the podium.

"Today," the speaker jumps in immediately. "We hear the final deliberations of each judge and close this matter for good."

If there is one thing to love about the Ophidians, it's their down-to-business nature. They don't drag out the proceeding or prolong it with pomp and dramatics. They get right down to it.

Right now, that's exactly what I need. My wobbly legs can't take an hour of speeches and grandeur.

"Judge Naes?" The speaker calls and he steps forward.

"My question was: If betrayed, how would you respond to maintain order while preserving strength?"

My breath catches in my throat.

"Your answer, while thoughtful, did not pass. Day one: fail."

He slides back into his place in line.

Holy shit. I failed the first day? That's it? His part is over?

"Judge Lious?" The speaker calls.

He steps forward. "My question was this: How will you deal with those who challenge your authority? Your answer was succinct, thoughtful, and wise. Pass."

Just as quickly as the first judge, he steps back.

Ok. I passed one. One pass, one fail. I just have to pass the last three.

I'm so warm and my legs wobble.

"Judge Columme." The speaker calls him forward.

This was the one I was truly the most concerned about. My fate will be decided right here. If I fail, it's over.

"My question was: Will you involve the Fenlands in decisions requiring delicacy, or will you relegate us to the outskirts of your vision?" He pauses.

Riven breaks his composure, reaching over to take my trembling hand. The gesture makes me feel taller.

"Pass."

I passed? No notes, no critiques, just a passing judgment.

"Judge Rena."

The fourth judge steps forward, his eyes meeting mine beneath his hood.

"My question was: How will you reconcile the predatory instincts of our kind with the cooperative needs of the society?" His soft voice whips through the room.

The corners of his mouth tug upward, barely, almost imperceptibly, but my whole body relaxes.

"I was impressed by your response. Pass." He bows and steps back.

"And finally, Judge Salus." The speaker calls.

My fingers tighten around Riven's, squeezing too hard, but I can't stop myself.

"My question was: How would you handle the policies on the use of venom?" He looks up, making eye contact with me. "Pass."

All the air is punched out of my lungs. One fail and four passes. I did it.

"The final count is four passes and one fail," the speaker announces, voice echoing through the chamber like a bell. "This Queen trial is concluded with a passing result."

For a moment, everything feels distant—like I'm floating just outside my body, watching this unfold from somewhere far away. My hands are trembling. My heart is pounding, but the rest of me is frozen, suspended between disbelief and over-whelming relief. I passed. I did it.

I didn't let him down. I didn't let myself down.

All the hours of studying, all the time poured into me by Riven, Sidra, Verrin… I did it.

Riven wraps me in his arms, leading me outside. The doors are wide open. A thundering sound from outside pulls my atten-tion. Bright golden light spills into the stone hall, warming my skin.

Then—boom.

A single, thunderous stomp of feet outside shakes the ground. The sound travels up through my heels and into my bones, vibrating in my ribs, and echoing in my skull. I stum-ble, breath catching, as another stomp follows, then another —dozens, hundreds—until the sound becomes a living rhythm.

Again and again.

I step outside and finally see them. Row upon row of people gathered at the foot of the steps. Their feet strike the ground in perfect unison, the heartbeat of a kingdom. A signal. A salute. A cheer of congratulations.

They came for me. Again.

My eyes fill with tears as I watch them.

A basin is being passed through the crowd. One by one, they slice the palms of their hands and add drops of their blood to the growing pool.

They're giving me their blessing, their consent.

"You are accepted. The people have given you their blessing, they stand with you." Riven whispers, pressing a kiss to my cheek.

The judges, now with their robes removed, walk out behind us.

Salus makes eye contact and gives me a nod.

CHAPTER 82

The drums begin at dawn.

Low and rumbling, they keep time like a heart beating, waking up the entire city. Sitting on the edge of the bed, I close my eyes and take a long, slow breath.

I still haven't really had time to process it all. I did it.

It's real. All of it is real. I passed the trials. I'm still breathing. And today, the entirety of the Ophidian kingdom celebrates.

Riven is awake, lying in bed, staring up at the ceiling.

"Are you ready for today?"

"Yes. Are you?" I turn to look at him. His relaxed body spread out on the sheets.

He doesn't answer with words, just a smile that stretches across his face.

Everyone is gathering. Things have already started, but we take our time. It's like we're alone in the world. We shower, I do my hair; we hold each other. There is no rush. This is our day.

Then there is a loud bang on the door.

Sidra.

She's radiant in a pale green gown, her silver hair braided and studded with tiny crystals that catch the light. Her scales are painted silver to match. She looks fresh off the runway, as usual.

"Ready? Her smile is so wide and full of mischief, I'm suddenly nervous about what I might be agreeing to.

"For what?"

"Your dress." She grabs my arm. "I'm stealing her, Riven!" She whisks me away before I can say anything more, pulling me into the hallway and toward the room that once was mine.

"Oh, my god! Sidra!"

I don't know why I'm surprised. She never fails, but this...

It's the wedding dress of my dreams.

She helps me step into it, pulling it up

It's better than anything I could have imagined. Pale ivory silk that clings to my waist before flowing out in layered panels, embroidered with threads of silver and gold that shimmer as I move. The bodice is intricate, almost like armor, but it twinkles like it's made of starlight—delicate, powerful, and elegant. She worked magic into the seams.

"You made this?" I whisper, turning toward her.

Her eyes are brighter than usual. "You earned it."

I reach for her hand. "Thank you."

"I doubted you." She laughs. "This is unlike anything we would wear, but it is lovely. Maybe humans aren't as misguided about fashion as I thought."

"Oh, no, we are!" I laugh. "But I think we got wedding dresses right."

"I'll send Riven in." She gives me one more look before slipping out the door.

Standing in the mirror, I stare, finding new details everywhere I look.

"Demi." Riven chokes. "You look–"

"You too," I whisper, his pristine uniform, all clean edges and precise creases hanging from his body.

"I can't believe I get to spend the rest of my life with you." He almost looks lost, emotion etched into his face more than I've ever seen it.

"I can't wait." I blink back tears. I don't want to be red and splotchy when we see everyone.

When I step outside, hand in hand, the streets are already alive. Thousands flood the bridges and roads, bodies pressed shoulder to shoulder, cheers echoing off the trees. Streamers dance from the balconies, and flower petals rain down from the windows built into the trees.

We push through the crowd, people parting as they recognize us. Everyone is buzzing. I can feel the excitement in the air. Children hold makeshift flags, some painted with their territory's symbols.

The parade winds through the heart of the capital. Each territory marches in turn—lines of proud warriors in gleaming armor, banners blowing in the breeze, and chants hum through the crowds.

I recognize the flags, The Fenlands, Elphdia, Inner Mornia, everyone is here.

I lose track of time, caught up in the rhythm of the drums, the way dancers twirl between the marching lines, and the endless food and drinks. A group of children spot me and start waving wildly. I wave back, smiling until my cheeks ache.

Hours have passed in celebration. There hasn't been a moment of quiet all day.

Riven pulls me into a pod, holding onto him. We don't speak, but the silence is comforting. It's just us, for a moment.

He drives us up to the end of the parade. A final decorated plaza with a podium erected in the center.

My breath catches. This is it.

The crowd falls silent as we step onto the podium.

Sidra and Verrin are already there, waiting for us.

My heart pounds. The weight of everything pressing down on me. I feel it in my bones. In my blood.

The officiant steps forward, voice calm but carrying. "Today, we honor not just victory, but commitment. Not just strength, but a bond. Before witnesses of the realm—before all territories, before all Ophidians…"

I glance to my side and meet his eyes.

Riven.

My partner. My savior. My impossible match. He reaches for my hand without hesitation. His grip is warm, grounding, steady.

The words blur. I hear them, but they melt around the moment. What I remember is the way he watches me—like I'm the only thing in existence that matters.

"I offer you my strength," his voice low but fierce. "My loyalty. My truth. My heart."

"And I offer you my choice. My life. My body and soul."

The judge turns. "Verrin Orlovs, do you accept this commitment?"

"Yes, I do." He nods, almost sternly.

"Sidra Garter, do you accept this commitment?"

"Wholeheartedly, I do."

"There is nothing here or anywhere that can separate you." The officiant smiles.

"Honored guests and witnesses, I present to you, forevermore, this pair, united."

The cheers rise again, louder than before. The entire planet must be shaking.

As the sun begins to sink and the plaza erupts into music and celebration again, I stand there in my wedding dress, my hand still wrapped in his, and I realize something: This isn't the end.

It's the beginning.

ABOUT THE AUTHOR

A bonafide motha' to five kids under the age of eight, Myranda requires no fewer than 2 cups of black coffee (2 sugars) each day to support her habits and has finally built up the courage to publish her work. She enjoys noise-cancelling headphones and long waits in school pick-up lines and can change a diaper one-handed while blindfolded.

ALSO BY MYRANDA RAE

Contemporary

When I Whisper His Name - A Big Brother's Best Friend Romance

Unplanned - A one-night stand turns into an office romance

Lewd & Lascivious - Lawyers, office politics, and a book boyfriend to die for.

The Void He Fills - An artist and her physical therapist do more than heal her body.

Pink - A workplace romance with a twist.

What's Done in the Dark - The Ruler of the Underworld finds true love in the Hades & Persephone retelling.

Paranormal/Shifter

Alphas, Kings & Playthings - She has trained for years to be the Alpha Kings breeder. But then she meets his brother…

Hardest to Love - A vampire prince falls for a human woman, and it's happily ever after—for a while.

NOTE FROM THE AUTHOR

Dear Reader,

I wanted to take this opportunity to thank you. Writing books is my dream, and knowing that you've taken the time to read them means everything to me. I can't express enough how grateful I am for your support. If you enjoyed the story, it would mean the world if you left a review. Your thoughts help other readers discover the book. Even a few words make a huge difference! If you're not able to, that's okay—I'm just happy you're here. Thank you for being a part of this journey with me. I appreciate you more than you know.

With gratitude,

Myranda